The Sound of Us

Titles by Sarah Willis

The Sound of Us

Sarah Willis

BERKLEY BOOKS, NEW YORK

THE BERKLEY PUBLISHING GROUP
Published by the Penguin Group
Penguin Group (USA) Inc.
375 Hudson Street, New York, New York 10014, USA
Penguin Group (Canada), 10 Alcorn Avenue, Toronto, Ontario M4V 3B2, Canada
(a division of Pearson Penguin Canada Inc.)
Penguin Books Ltd., 80 Strand, London WC2R 0RL, England
Penguin Group Ireland, 25 St. Stephen's Green, Dublin 2, Ireland (a division of Penguin Books Ltd.)
Penguin Group (Australia), 250 Camberwell Road, Camberwell, Victoria 3124, Australia
(a division of Pearson Australia Group Pty. Ltd.)
Penguin Books India Pvt. Ltd., 11 Community Centre, Panchsheel Park, New Delhi—110 017, India
Penguin Group (NZ), Cnr. Airborne and Rosedale Roads, Albany, Auckland 1310, New Zealand
(a division of Pearson New Zealand Ltd.)
Penguin Books (South Africa) (Pty.) Ltd., 24 Sturdee Avenue, Rosebank, Johannesburg 2196,
South Africa

Penguin Books Ltd., Registered Offices: 80 Strand, London WC2R 0RL, England

This book is an original publication of The Berkley Publishing Group.

This is a work of fiction. Names, characters, places, and incidents either are the product of the
author's imagination or are used fictitiously, and any resemblance to actual persons, living or
dead, business establishments, events, or locales is entirely coincidental.

First edition: June 2005

Library of Congress Cataloging-in-Publication Data

Willis, Sarah.
    The sound of us / Sarah Willis.—1st ed.
        p. cm.
    ISBN 0-425-20302-6
    1. Custody of children—Fiction. 2. Cleveland (Ohio)—Fiction. 3. Single women—Fiction.
4. Child abuse—Fiction. 5. Girls—Fiction. I. Title.

PS3573.I4565557S68 2005
813'.54—dc22
                                                                    2005041103

PRINTED IN THE UNITED STATES OF AMERICA

10 9 8 7 6 5 4 3 2 1

For Matt and Moira,
with all my love.

The Sound of Us

Sarah Willis

Chapter One

The girl lying on the exam table is fourteen and bone thin, elbows and knees like pipe fittings. Her mother stands in a corner of the small room, arms crossed. When she first dragged her daughter into the clinic she said, "I want to know if my baby's pregnant," but she has hardly said a word since then. The information that I got from the Hearing and Speech Center was that the girl, Beatrice, is deaf and uses ASL at the school she attends, but that her mother only knows a few signs. At this moment every inch of her face is tight with anger. I have just signed the words *Test exam same. Pregnant you. Eight weeks, ten weeks, between.*

"You can sit up now, Beatrice," Dr. Franklin says, and again, I interpret. The doctor switches off the lamp, swiveling it out of the way. With four people in the room there's little space left to move around and it's uncomfortably close.

Beatrice points to the doctor. *Sure?* Her eyes are tearing up.

I want to look away. Most of my interpreting jobs are at schools and colleges. This is the first time I have had to tell a child that she's pregnant. And her mother's certainly not helping me any. I ask the doctor Beatrice's question, and he nods.

"Sorry," he says. "I'm quite sure."

As I sign *sorry,* I feel the word inside me.

I can't help thinking that this girl should have been under better supervision, and not because she's deaf, but because she's at such a vulnerable age. If I can see the danger she could get into, why couldn't her mother? If I had children, I'd know where they were at all times.

Beatrice sits up awkwardly, making sure the blue paper robe covers her thighs. I hear the sound of the paper crinkling and wish this clinic had something soft and warm to cover this child.

"We'll give you a prescription or prenatal vitamins," Dr. Franklin says, "so Medicare will cover it. You need to make monthly appointments for the first five months, then we'll see you—"

Beatrice's mother bumps into me as she moves between the doctor and the exam table, her back to her daughter. "My baby will need an abortion," she says to Dr. Franklin. The minute I start to sign she turns and grabs my hands. Her grip is tight. "Don't you signify what I'm saying, lady," she says. "He can hear me just fine."

It happens so quickly. I try to pull my hands away, but she holds on tight. I am completely freaked out by this woman grasping my hands. "Let go of me! This is my job!"

Her face is inches from mine. I can smell her. "I'm talking to the doctor. This is my baby we're talking about. You understand?"

My heart pounds in my chest. I hear Dr. Franklin say, "Hey! Hey!"

"Let go of me!" I tug harder, and she lets go so quickly that I fall backward against a cabinet. Something clatters to the floor. Dr. Franklin steps between us. It's so crowded, our movements seem like some strange dance, as if we're caught in a savage box step.

"Don't you *ever* do anything like that in here again!" Dr. Franklin says. "Do *you* understand? We'll leave the room now and let Beatrice get dressed. We don't do abortions. If you'd like to come for prenatal care, make an appointment with the receptionist."

I'm still thinking about this woman grabbing me, and can't think straight. What did he just say? How can I interpret it? My hands are shaking. I've *never* not signed what I should have.

"Yeah, you go on," Beatrice's mother says, motioning me with her head to get lost. I want to give her the finger, but I'm not that stupid.

I look at Beatrice. She looks horrified. I raise my hands and point to the doctor. *He say we all leave room now. Clothes-on you now.* My signs are slow and deliberate. Her mother watches me carefully. I could say something nasty to her that I bet she *would* understand, and the doctor would never know.

Beatrice nods slowly, obviously confused by what's happening. Dr. Franklin and I leave the room, closing the door behind us.

In the hallway, a nurse walks by with a specimen slide, and at a small desk a physician's assistant takes an old man's blood pressure. I feel as if I'm in one of those movies where meteors are about to destroy the earth, but no one has been told. I want everyone to know what just happened to me.

"I'm sorry," Dr. Franklin says, putting a hand on my shoulder. I hate being touched and he must sense this because he takes his hand away. "Are you all right?"

I'm shaking and furious, but not hurt. Still, I rub at my wrists. "I'm okay, but, Jesus, she wants her daughter to get an abortion without telling her. Can she do that?"

"Let's hope not."

"Isn't there anything you can do?" I ask.

He shakes his head.

I want *him* to do something, because I can't. Ethically, I can't pull Beatrice aside and tell her what I think her mother might do. I spent years at Gallaudet getting my masters in ASL Interpreting, taking two different classes on ethics alone: *I am not to get involved, only interpret accurately.*

"I'm sorry she did that," the doctor says again. "You're all right?"

I nod, and he walks off. I have to wait here for Beatrice to come out in case she has some questions, which I doubt, but my job is to interpret for her until she's done at the clinic. After Beatrice leaves the building, I'll be free to go wash my hands, physically and figuratively.

The door to the exam room opens and they come out, the mother holding her daughter's thin upper arm so tightly that I bet it'll leave a mark. Pulling Beatrice down the hallway, she looks right into my eyes as she passes, silently daring me to say anything. What can I say? *Hey, bitch, you're a lousy mother?* They didn't have to tell us in ethics class that we weren't to call our clients bitches. Then again, Beatrice's mother isn't my client.

Just before they turn into the next hallway, Beatrice looks back at me. She's in tears, and then she's gone.

. . .

Outside, it's hot and humid, and when I open the door of my Corolla, which has been parked in the sun for two hours, the pent-up heat is stifling, the steering wheel too hot to touch. Turning on the car and starting up the air-conditioning, I sit on the edge of the seat, leaving the door open, my feet on the sticky pavement. My hands still tremble as I take out my cell phone and call Polly at work. I'm not supposed to talk about the details of an interpreting job to anyone except my supervisor, but Polly's my best friend. I need to talk to her. My supervisor is only going to be upset at me for not signing something I should have.

"Jesus, Alice," Polly says after I tell her what happened. "What a wacko. That poor girl. I know you wanted to do more, but, really, there's nothing you could do but get out of there. I'll come over after dinner." She's speaking in a rushed whisper. I hear phones ringing, people talking. She's the assistant to the mayor of Cleveland.

"No, no, I'm okay. Don't bother. Really. I'm fine." Polly's daughter Rachel is heading back to Boulder in two days, and I don't want to take up time they could spend together. "I have to finish reading that book for my book club."

"You sure?"

"Yeah."

"Well, call me, if you need me."

"Tell Rachel I said *Love*."

"I will."

Rachel's deaf. I met Polly when she and her husband, Patrick, came to the Cleveland Hearing and Speech Center where I was teaching sign language classes when Rachel was first diagnosed.

Now Rachel attends the University of Colorado. She's smart, just like her sister, Nora, who's not deaf. Polly's going through that empty-nest syndrome thing. I miss her kids, too.

Next I call my supervisor, Elaine, to report the incident. "You should have signed even if your hands were shaking," she says.

I say, "I know," hang up, and throw the phone against the backseat. Screw her. She wasn't there.

The car has almost cooled down. It's three o'clock on a Thursday afternoon in mid-July. This is really my vacation time, but I'm through going on vacations by myself, trying to pretend I'm thrilled to learn about the mating habits of whales or hiking with strangers in the Grand Canyon. Now I just stay here, where my friends are, take on a few jobs until the schools start again.

I drive home, my teeth tight, unable to shake off the experience at the clinic. But turning the car onto my street comforts me, the sight of my house loosening my hunched shoulders. It's a plain white colonial, but it's mine and I've lived here for ten years now. The front lawn is perfectly green, the hose roping across the grass, the sprinkler a metal frog lying on its back, an odd little thing I found in an odd little shop last week. I need to move it to the back lawn, get the ground good and wet. I've got three dozen perennials in pots to plant back there. It's not the right time to plant them—early spring or late fall would be best, the man at the garden center told me—but I've got it in my head to plant a perennial garden, and I don't want to wait.

Across the street, the widow Mrs. Myerson's daylilies are a wide band of orange trumpeting summer. Along the sides of her walkway is a rainbow of snapdragons, and both trees on her lawn are surrounded by yellow marigolds. My garden is going in the backyard where no one can see it. I need to see how I do with this flower thing before I put it on display.

The man with the horse dogs and the baby is just crossing my drive, and I wave hello. He has two Great Danes, and a new son, whom he carries in a pouch across his chest. I never see his wife, just him and the dogs, and now him and the dogs and the baby. We have said hello for years—he lives a few streets over—but I don't know his name. He is just the man with the horse dogs, as Vince's son Bruce nicknamed him. Seeing the horse dogs reminds me of Bruce, which reminds me of Vince. I miss him so badly.

As I park my car and get out I hear the sounds of my neighborhood: the muffled afternoon soaps coming from Mrs. Linley's window, which looks out over my driveway; the *shush, shush, shush* of the sprinkler in the yard to the left of my house where the Boncheks live; the annoying loud drone of a leaf blower somewhere; the faint sounds of children calling each other. My hand spells *Come on!* and I know I must have heard those words, although I wasn't aware of it.

There are in this neighborhood the man with the horse dogs, the widow with the daylilies, the Orthodox Jewish family with five kids, the college kids who rent the side-by-side duplexes, the old retired couple, the man and woman from Hungary who grow tomatoes in their front yard, and me, the tall, white-haired lady without kids who occasionally sits on her front porch in the white wicker chair, reading a book.

Some life, Vince says.

Shut up, I say. *It's my life.*

Yeah, like I said. Some life.

Even when he was alive he never shut up.

When I was fourteen, I got a book at the library about the life of Helen Keller, and learned the manual alphabet that was printed in the back. I began finger-spelling people's names as I met them, words on signs, things I was thinking, forming the letters with my left hand down by my thigh like signing a secret. When I was young, my hand would ache at night when I went to bed and I'd tell myself that I had to stop this, as if I had picked up a bad habit like smoking cigarettes. But the habit stuck. When I entered Gallaudet, I could finger-spell like all get out. At least I never took up smoking.

Growing up, I took ballet lessons, painting lessons, acting lessons, always moving on to the next thing within a year, believing I could never be great at what I was trying to do, but that I might be great at something else. At Ohio University, I majored in English for no particular reason, and minored in dance. After college I danced in a small company that paid almost nothing, and worked mornings as a secretary in a real estate office. I was neither a great dancer nor a great secretary. It wasn't until my midtwenties that I went to a play where an interpreter signed, and it occurred to me that signing for the deaf was an occupation, and one my hand had been training me for all these years. I was accepted into Gallaudet, where I found that sign language came naturally to me. Suddenly, I had a skill, a career, a passion, and a feeling of power.

Standing in line at the grocery store, I felt special. I knew something no one else knew.

I moved to Cleveland, following a man I thought loved me. We had lived together in Washington, D.C., for almost three years while I was at Gallaudet, and as well as I had learned to read faces, I ignored that quick moment of surprise on his when I told him that I'd move with him to Cleveland, where he had just gotten a job. Six months after we moved here, he left and I stayed. Cleveland is only a few hours from Columbus, where my parents still live in the same house I grew up in. Housing is cheap, and there's a good, strong, Deaf community with plenty of jobs for an interpreter. His name was Jeff. I've dated two Jeffs since then, and men with other names, too.

Yeah, all hands-off stuff, Vince says.

My brother just won't give it a rest.

I'm a twin, but not identical, although I once wished I were. When Vince and I were six, I'd make him wear my clothes, little pink dresses with crinoline slips and pinstriped pinafores. We could make each other do anything. Together we were fearless; a competition and a team all in one. When we were eight, Vince cut my hair as short as his and rubbed my father's brown shoe polish into my lighter, dirty blond hair. I thought it looked great. My father grounded us, but my brother loved me for it.

My hair turned white when I was thirty-three. Vince teased me for a year until he suddenly went white himself. It looked good on him. It made him look more serious than he was, smarter, like wearing glasses might for some people.

He was hit by a car and killed five months ago on Valentine's Day, at age forty-seven, while walking across a busy street, sipping steaming hot hazelnut-flavored coffee out of a paper cup. There was a slash of burn across his right cheek that might have scarred him if he hadn't died. The car hit him at fifty miles an hour in a thirty-five-mile-an-hour zone.

Vince had been married twice—the second time, he had two sons, Bruce and Dylan. When he got divorced, his ex-wife Cindy left the boys with Vince so that she could go to Hollywood. She made two commercials in two years, then married someone else. The someone else didn't want someone else's kids, although

Bruce and Dylan visited her occasionally. Now, of course, they live with her in Arizona. Vince made a living painting houses during good weather. In winter he plowed driveways. He drank and smoked pot, and always called me after he'd done one or the other.

"You need to get married, sister of mine," he said in that last phone call. "There's got to be someone out there for you besides me."

The last thing I said to him on the phone was, "Oh, just shut up and leave me alone."

But he still talks to me even though he's thirty miles away and only ashes in the bottom of a pond.

I start digging a plot for my perennials, not bothering to water the backyard first. The ground beneath the first two inches of earth is all clay, but this is exactly what I need to be doing; I think less when my hands are occupied this way. Blisters begin to form even beneath the gloves, but I don't stop until my stomach growls. It's seven-thirty. Reheated pasta from the night before takes less than ten minutes to eat, and I'm digging again until it's too dark to see. After taking a shower, I go to bed with the book for my book club.

Long after I fall asleep, in the middle of the night, my phone rings.

Chapter Two

I wake with a start, the phone ringing less than a foot from my head. Before I even say hello, I imagine my mother's sobbing voice telling me that my father's dead.

"Hello?" I say.

"Auntie Teya?" A soft, timid voice. A child. I can hear the waver of tears behind those two words. It takes me a few seconds to clear my thoughts.

"I'm not your Auntie Teya, honey," I say. Even awakened abruptly from sleep, my left hand tries to figure out how to spell *Teya*.

"Where's Auntie Teya?"

It's a girl's voice. She's crying now with little hiccup breaths. "You have the wrong number, honey. What number are you calling?"

There's a short silence, then the child says, "371-4569," as if she's reading it off a piece of paper.

"I'm 4566," I say, thinking, *Oh, I shouldn't give her my number.* "Isn't there an adult there who can dial the phone for you?"

"No." A hesitant no. A scared no.

"Are you all by yourself?"

She doesn't answer. She's probably been trained to never say she's alone, just as I was trained to never give out my number to someone who called the wrong number.

"Sweetie, isn't your mother home? It's pretty late at night."

I hear her sniffle, then a sound like a moan. Goose bumps rise on my arms.

"Is there something scaring you? You should call 911. Can you do that?" In her upset state, she might keep dialing her auntie's number wrong. Dialing 911 should be easier. "Is there a fire or anything like that?" I shake my head. What is *like* a fire? My brain's waking up, rebuking me for word choices.

"Un-unh."

"But no one's there?"

She hangs up. Shit.

In the dark, lying in my bed, I pretend I'll go back to sleep. A minute later I sit up, dial star 69. A calm, machine-made voice gives me a phone number, and I write it down on the notepad I keep on the table by my bed.

What now? I should call the police, but maybe the girl has reached her auntie by now. I should stay out of this.

I dial her number.

She answers on the first ring. "Mommy?"

"It's me," I say. "The woman you just called. Did you reach your auntie?"

I can hear her breathing, but she doesn't say anything.

"Honey, I'm worried about you. It's . . ." I look at the clock. "Two-thirty at night. Someone should be home with you. Do you know where your mommy is?"

"No."

I'm using a calm, gentle voice, trying hard not to show how nervous I am, trying to keep her talking. I don't know how talking to me will help, but I'm apparently all she has at the moment.

I have to think about what to say. *Has your mother ever done this before, left you all alone?* seems too personal. "Is there anyone I can call for you?"

"My auntie." Then, with a plea, "I want my mommy."

"Okay. I remember the number. It was a nine at the end, not a six, like mine. Should I try calling her for you?"

"Uh-huh."

"Okay. I'll do that. Someone will call you right back. Maybe me, maybe your Auntie Teya, right?"

"Uh-huh."

"Okay, I'll call her."

I hear the phone click.

I can't remember the last time I was so completely awake at two-thirty in the morning. I pick up the phone and dial her aunt. A deep-voiced woman tells me she can't get to the phone right now and to please leave a message. I hang up, call again, then hang up when I hear the recording again. If she were there, wouldn't she answer the phone with it ringing so many times in the middle of the night?

I call the girl back. She picks up the phone, but doesn't say anything. Once again, I can hear her breathing.

"It's me. I'm sorry. Your auntie didn't answer the phone. It's just me. My name is Alice Marlowe. I think maybe I might live near your auntie, since our numbers are so close. I live in Cleveland Heights. Do you know where that is?"

"Uh-huh. Auntie Teya lives there."

Oh, it feels so good to get a full sentence. It's as if I'm interpreting for someone who won't talk to me. "Oh, good. It's a very nice place. I live by Severance Town Center. I go grocery shopping at Tops." Actually I hardly go there at all, since I get most of my food at the Food Co-op, but instinct tells me to mention someplace common.

She doesn't say anything for a few seconds, but before I can figure out what to say next, she speaks up. "We go there. Mommy and me, and Auntie Teya." She pauses. "I want my mommy." She's on the edge of tears again. I don't want her to cry.

"I'm sure you do. When was she supposed to be home?"

Nothing. I probably shouldn't have asked her that. Still, something has to be done. I press my luck. "Sweetie, I just want to help. Do you know when she was supposed to come home?"

"Yesterday."

Something is terribly wrong. "Honey, do you mean the day that just ended? Thursday? Or Wednesday?"

"Yesterday."

"Sweetie, how old are you?" Jesus, I've never said *sweetie* or *honey* so many times in my whole life. I didn't even know those words were in my vocabulary.

"Six."

I'm sitting on the edge of my bed, but now I begin to pace around my bedroom, touching things; the smooth top of my bureau, the windowsill. "Is there anyone else you can call besides your Auntie Teya?" *Auntie* isn't my word either—I always say

Aunt—but I'm using her terminology, trying not to sound too white. As if being white might frighten her off.

"Uh-unh."

"No one? A neighbor, a teacher?"

"We just moved here, be with my Auntie Teya."

"Does your auntie live near you?"

"Uh-huh."

So this girl doesn't live that far from me. "Honey, we should call the police."

She hangs up, the *click* like a slap.

I feel so completely alone. I should call the police, but I don't want to. I want to help her myself. I imagine telling Polly tomorrow how I talked to this little girl until her mother came home, a voice in the dark. But maybe her mother isn't coming home.

I call her back. "Don't hang up," I say. "I promise I won't call the police or even mention them again. Just stay on the phone. We'll talk until your mommy comes home. That way, if something scares you, you can tell me. I'll be right here? Okay?"

A long pause, then, "Okay."

I try to think of something to say. "What's your favorite food that you and your mommy get at Tops? Mine's raspberry sorbet. What's yours?"

She doesn't answer right away, but this time, when she speaks, her voice sounds less frightened. "Snowballs. Pink ones."

I laugh. I'm not someone who laughs out loud often, and the sound is strange in my empty bedroom. "I haven't had those in a long time. I used to like them a lot. And elephant ears. Those were my favorite. Do you like elephant ears?"

"Un-unh."

"They're big and funny-looking, flat, with cinnamon and lots of sugar. I don't think they sell them at Tops anyway. But I liked them." I can't believe I'm talking about snowballs and elephant ears to a six-year-old girl whom I don't know at almost three in the morning. "Do you have food? Are you hungry?"

"Un-unh."

"You sure? Have you eaten today?" *Today* seems like the wrong word. The darkness outside and the situation make it seem as if I'm occupying a lost time, neither day or night; a time held separate except for our voices on the phone.

"Uh-huh."

"Okay. Good."

My cat, Sampson, wanders into the room to see what all the commotion is about. He looks up at me standing by the window, talking in a dark room. He jumps up on the bed, waiting for me to get some sense and lie down. "Do you have a cat?" I ask.

"No."

"I have a cat. Sampson. He's a tiger cat, but really he's just a big, fat, lazy lap cat. Do you like cats?" What I really want to say is, *What is your name?* How long will it take before she won't hang up if I ask her that?

"Uh-huh."

We talk for over half an hour. A harmless question, then a *no* or a *yes,* or more specifically, *un-unh* and *uh-huh.* Holding the phone, I begin to wander around the house, moving things around: a magazine into the garbage, a cup into the dishwasher. Finally I sit on my couch.

"Honey, it's almost four in the morning," I say after she answers *uh-huh* to my question about Barney. "Your mother hasn't been home for almost two days. We have to do something about it. Now don't hang up on me, just listen to my whole sentence first, okay?"

"Uh-huh."

"Either I have to come there and see how I can help you, or we have to call the police. Me, or the police. What should we do? Who should come help you?"

A pause. "You."

I manipulated that, but if I had said I was going to call the police, she'd have hung up. And then I *would* have to call the police. But it would be all over, just a story to tell Polly.

"Okay. I'll come there and we'll keep talking, okay? So someone can be with you until your mommy comes home. But you have to tell me where you live. Can you do that?"

"Uh-huh." She recites her address. It's on a wide busy street with a division down the center. It traverses three cities.

"Is it near any stores? Something I might know?"

"Burger King." And that does it, I know how close she is, only a few miles away in East Cleveland. Not the best neighborhood, but not too bad. By now, there's a false dawn in the sky, a barely perceptible lightening that will go away, then come back as morning. The false dawn makes it easier to imagine leaving my house, driving to a stranger's. I ask her apartment number, tell her I'll be there in ten minutes.

"Okay?" I ask.

"Uh-huh."

I never even asked her name.

The entire drive there, my hands sweat and I have to keep wiping them on my pants. What if her mother *does* come home while I'm sitting in her apartment? What if her mother's dead? How long should I wait? What if I get to the apartment building, but am too afraid to get out of my car?

You need to rescue this kid, Vince says.

Oh, you think so, huh? Easy for you to say.

Just do it, he says. Don't wimp out on this, Alice.

If we were on the phone, I'd hang up now. He's right, fuck him. There are too many things I've said I was going to do and never did. My fear of failure drives me on.

Chapter Three

When we were ten, Vince created a detective agency, making business cards by drawing an eye over the picture of a pie on my mother's recipe cards. He assigned lookout stations to the neighborhood kids, placing us near the homes of people on our street who had left on vacation. "Burglars know these things," Vince said. "They'll be here in droves." Vince assigned me to the backyard of the McHughs, who had gone to Nags Head for two weeks. The McHughs lived next to the deaf boy.

The first day of my assignment, I sat behind the McHughs' house between the back porch and a bush. That my brother thought burglars might come in the middle of the day made me question his intelligence, which, in turn, made me question mine. We liked the same foods, could talk in unison, and thought the same things were stupid, but now I thought *he* was stupid.

After sitting next to the bush for a while, I began to get edgy.

What if the McHughs had *already* been robbed, and here I was leaving my footprints in the dirt? As stupid as this whole thing was, I was determined to be the best detective in the agency, so I got out of my hiding place and circled the house, keeping my eyes open for signs of a break-in.

The back door was still locked. No broken basement windows. Cupping my hands around my face, I peered through the large oval window on the front door and jumped a foot when I saw a face peering back at me. It was me, reflected in the mirror on the McHughs' closet door. Feeling pretty stupid, I came around the other side of the house just in time to see the deaf kid watching me through a window. Henry. We all knew his name, that he talked with his hands, and that his parents sent him to a special school. When his family had moved onto our street a few years before, my parents took us over and introduced us. Henry, a toddler with curly hair, stood behind his mother. Vince and I didn't believe he couldn't hear. We couldn't imagine that at all.

Seeing Henry at the window staring out at me, I was so startled that I automatically waved to him. He jerked backward as if I had shouted at him, and I wondered if I had said something wrong with my wave. But then he leaned forward again, a big, goofy smile growing on his face. He waved back.

I ran back to my spot between the bush and the porch. I wasn't supposed to be seen snooping around the McHughs'. What if he told his mother? Could he say that with his hands? But what really scared me, what made me run, was that I had waved to Henry, and he waved back. Now I would be expected to do so every time I saw him. That smile on his face: I knew now what it meant to him to have someone wave to him. I promised myself I would. I would even go out of my way to make friends with him.

Sitting on the hard ground, my face hot, I took out my notepad and pencil and began to sketch pictures of dresses that would someday make me famous. In less than a minute, a door slammed. It was Henry's door. Through a border of tall, staked marigolds, I watched Henry come out into his backyard. He looked around. Was he looking for me? Ducking down, I kept my eyes on him through an opening in the bush.

How would he play all by himself? When I was by myself, I always had a conversation going on in my head, as if I were talking to someone. Even reading, I heard the words. How did a deaf kid think without words? Did he see hand movements in his head? Was it like watching ballet without the music?

Henry got on the swing that hung from a big tree and swung back and forth, staring up at the sky. There was this look on his face, a distant look, as if he weren't really on the swing at all, but someplace else, and that felt familiar to me; that was how *I* felt on a swing. Finally he jumped off and went over to a sandbox with trucks and old pots and pans. He stood there, looking down at the box, then started moving his hands in sharp, quick motions. His back was to me, but it was obvious he was angry. Then I got it. He was yelling at his sandbox and his trucks. A deaf person could yell his guts out with his hands and no one would hear.

Was he mad at me? That I had waved then run away? I couldn't watch his silent, painful anger, and I looked back down at my drawing, the same skirt I always drew. But a minute later, I heard a loud, high-pitched cry. I lurched forward from my hiding spot to see what had happened, landing on my hands and knees. Henry stood where I could see him perfectly, right between the end of the flower bed and the garage. He looked right at me. We both froze, but even holding his body still, so much was on his face. I saw surprise and questions and worry. He must use his face as much as his hands, and when he thought, his face just went into action. What would it be like to have your thoughts exposed like that? How would you tell a deaf boy to be careful what his face showed? Then suddenly he hooted like an owl. I swear he said *who,* but really he was just letting his breath out and shouting at the same time. Then he ran across the backyard to his house, and the door slammed.

My heart was beating a hundred miles an hour, just as if I had seen a burglar. But he was only a deaf boy.

I never made friends with him. I never even tried. He's not even why I became an interpreter. I got the book on Helen Keller because it was assigned in school, learning the manual alphabet because it was cool and I could talk in secret with my friends. I became an interpreter because it was something I could do well.

Not doing anything for Henry is one of the things that comes to me whenever I begin the list of my regrets—a long list I will now end by saving this little girl.

Chapter Four

The apartment building is an old four-story brick on the corner of Superior and Hanson. There's a center doorway set back deep in between the two sections of the building, and the street lamp casts shadows of trees against the brick walls. Only the archway is lighted, and one set of windows on the third floor. I think about those movies with abandoned castles and the strange men who always open the front door. What the hell am I doing? I park right in front under that street lamp. A sign reads NO PARKING, 7:30 A.M.–9:00 A.M. Seven-thirty is hours away.

I reach for my purse and it's not there. I spell *shit* with my hand, and say it out loud. If I go home for it, I'll never come back.

Looking around first to make sure no one is lurking in the bushes, I get out of the car, making sure all the doors are locked. The false dawn is gone. It's dark as hell.

With a tight fist, I hold my keys so the car key sticks out

between my fingers, ready to jab someone. *Good thinking,* Vince says.

Hey, I think back to him. *First you tell me I have to do this, then you tell me to watch out. Make up your mind.*

Do both, he says. *Just do it right.*

Inside the doorway are two sets of buzzers and two doors leading to the two sections of the apartment building. I press 305, on the left. It's so quiet. If I scream, I'll wake up the whole building. The thought doesn't comfort me; the idea of having to scream overrides the idea of help coming.

The door buzzes and I tug it open, then stand there. In the stairway, the second bulb up is broken; shards of glass dully gleam on the steps. Wouldn't it have been cleaned up if it had been broken for more than a day? With the key stretched out in front of me like a gun, I go up the steps. For a second I'm glad I'm alone so no one can see me looking so stupid.

More lights are out, but not broken. Each floor has two doors. On the third floor, I knock on door 305.

There's a scraping sound. What in God's name is that? Then the light behind the peephole changes, as if it's blocked. She must be looking at me; the scraping noise was her dragging over a chair so she can look out the peephole. *Good girl. Don't open your door to strangers.* As if I'm not one. I try to smile.

"Hi, it's me, Alice Marlowe, the lady on the phone."

The scraping noise again, then more sounds: locks being turned, a chain being unhooked. The door opens. She stares up at me.

She's beautiful.

We look at each other for a few seconds, then she moves back and I step into the apartment and close the door behind me.

I'm in a dining room. In the center is a thick-legged table covered with papers and bills in neat piles, although at one end everything is pushed back so there's a small, clear area. At that end is a chair with two phone books on the seat. This is where she ate whatever she's eaten in the past two days. The surface is wiped clean.

The child is walking backward, eyes on me, until she's standing near the archway into the kitchen. Her thumb's in her mouth, and she's holding an obviously well-loved stuffed rabbit to her chest. She's wearing pink pajamas with some cartoon character design. Her ears are pierced and she's wearing stud earrings that look like diamonds, although I assume they're just rhinestones. The pink pajamas and the stud earrings are such an odd combination that it bothers me. I didn't get my ears pierced until my twenties.

I look away. Just behind her, in the kitchen, I see a stove, a countertop, the corner of a refrigerator, a green linoleum floor, and a cardboard box. Every light in the apartment is on. With all the lights on, there is an eerie feeling, like an overlit movie. The darkness outside seems absolute.

She's so small, and I'm so tall. At five-ten, and with my short-spiky white hair, I imagine I look imposing to a child—and, apparently, to some men. I try smiling again. She doesn't smile back, just looks at me with those big dark eyes.

Her skin is the color of strong tea and glows as if she's the picture of good health. I was worried she might look sickly, unkempt, maybe ill—after all, she's the child of a woman who has left her alone for two days. One side of her head has braids with pink beads at the ends. The hair on the unbraided side is long and curly. Her half-braided head reminds me of those empty ships that were found with plates of food waiting to be eaten.

Her face is round and her eyes huge. They're the largest eyes I've ever seen on a child. Unfortunately, that's because she's looking at me as if I might be a werewolf.

"I don't suppose your mother came back while I was driving here?"

She shakes her head no. I nod. Deaf people and interpreters nod a lot. It means *I got what you were signing,* but it does not necessarily mean *I understand.* It feels very appropriate right now. I know that her mother isn't here, but I certainly don't understand it.

I don't move any farther into the room, although I wish that I were closer to something I could lean on. "Please call me Alice," I say. "And you are?" My eyebrows rise with the question. Habit.

She just stares at me.

"Could you tell me your name, honey?"

She looks around the room as if needing someone to give her permission to answer. Her lips quiver. "Larissa," she says, then her thumb is back in her mouth.

"What a lovely name. Hello, Larissa."

Now tears spill from the corner of her eyes. I know she needs to be hugged, but I can't do that. "Everything's going to be all right, Larissa. Your mother will probably be home soon. We'll just wait for her. Do you know where she was going when she left?"

She nods.

"Where? Where did she go?"

She takes her thumb out of her mouth but keeps it close to

her chin, ready to pop it back in. Her top teeth are all pushed forward. "She go find a job."

"She didn't have a job?"

Larissa shakes her head no. Damn. No workplace to call. "Do you have a daddy?"

Larissa nods yes, and I sigh, both glad she has a father, and frustrated; it's like pulling teeth to get her to answer a simple question.

"Where is he?"

"My daddy's in heaven." She looks up at the ceiling, then back at me.

The apartment is sweltering, all the windows closed. I need to sit down, but I'm afraid to in this stranger's apartment. There are no family portraits on the walls, and I keep picturing Larissa's mother as the mother of the deaf girl, Beatrice. It makes me nervous, imagining Beatrice's mother coming home, finding me here. My brain is working about as well as my legs.

In the living room I see more boxes, a couch, a plain wooden chair, and part of a mantelpiece. Maybe there will be pictures on the mantel.

"I'm sorry about your daddy," I say. "Do you have any pictures of him or your mommy?"

She nods slowly.

"Could I see them?"

With her eyes still on me, Larissa backs into a hallway that must lead to the bathroom and a bedroom or two. She disappears to the right. When she comes back, she's carrying a framed picture, the kind that sits on a table. She hands it to me, then quickly goes to the same spot where she stood before, glancing into the kitchen. I'm willing to bet there's a back door there, that she's eyeing her retreat. Smart kid.

The picture is of a young black man, mostly just his face and shoulders. It's a professional portrait with a blue background. He's smiling, a happy smile that makes me want to smile back.

He looks no more than eighteen. He has Larissa's round face, but his skin is darker and it looks as though he had a bad case of acne once. How did he die? How could someone with that smile be dead? Now I'm sad for two people: this little girl and this young man. I have no sympathy for the mother.

"Any pictures of your mother?"

Larissa shakes her head no. From somewhere below there's a loud bang and I flinch, turning toward the door. For a whole minute the two of us stand perfectly still, listening for footsteps. Nothing. My legs are about to give out.

"May I sit down?" I ask when no one comes barging in the door asking who the hell I am. "Would that be all right?" All I really want to do right now is pick up a phone and call the police, exactly what I should have done in the first place. Larissa nods that slow nod and sidles into the living room, keeping as far from me as she can. She glances at a cushioned rocking chair in the far corner, showing me where I should sit, but I don't want to sit there. I won't be able to see the door. "May I sit over here?" I ask, pointing to the plain wooden chair. She nods once.

On the mantel is a framed picture of Larissa, also professionally done. The beads in her hair are different colors, her hair is shorter, and she's smiling, showing those crooked teeth.

She stands by the couch, wary, watching me. Her eyebrows are dark and straight, low against the top of her eyes. They make her look pensive, somber. They're a bit off-putting on such a young child.

"Okay, Larissa," I say, sweetly, trying to lighten my mood, "we need to figure some things out, I guess. Your auntie's not answering the phone, and your mother's been gone for two days." I almost add, *and your father's dead.* "Isn't there anyone else we can call? Think hard."

"Un-unh."

"When did you move here?"

She looks up and to the right, trying to figure it out. Tears well up in her eyes.

"It's Friday, July nineteenth," I say, trying to help. "Do you know the name of the month you moved here?"

She nods and slips her thumb out of her mouth to answer me. Oh, how I want that thumb to stay out of her mouth! I imagine her mother does too, and for the first time since my phone rang, I see the mother as a human being. Not a very good human being, though. "June."

"Where did you move from?"

"Cincinnati."

What a big word to come out of her! My hand automatically spells it. Her eyes widen.

"I spell words with my fingers," I say. "I just spelled *Cincinnati.* See?" I hold up my hand, spell *Cincinnati* again. "I can spell your name, too, with my hand, but I'm not sure how you spell it. Can you tell me?"

Along with the invariable nod, she spells her name. "L-a-r-i-s-s-a."

I spell it with my fingers, saying the letters as I go. "And your last name?"

"Benton." She slips up onto the couch, scrunching up into the farthest corner.

I spell out *Benton.* She squints one eye, doubting me. "I can sign words too. You are a *girl.*" I sign *girl,* my thumb tracing the curve of my cheek. "What's your bunny's name?"

She pulls it tighter to her chest, as if I might take it from her. "Lucy."

"This is how you spell *Lucy,*" I say, and spell it out very slowly. "Would you like to try?"

She shakes her head no. At least she isn't looking at me with quite the same amount of fear now. I'm strange, but probably not going to hurt her.

It's almost five. At eight, I'm calling the police. Until then, I'll just sit here, as I told her I would. Keep her company. There doesn't seem to be a TV. Maybe in a bedroom, but I'm not going to go into a bedroom.

"This is the sign for *bunny,*" I say, and do it twice. "This is how you say, *I love my bunny.* This is how I spell my name. *Alice Marlowe,* remember?" To everything I say, she nods slowly. I keep showing her signs and making sentences with the words I've shown her. At some point while I'm showing her how to count in sign language, she lays her head against the soft curve of the couch's arm. As I'm signing *This is your apartment,* her eyes close, and she falls asleep.

I want to fall asleep myself. In my own bed. What the hell am I doing here, and where's the phone? I need to look around, see if I can find it, but what if she wakes up and I'm snooping around?

Now that I've stopped talking, I hear birds chirping madly outside. Morning is lightening the sky for real now, another day beginning—another hot day—and it feels at least eighty in this closed-in apartment. If I don't open a window, we'll suffocate.

I get up slowly so my movements won't wake Larissa. The only windows in the living room are behind the couch Larissa sleeps on, and two small, hinged windows on both sides of the fireplace that look painted shut. In the dining room, the windows don't have screens. Still, I wiggle one open a little, hoping none of the chirping birds will fly in.

I need to find the phone.

It's not in the kitchen, which is clean even though the linoleum's stained and curling up at the edges and the cupboards are nicked and scratched. I open a cupboard. There are cereal boxes and cans of soup, and in the refrigerator there's milk, butter, eggs, and covered containers. Instinct tells me to see if the stuff in the containers has gone bad so that Larissa won't get sick, but that's stupid—it's not as if she's going to be staying here alone.

Peering into the narrow hallway that leads to the bedrooms and the bathroom, I see three open doors, and once again, all the lights are on. Thank God. I'm not about to walk into a dark room hunting for a switch.

The bathroom is the first door on the right, and I only glance in. Even if I have to go, I can't imagine my going in there, closing the door behind me. What if the mother comes home while I'm in there? Of course, thinking about going to the bathroom makes me feel that I have to.

The next room on the right is obviously Larissa's. There's a toy stove made out of heavy-duty plastic, and next to it a sink to match, with an assortment of plastic plates and cups in the dish drainer. The surface of the stove and sink have been crayoned on, her name written in a waver of capital letters. There's a stack of books near the bed, *The Cat in the Hat* on top. They're still reading that? On one wall is a poster of a fish with silvery blue and purple scales. In the far corner there's a cardboard box turned upside down on top of newspapers spread out on the floor. On the box are two jars of finger paints and a sheet of

paper with a small red handprint. On the bed are stuffed animals, one a banana with a face and arms. My favorite stuffed
animal was a tiger named Tiger.

The room across the hall is her mother's, and I step into it on
tiptoes as if land mines might be buried under the floorboards.
There's the phone on the table by the bed. It's a portable, and I
pick it up, listen for a dial tone. Larissa must have called me on
this phone, but I just have to hear it, that sound that connects me
to help.

Her bed's made and the room clean, almost void of personal
effects; still there is that smell of someone else. I back out, carrying the phone, going into the more familiar dining room. All I
know about this woman now is that she has food in the refrigerator, her daughter has toys, and she keeps her place clean.

Larissa is still sleeping, and I sit back down on the wooden
chair, perched there with the phone in one hand, ready to jump
up if I hear footsteps or see the doorknob turn. The slightly
opened window in the dining room does nothing to help; there's
a sheen of perspiration on Larissa's forehead. She sleeps with her
thumb in her mouth, her legs folded up under her like a foal's.
Doesn't it hurt to sleep on those beads?

In a half hour, as my eyes begin to droop, I know I will betray her. It's a little after seven o'clock and it's day outside now.
Her mother is not returning. What else can I do? Take her home
with me?

I consider that only for a moment before I get up and go into
the kitchen, dial 911.

Chapter Five

The East Cleveland police officer sounds more than a bit confused when I explain the reason for calling. When he finally gets the facts straight—that I don't know this girl from Eve and yet I'm in her apartment—he has me give him the address and phone number and spell my name, then tells me to stay exactly where I am. Suddenly, I have become a suspicious character.

"Make sure a woman police officer comes," I say, my voice calm and authoritative, but when I hang up the phone, my hands shake. I need to wake up Larissa. It won't be good for her to be awakened by police banging on her door.

"Larissa," I say. "Larissa. You need to wake up, honey." I say this so softly she doesn't even twitch.

I don't want to touch her. I want to be able to tell the police that I never touched her. Suddenly it's clear that I'll have to answer a lot of questions—that they won't be taking this as kindly as I meant it. "Larissa, wake up, please," I say louder. "Larissa. Wake up. The police are coming."

That does it. Her eyes fly open. "No!" She takes a gasp of air. "No! No! No!" She sits up on her knees, no thumb in her mouth now.

"I had to, honey. Your mom might need some help. They can help her."

"Liar!" she spits at me. "Liar! You said you wouldn't. You said! Liar!"

She's furious, her nostrils flared, her eyes narrowed, and there is this look on her face that stuns me. She is suddenly not a child. She is just as old as I am, just as self-aware, just as smart, and she scares me; it's as if she sees me clearly and knows I'm a liar, that we both know each other very well.

"I had to," I repeat. "We need some help here. Someone who can find your mother."

She jumps off the couch and runs to the front door. "Go away! Go away now!" And now she is a child again.

I have to stay, not just because the policeman said so. If I leave, she'll lock the door and the police will have to break it down. She might even run out the back door, down the fire escape steps. "I have to stay," I say. "I have to stay and wait with you."

"No! Go away! Get out!" She points to the door, stamps a foot on the hardwood floor. "Go away now! Go away! Liar!"

"The police will help you find your mommy. Don't you want to find your mommy?"

She holds still, hearing what I said. She's only six, but she can tell I have a point. Her thumb goes into her mouth and she moves her other arm around her waist. A flash of shock goes across her face, and she looks back at the couch. I'm standing between her and her stuffed bunny, but she is not about to come anywhere near me now. I go over to the couch, pick up Lucy, and hand the bunny to her. She snatches it from me.

"Go away," she says. Plain and simple. Then she bursts into tears.

What have I done? "Oh, honey, I just want to help you. We need to find your mommy. I'm not a bad person." I kneel down, wanting to be on her level. "I'll stay with you, okay? I'll stay with you until they find your mommy. Your mommy loves you. We'll find her."

Oh Jesus. After so many years of being so careful about every word I ever use, here I tell this child that I'll stay with her until they find her mommy.

"Larissa, honey, it's okay. I'm your friend."

She's crying, her shoulders hunching up and down with her sobs. I hold out my arms. "I'll protect you," I say.

The buzzer rings, a sharp, harsh sound, startling us both. Before I know what happened, she's in my arms, the bunny pressed between us. "Don't let them in, don't let them in." Her tears are falling on my bare arms. I know better than to make any more false promises, but I hold her tightly to my chest.

"I'm your friend," I say. "No one will hurt you." *Please let that be true,* I think. I stand, still holding Larissa in my arms, and walk over to the speaker by the door.

"Hello," I say, holding down the button.

"East Cleveland Police, ma'am," a male voice answers.

I press the buzzer. "We'll be okay," I whisper to Larissa. "We'll be okay." Her skin is warm against mine. It's been a very long time since I've held anyone like this.

. . .

One of the two police officers is a woman. "Thank you," I say as I let them in.

They're both in uniform, wearing thick belts with guns and phones and nightsticks.

"I'm Officer Robert," the policeman says. "And this is Officer Shelley. You are . . ." He looks down at a pad of paper in his hand. "Ms. Alice Marlowe?" He's a large black man with a high forehead, the brim of his hat tipped backward as if it doesn't quite fit him. Officer Shelley is white. The uniform and the heavily laden belt make her look quite solid and strong.

"Yes, I am," I say. Larissa still clings to me, her face pressed into my neck. "This is Larissa Benton." I turn sideways so they can see her better, but she turns her head away. I can feel the softness of her hair against my neck, the unbraided side. *Just go away and leave us alone,* I think. *I'll take care of her.*

"Would you spell your name?"

I do. My hand wants to join in, but I'm holding Larissa. Then he asks for my address and phone number, which I give, getting more nervous. Have I broken any laws? When he asks for some identification, and I tell him that I left my purse at home, the woman police officer makes a noise in her throat. I interpret it as, *What a fool.*

"Would you tell us why you called?" Officer Robert asks. "I'm not sure I understand. You don't live here? What exactly is your relationship to this child?"

"No, I don't live here. I just gave you my address. I came here around . . ." I can't think. It seems like so long ago. "Three hours ago. I never met Larissa before." I explain about the phone call, dialing star 69, convincing Larissa I should come and be with her. The officers look at each other.

"You should have called us first," Officer Shelley says. "This was not a smart thing to do."

"I know. I know. I'm sorry. But I'm here now, and her mother hasn't shown up. She said her father's dead. Her Auntie Teya's not answering the phone. Something must be . . ." I stop what I'm about to say, which is *something must be terribly wrong*. I can feel Larissa listening, tense in my arms. Officer Robert nods, seeming to understand.

"Larissa," Officer Shelley says, softening her voice. "Could you look at me? So we can talk?"

She doesn't budge. "She's afraid of the police," I say. "She made me promise not to call, but I did."

Officer Shelley continues, ignoring me. "We need to know where your mommy went, Larissa, so we can look for her. Do you know where she went?"

She shakes her head no. I'm oddly smug that she isn't talking to them.

"She said her mother went out to look for a job. I think that was Wednesday morning, but I'm not sure."

"And you've been here all alone since your mommy left, Larissa?"

Larissa nods yes against my neck, but she still won't turn to look at them.

Officer Robert, who's been writing all this down, tucks the notepad into his back pocket. "We'll have to look around. Do you understand, Larissa? We're going to look around your place to see if there's something written down about that job—a phone number, or a name. Okay?"

She shakes her head no. She's a tough little kid.

"Well, we'll have to anyway. I'm sorry."

As they enter the interior of the apartment they move with such confidence—as if this is an ordinary thing, just part of the job. It's one of the hugest things that has ever happened to me. I want to believe it isn't ordinary.

"When was the last time you tried the aunt?" Officer Shelley asks me as she lifts papers off the dining room table. She's not looking at me, but I can tell she's talking to me just by the disdain in her voice. I am someone she can easily dismiss, just some foolish woman. I am bound and determined to prove her wrong.

"At three forty-five A.M.," I say, as if I actually know the exact time.

"And that number was?"

I tell her. I'll remember that number forever.

"The phone is?"

I point to where I left the portable by the chair. She goes to the phone and dials the number. Hangs up. "Do you have any idea where your auntie is, Larissa?"

A shake of her head. My arms are beginning to ache. I lean back against the surface of the dining room table, thankful for its thick legs.

"Will you please talk to the police officers?" I say softly to Larissa. "They're just trying to help you."

Another no against my neck. I hold her as they look around, go into the bedrooms and the bathroom. "It's okay," I whisper to Larissa. Whispering feels like we're in a conspiracy. I say it louder. "It's okay."

Finally Officer Robert approaches us and smiles gently, tilting his head, trying to get a look at Larissa then shrugging as if it doesn't matter—he can do his job, even if he doesn't know what she looks like. She's beautiful, I want to say.

"Nothing." He shrugs his large shoulders. "No phone book,

names on papers. We haven't gone through the unopened boxes, and we're not going to do that. We'll have to canvass the apartment building, see if her neighbors know something. It may take a while. You'll stay here?"

"Yes. Of course."

"We'll be back as soon as we can, but you might want to sit down."

I smile at him, grateful for a little consideration. "I will. Thank you."

"Larissa," he says, tugging at his ear. "Do you know any of the neighbors?"

She shakes her head no.

"Thought not," he says, but nicely. The police officers leave. I can hear them knocking on doors.

Carefully, still holding Larissa, I move back into the living room and look out the window over the couch, hoping to see a woman running down the sidewalk toward this apartment building, worried and terrified. I want her to be terrified. Plenty of cars, but no black woman running toward home. I turn around and sit on the couch, shifting Larissa so she's on my lap when I sit down. "They're going to help us," I say. *Us?* How did this child and I become *us?*

Larissa slides off my lap and moves over on the couch, back to her corner, chin up, thumb in mouth, Lucy tucked to her chest. She won't look my way when I speak to her. A little more than twenty minutes later, the police officers come back. They knock on the door, and I get up to let them in. When I turn back from the door, Larissa is standing right behind me and I nearly trip over her. I offer out my arms, but she steps back one step. She doesn't want to be picked up, but she wants to be near me in case she needs to be picked up, and then I'm the best bet going.

"We didn't find out anything helpful," Officer Robert says. Sweat trickles down from his hairline and he swipes it away. "The neighbors say Mrs. Benton and Larissa moved in less than a month ago. That they kept to themselves. No one remembers any visitors, anything out of the ordinary. We'll have to contact Children and Family Services."

"And that means?"

"They'll come here, pick up Larissa, and place her in temporary custody of the county. She needs to be someplace safe while we look for her mother."

"I could take her to my house," I offer, knowing they won't let me.

Officer Robert smiles kindly. "Sorry, Ms. Marlowe, we can't let you do that. I understand how you feel, but that would be impossible."

"I know," I say. I don't want him to think I'm stupid.

"We'll just make that phone call?"

"Yes. Okay." I move so he can get by me to the phone. Officer Shelley stays right by the door, as if she's guarding it.

Larissa doesn't move. She stands in her place, glaring at Officer Robert, then at me. "I hate you," she says. I think it's Officer Robert she means. He takes the phone into the kitchen. I hear, "Abandoned . . . This lady . . . No one knows . . ."

"They're sending someone out," he says when he comes back in. "They should be here soon. You can go now. She'll be safe with us."

I freeze. I can't just leave. I promised her. I look at Officer Robert. "Can I stay? You can see she trusts me. I'm a familiar face. Can't I stay?"

Officer Robert waits a beat, then nods.

"Christ," Officer Shelley says under her breath, but loud enough for me to hear.

"Thank you," I say to Officer Robert. Then, "Can I ask another favor?"

He cocks his head. "Such as?"

"Would you watch her while I go to the bathroom?"

He laughs. "Yes. Certainly, go right ahead."

I don't sit down on the toilet, just crouch above it as if I'm in a public restroom. I wash my hands, but am too afraid to dry them on the green hand towel, even though it looks perfectly clean, so I wipe them on my slacks. The shower has a glass door, slightly ajar, and I peek behind it. What if her mother is dead in there, and no one knows?

Then, very quietly, I open the cabinet above the sink. There are all the normal things one might find, and some pill bottles. None are facing out and I'm afraid to touch them. The police might fingerprint the apartment and I'm obviously a bit suspect already. Still, I can see a bit of the label and can tell they're CVS bottles. Just like mine. I might have seen this woman at CVS, seen Larissa. Two people who meant absolutely nothing to me. Who could imagine that right now I really *do* want to grab Larissa and run?

I did an interpreting job down at Children and Family Services once. I interpreted for a deaf mother who lost temporary custody of her child. Temporary turned out to be more than two years. Maybe if I'd stayed out of it, Larissa would have reached her aunt today. Which makes me think; maybe as soon as they find her aunt, they'll let Larissa stay with her. The idea of foster homes sends a shiver up my spine.

I come out to find Larissa standing just outside the bathroom.

I walk over to the wooden chair where I sat all morning, and she follows me.

"Would you like to sit in my lap?" I ask.

Of course she shakes her head no.

"She can talk," I tell Officer Robert and Officer Shelley, who stand in the dining room. "She's quite bright." I feel like I'm bragging about my own child, and blush. I'm so hot, I think I might pass out. I've never fainted in my life.

"Would you like to sit down?" I ask them.

"I'm going back out to the cruiser," Officer Robert says. "But Officer Shelley will stay here with you."

She pulls out a chair from the table, turns it toward the front door, and sits down, legs splayed out, feet firmly on the ground. She doesn't even look my way. Officer Robert leaves, giving me a nod. He's okay. I'm the one who asked for a woman officer.

We wait.

I want coffee so bad, I can taste the absence of it in my mouth. And I'm hungry. I want Children and Family Services to come soon, and I hope they won't come at all. Larissa sits on the couch and looks at me, not glaring now; she has a pleading look that makes me sick to my stomach.

If her aunt can't take her, I will.

Chapter Six

The buzzer rings and I stand, but Officer Shelley shakes her head; answering the door is no longer my job—if I ever thought it was. The woman from Children and Family Services comes in and shows the policewoman her badge, then asks Officer Shelley to sign a piece of paper on her clipboard. When they're done with the formalities, they both walk into the living room.

Larissa is pressed against the back of the couch, knees drawn up.

The woman looks at Larissa, then nods to me. "I'm Yolanda Walker, social worker with CFS." She's black and probably in her early thirties. Her hair lies against her head in flattened waves, and her makeup is precisely painted on; her lips outlined, a careful sweep of eyeliner, a perfect swatch of blush. She carries a clipboard and a white canvas bag with the words *Department of Children and Family Services* written on it in stark blue letters.

"I'm Alice Marlowe," I say.

"Yes, I know. And this must be Larissa. Hello, Larissa." Larissa glowers at the social worker. "I'm Mrs. Walker. I'm here to take you to a safe place, where there are people who can help you."

"Go away."

Yolanda Walker kneels down in front of Larissa. In her pressed black pants and fitted jacket, her pressed hair and perfect nails, she looks polished, almost glossy, but her voice is kind. "I know this must be very hard for you, Larissa, but you can't stay here without an adult. You must have been a little scared, being here all by yourself. We don't want you to be scared. We want to help you. Are there some special things you want to bring along? If you show me your favorite clothes, we'll bring those, and you'll feel more comfortable."

"Go away. I hate you."

The social worker smiles gently at Larissa, as if this is just what she expected. She doesn't seem to take it personally that Larissa hates her.

"I'm sorry, Larissa, but you'll have to come with me. It's the law, but it's also because we care about you. Can you show me your room, please, so we can find some of your favorite things to bring along?"

"Go away!" Larissa's close to tears, but she looks too mad to cry.

"Her room's this way," Officer Shelley says, pointing to the hallway.

Mrs. Walker smiles a little less gently at the policewoman. "All right, thank you." She turns back to Larissa. "I guess I'll just have to go and see what I can find by myself. Looks like you have your favorite bunny right there."

Larissa curls into a ball around the stuffed rabbit and tucks her head down.

"Oh, Larissa, I don't want to take your bunny. You hold on to it while I find you some clothes. You can stay in your pajamas if you like." She stands up, unfolding from her kneeling position with ease. She and Officer Shelley disappear into the hallway.

"I'm so sorry," I say to the curled shape of Larissa.

She doesn't tell me to go away.

When Yolanda Walker comes back into the living room carrying the canvas bag now filled with Larissa's clothes, Officer Shelley heads straight for the front door.

"Time to go." Sweat beads on her forehead. It's so hot in here it makes me queasy thinking of Larissa waiting for days in this sweltering apartment for her mother.

Where *is* her auntie? Has this girl's whole family fallen right off the face of the earth?

"Could I talk to you just a minute?" I ask the social worker, tilting my head toward the kitchen.

She looks at me for a moment. "Certainly."

"I'll be right back," I tell Larissa.

"Look," I say when we get into the kitchen. "Maybe I've gotten involved when I shouldn't have, but I'm here now. Can I come along with you, wherever you're taking her? Please? I think she trusts me. I could help, any way you want."

She studies me for a while, thinking. She has a patient air of authority, that take-charge attitude I admire in a woman. In men, it always seems arrogant.

"All right," she says, nodding slowly. "*If* Larissa agrees. We'll be going to the hospital for an examination. If you want to come along and wait with us in the waiting room, that'll be fine. It can be a long wait, we won't be a priority. You'll have to stay out in the waiting room while she's examined."

"Yes, of course."

"After, you can come with us downtown, but you'll have to say good-bye to her there. You can't come into child care. No one can. Not even her mother."

"Thank you." I sound a bit weepy. I'm bone tired, emotionally exhausted, and I should go home, but I haven't done anything I ought to yet; why start now?

I feel Vince grin.

Oh, shut up, I tell him.

"It's up to Larissa," she reminds me.

"I know." I'm betting that Larissa's agreeing will not be the biggest problem in the next few minutes.

I'm right. She won't move, no matter how many kind words Yolanda Walker uses. Even the offer of my coming along has no effect. Larissa stays balled up, coiled like a snake. Finally, when Yolanda tries to take Larissa's hand, Larissa kicks her right in the crotch. I don't think Larissa was aiming for that particular spot; it's just blind luck. Yolanda gasps and bends over double. This pisses off Officer Shelley to no end.

"Enough of this. You will have to vacate the apartment now."

Vacate? What kind of word is that for a six-year-old?

Larissa glares at us from under one arm. I decide I'll wait for someone else to try to pick her up. Officer Shelley decides that will be her.

"We can't wait here all day. I'm sorry, either you get up off the couch and walk out of the apartment with us, or I'll have to carry you."

"Fuck you," Larissa says.

That stops us all dead. I quickly cover my mouth with my hand. I don't want Larissa to see me smile. Officer Shelley doesn't think it so funny. More quickly than I thought possible, considering all that equipment and heavy clothing, she grabs Larissa and picks her up, managing to wrap one arm around both of Larissa's drawn-up legs so she can't kick out. The officer's other arm comes around Larissa's shoulder, holding down at least one of her arms. The arm not held down is holding Lucy.

A look of horror crosses Larissa's face, understanding that if she uses her free hand to fight back, she'll lose Lucy. Still, she struggles, shaking her head and screaming, a wail of no's and sobs so painful it catches my breath.

"Careful," Mrs. Walker says to Officer Shelley. "Careful. Don't hurt her. Oh, Larissa, it's all right. It's okay. We'll take good care of you."

Officer Shelley begins walking toward the front door, and Larissa's screams get louder. It has to hurt the policewoman's ears. "No! No! No! Go away! Go away! I hate you!" Her words are shouted through sobs, and tears run down my face.

"Get the door," Officer Shelley orders, and Yolanda Walker does, balancing her clipboard and the canvas bag in one hand. I haven't moved since Larissa started screaming, but now I force myself to follow them. Mrs. Walker closes the apartment door behind us, turning to tape something on the outside of the door. Larissa's screams echo loudly, the acoustics of the stairwell trapping the sound and amplifying it. Her cries are making it hard for me to breathe. I stumble, stepping on something soft. It's Lucy, the bunny. Larissa has dropped Lucy—or did Officer Shelley tear it from her hands in retribution for Larissa breaking her eardrums? I pick up Lucy and continue down, holding on to the banister as if at any moment I might fall.

At the bottom of the stairwell we get blocked inside by an elderly man trying to open the door from the other side of the foyer. Officer Shelley stands at the bottom of the stairs next to Mrs. Walker, who is trying to tell the startled old man to back up, but he's alarmed by Larissa's screaming. Maybe he thinks we're kidnapping her. He probably can't see the police officer's uniform through the frosted door with Yolanda Walker standing there.

Just as Yolanda pushes the door open, causing the old man to back up while shouting, "Stop that, leave that girl alone," I reach out to hand Larissa back her bunny. She twists, turns, and throws herself into my arms. Suddenly I'm holding Larissa and her bunny. Officer Shelley must have lost her grip in the confusion. As we walk out of the apartment I am carrying Larissa, who now sobs against my shoulder.

Tears run down my cheeks but I can't wipe them off. I've never held anyone so tightly in my arms before. As we walk toward the street, I wonder which is Yolanda Walker's car, and if Larissa and I can get one seatbelt around the both of us.

My car has a ticket.

I leave the car there. I don't even mention to anyone that it's my car. They can tow it if they want. It's just a car.

The wait at the hospital is forever. There are so many people that we're lucky to find two chairs together. Larissa falls asleep in my arms, and as uncomfortable as I am in this too-small, molded plastic chair, there's a physical and mental warmth from holding Larissa that feels so good, I don't ever want it to stop.

"If the police can't find her mother," I whisper to Mrs. Walker over the top of Larissa's head, "what will happen to her?"

"She'll be placed in a foster home," she whispers back. "As a matter of fact, she'll probably be placed in a foster home in the next few hours."

"Then what? What if they do find her mother?"

She leans her head toward mine. She wears some kind of perfume. I haven't worn perfume since I was in my early twenties, so I don't know what kind it is, but her perfume, the hospital odors, and the warm smell of a child in my arms disorient me. Is it really me sitting here?

"It goes like this," Yolanda Walker says. "As soon as we took her from her home, temporary emergency custody went into effect. In the next seventy-two hours we'll have to go to court, ask the judge to agree to put her into emergency custody, which he will unless Larissa's mother has been found and has a damn good excuse for abandoning her, such as she's in the hospital comatose, or was kidnapped." Her tone is not sympathetic. It sounds as if Yolanda Walker doesn't think Larissa's mother will turn up with a damn good excuse.

"After that," she continues, "Larissa will be appointed a guardian ad litem—a lawyer who will act only in the child's best interests—and in about three weeks, there's a hearing with the magistrate, the GAL, the assistant prosecutor from CFS, me, and Mom, if she's found. Mom can also have her own lawyer. Then the magistrate will proceed with the case. Amendments can be made, legal custody can be awarded, whatever needs to be done at that time. It's possible even if Mom is found that she won't come to the hearing. It happens more than you'd think." All this is said flatly, as if she's been over this a thousand times.

"What will her mother have to do to get her back?"

"Parenting classes, counseling, a drug abuse program, whatever the judge decides she has to do to prove to the county she's a fit mother. It could take six months to a year. If she doesn't comply, in a year there's another hearing, and Larissa could go up for adoption."

"She has an aunt," I say. "Maybe she'll take her?"

"She could. A child always goes to a relative first, before another party, unless there's some reason not to."

"A reason? Like what?"

She presses two fingers to her temple. "Lots of reasons. If her aunt has a history of child abuse, endangering, a drug or alcohol problem. Or something beyond her control. A high-rise where the lease specifies no children. Something like that."

All around us are mothers with their children, waiting for the doctor. I've been here before, interpreting. I always came down with a cold the next day. "Let's say the aunt can't take her. Can I? Can I be her foster parent, while her mother takes those courses?"

She almost smiles. Just the corner of her mouth turns up. Adjusting herself in her seat, she says, "You could apply to be an interested individual. If the aunt can't take her, they might let you, seeing she has a connection to you already. They'd have to do a background check and take your fingerprints. You'd have to take foster parenting classes."

"I could actually do this?"

She nods.

"I want to do that, then. That interested individual thing. If her aunt doesn't take her." I pause, feeling the weight of Larissa in my lap. She breathes with her mouth open, her thumb nearby. "I hope her aunt can take her, or that her mother shows up with a damn good excuse, for Larissa's sake. But if not, if she has to go to a foster home, I want to be it. I want to apply."

"When you get home, call and they'll get you started."

"And you'll be her social worker?"

"For about the first thirty days. I can try to keep her under my care for a bit longer than that, but not much."

"She won't get lost in the system?"

She starts to say something, then stops. "No. That won't happen." I nod, taking her answer for what it's worth.

Finally they call Larissa's name. Mrs. Walker stands up and holds out her arms. I am to hand Larissa over, and wait here. As the social worker carries her away, Larissa wakes and begins to struggle again. "No! No! No! Let me go!" I'm glad I'm not the one carrying her in for her exam, to some strange doctor undressing her, nurses holding her down. By the time they come back, more than a half hour later, Larissa is as limp as her stuffed bunny. She's wearing a pair of white tennis shoes. Mrs. Walker must have put them on Larissa in the exam room, when she finally quit struggling.

She hands Larissa back to me. Larissa doesn't protest. Her face is wet with tears, her cheeks flushed. My hands are occupied, holding Larissa, or I would wipe away her tears. I need three hands. Not the first time I've thought that.

Larissa seems lighter now, so slight. As I place her in the backseat and buckle her up, she looks dazed and withdrawn. Is this the same little girl who said *Fuck you* to a cop? I sit next to her, but I doubt she even notices.

We drive off to Children and Family Services.

Chapter Seven

Children and Family Services is a long, low building with three floors of flesh-colored bricks and unbroken rows of dark glass windows. Those windows don't seem to let anything in, or out. The overall impression is so stark. Couldn't they put some smiley-face stickers on those windows? Balloons? Bunny faces? "You won't be able to stay long," Yolanda says, as we walk to the building from her car. "But while you're here, you'll need a name tag."

Larissa holds my hand. I don't think she knows whose hand she's holding. The street is busy. She holds someone's hand. It just happens to be mine.

The sign-in desk and waiting area are in a large, open atrium, sunlight streaming through the upper windows. A red carpet leads up to the sign-in desk, which seems a bit much. This is not a red carpet event. To the right of the desk is a bronze life-size statue of a woman holding a large bat, which on a closer look turns out to be a sheaf of rolled paper. Larissa doesn't even glance that way. For the best, I think.

Yolanda Walker signs me in and hands me a badge with my name on it. "I need to place Larissa in child care while I find her a temporary foster home. It's just down the hall. You can walk with us."

"Can I sit with her, just a little, try talking to her?"

"Not in child care," Yolanda says, looking down the hall. She holds herself so straight; she looks like someone who walked around with a book on her head, like someone who wanted to be Miss America. "The waiting room. For a few minutes."

The chairs in the waiting room have cushioned seats and backs with the look of red leather. I suppose they don't want upset parents fidgeting around in uncomfortable plastic chairs. I sit down and tug gently on Larissa's hand. She sits down next to me.

There are a few groups of people, mostly women with young children. They look tired, as if it isn't morning at all but the end of a long day.

"Larissa," I say, keeping my voice low. "I have to break my promise. I can't stay with you until they find your mommy. I shouldn't have promised you that. I'm sorry."

Nothing. Not a blink or a frown.

"Mrs. Walker seems like a nice lady. She's your social worker. She'll take good care of you, I'm sure she will. It's her job to take good care of little kids like you. And the police are looking for your mommy. You're not alone anymore. There are big people trying to help you now. You should let them help you. Okay?"

She doesn't say anything, but I think she's listening. When I said the word *mommy*, I saw her tense. She's tired and stunned and she isn't going to talk anymore. If she cries out for her mommy, her mommy's not going to answer, so silence is better. In a class at Gallaudet we discussed the power of words, and of silence. Those in the Deaf culture refuse to even try to speak—it would lessen the authority of their own language, their own culture. I always came down on the wrong side. Why not try? I thought. Why draw lines in the sand?

Someone up at the check-in desk shouts something. I can't make out the words, only the tone: frustration and anger. A security guard approaches the desk. The words grow louder. Something about a brother and a stolen car. "Hey, it's not my fault," the angry woman shouts. "He was with her, not me!" Now another person approaches, and more words are said, calm words. The angry woman is ushered off somewhere. Larissa hasn't looked up from her feet.

"Larissa. This is the sign for *mommy*," I say, making the sign for *mother,* an open hand, fingers spread, thumb tapping my chin. "It's a way to say *mommy,* just to yourself, and no one will know but you." She looks at me. I feel such relief in that slight movement of her head. "Like this," I say, making the sign again.

She takes her thumb out of her mouth and makes the sign, just a small motion of her hand, like a whisper. "Yes, that's it," I say with such pride, as if I'm Annie Sullivan and have just taught Helen Keller her first word. *Pull yourself together,* I tell myself.

"Deaf people have special signs for their friends and the people they love. I'll make a sign for you that only I know. You'll be an *L,* to my chest, because I care for you." I tap an *L* at my heart. She doesn't nod or smile, but she watches me. "That's my sign for you. And I can be an *A,* for Alice. It's easy. You just make a fist, with your thumb stuck up, like this, remember?" I make an *A.*

"You don't have to put the *A* to your chest for me. An *A* down to your side can be your sign for me, because I'm going to be by your side. I'm going to help you. I'm going to try very hard to help you. Do you understand?"

She just looks at me, waiting to hear what she needs to hear, not what I'm saying.

"They won't let me come into the child care room with you. It's just for very special people and very special children, but Mrs. Walker's going to help me stay in touch with you. I'll be helping you as much as I can." Polly is the assistant to the mayor, and if I have to, I'm going to use her connection. If I have to, I'll write to the president.

Yolanda Walker nods to me from across the room.

"Larissa, Mrs. Walker needs you now. I'm really sorry about all this. I know it's scary, but you're a tough girl. You're going to be fine. You have Lucy, and Mrs. Walker, and all the good, kind people here. And when you want, you can make the sign for *mommy,* and maybe that will help you too."

I don't know what else to say. I look over at Yolanda. She crooks her finger, beckoning me. I get up and go over. Larissa stays in her seat. I don't think she will refuse to get up; she just hasn't been told to do so yet.

"Thank you for giving us that time," I say.

"I have to tell you something." She glances around as if she wants to make sure that no one can hear. She looks so official in her professional clothes. I must look a mess. I run my fingers through my hair.

Yolanda Walker hands me a piece of paper. "I just want to tell you, I think you did a brave thing."

I look at her, surprised, ignoring the paper.

"No one here would tell you that," she continues, holding

my gaze. "We follow the rules, and we still screw up. But I follow them. Every day, every child, for seven years now. Sometimes the only way to get through the day is just follow the rules." She takes a breath, shakes her head.

"Anyway," she says. "I admire what you did. People give you flak for it, I just want you to know what I think. That's the number to call, to start the process we spoke of. I'll help you any way I can."

I have to swallow first. "Thank you."

"Go and say good-bye," she says. I nod and walk back over to Larissa.

Kneeling down, I say, "Good-bye, Larissa," tapping an *L* handshape at my heart. "I'll see you again." Yolanda Walker's kind words make it actually seem possible.

Larissa looks at me with half-lidded eyes, but I see in them a pleading that I can't bear. I look down at the floor. Yolanda comes over and takes Larissa's hand, gently pulling her to her feet. Larissa doesn't say good-bye, or nod, or smile at me, but as they walk away, down the wide hall with a dozen closed doors on each side, I think I see her make an *A* with her hand. That, or she just has one hand in a fist.

I walk out of the Children and Family Services building, thinking, *Where did I park my car?* Then it hits me. My car is in an illegal parking zone, miles away. I have no way home. And I don't have my purse or my cell phone.

I turn toward downtown and begin walking. Polly will be at work. It's only thirty short blocks.

I arrive at City Hall, and the guard calls up to Polly's office.

"Would you ask her to come down and meet me?" I ask, too

tired to walk another step. He nods, pointing to a bench where I can wait. I almost fall asleep in the five minutes it takes Polly to come downstairs.

"What is it?" she says, sitting down and putting one arm around my shoulder. She knows there's something very wrong, or she would never do this. Her concern makes my eyes get hot and damp.

I tell her everything in a long, confused gush of words. I keep missing parts of the story and going backward. I doubt I make much sense. She asks me several times if I'm kidding her.

"I can't believe it," she says, finally believing it. "Are you okay? I mean . . . You don't look so good."

I smile. "I'm okay. It's Larissa I'm worried about. I have to do something."

Polly stares at me over the top of her half glasses. She's the assistant to the mayor, but she has no sense of style; she wears clothes that always look as if she's gotten the wrong size by mistake. "It looks like you *did* do something. Thanks to you, that girl isn't all alone in some hot apartment. She could have gotten into all sorts of trouble. I could just kill her mother."

"She could be dead already," I remind her. "Maybe you could call the police? See what they know? Or I could call some hospitals. But I don't even know her name. Could you find out her name?" I'm trying so hard to figure out what to do next. Maybe I should go back to Children and Family Services, apply right now for that interested individual thing?

"Alice, you have to go home. Go to sleep."

"But maybe I should go back—"

"No, go home. Sleep. Things happen really slowly with this stuff. Give them some time to find her mother first."

I nod. She's right. I have to get some sleep. "Can you take me home?"

Polly looks at her watch. "Oh, God, I'm sorry, I can't. She has a meeting . . . I have to be there. I can't get out of it, Alice. I'm sorry. I'll give you money for a cab. Wait here, I've got to get my purse."

By the time she gets back, I'm asleep, my chin dropped down to my chest. When she says my name, I feel my head jerk, and open my eyes.

"Here's forty. Go home and go to sleep. Call me when you wake up. I'll get off early. I'm coming straight to your house. I'll bring pizza. You're going to have to tell me this all over, in some kind of order. You're really okay?"

"I'm fine," I say. "Nothing bad happened to me. You have to help me, though. I want to be her foster mother."

"Go home," she says. "Get some sleep."

"Doesn't Rachel leave tomorrow?"

"I'll be at your house at six. Period."

"Will you help me?"

She nods. "Go home."

I leave, and find a taxi. I go home.

In my own living room, I stop and look around, taking in the calm muted colors of the walls, the Mexican prints of horses, posters of buttes and desert landscapes, dozens of pieces of pottery I brought back from Arizona and placed in pleasing spots to tie it all together. And then there's my collection of classical music: Vivaldi, Beethoven, and Mozart, music without words so I can sit still, relax my hands and my mind. I try to imagine Larissa sitting on my couch, watching TV. Even in my own imagination she looks uncomfortable and out of place, her hands folded in her lap. This is a house that belongs only to me.

I'll buy toys. A plastic stove and sink. We can make pretend cookies. Real cookies. Put up pictures of silvery blue fish. I close my eyes. My house is so quiet. It's a morgue. Larissa will hate it.

Upstairs, I take off my clothes, put on the old, soft T-shirt I sleep in, lie down on the bed. *Well, I did it,* I think.

Proud of you, sis, Vince says.

Thanks.

Anytime.

God, Vince, I'm tired.

This ain't nothing yet, he says. I know he's smiling, wherever the hell he is. I fall asleep with a smile on my face, not sure why.

At six o'clock sharp, Polly wakes me, standing next to my bed and softly saying my name.

"Hi," I say.

"Where's your car?" she asks.

"Oh, Jesus, my car!" I sit up. "I was so tired I did just what you said. I took a taxi home. You said *go home.* I did. My car's parked in front of her apartment. Or towed."

"We'll get it back," she offers with a nod. I understand her easy nod. Getting my car back will be a whole lot easier than helping me adopt a kid.

"The pizza's on your kitchen counter. Come on."

It's white pizza with artichokes, my favorite, and I'm so glad I have a friend who knows what my favorite pizza is. I eat quickly, finishing two pieces before Polly's done with her first. I wonder if Larissa likes this kind of pizza. A pizza called *white* pizza?

"You know," Polly says, "you should have called me before you left the house."

"At three in the morning?"

"Yes, at three in the morning, or four, whatever. You shouldn't have done that alone."

"You would have gone with me?"

She laughs. "Hell, no, but I would have talked you out of it."

I'm quiet for a minute, thinking. She might have.

"You done?" she says, pointing to my plate. We're sitting at my kitchen table, the overhead fan slowly sweeping warm air around us, the smell of someone's smoky grill easing in the window. The beginning of a summer evening when mosquitoes bloom like magic in the air, carrying West Nile virus. I'll have to get plenty of insecticide. Children and older people are most prone to getting the virus. I can pretend I'm not in the latter category, but I will have to think about a six-year-old child.

"That was good. Thanks. What do I owe you?" I ask this only to be polite. She shakes her head.

"Okay, listen," she says, pushing her plate aside. "I called Children and Family Services. Larissa Benton was transferred to a foster home this afternoon."

I try to take this in. "Already?"

"Yeah. They don't want kids sitting around downtown in the child care room for too long. She's in a home. I can't tell you where. I don't know."

I nod. Polly would have spent some time finding all the facts, using her professional voice and position, but not abusing either. Just like my car. She'll make it easier for me to grease the wheels, so to speak, but I'll still pay the fine.

"What I can tell you is that her mother has been found."

I gasp. "Is she alive? Dead? What?"

"She's alive. She came down to the county building a little after they took Larissa to the foster home. She was angry, loud, and upset. Most people are. They handle that very well down there."

I remember the raised voice, the way someone was led away.

"She says she was gone only nineteen hours." Polly rolls her eyes. "As if that makes it all better."

"I thought she had been gone for two days. Why was she gone?"

"Oh, who knows. Probably she has some stupid, half-assed excuse. But she wants Larissa back."

The pizza feels heavy in my stomach. I ate too fast. "Will they give her back?"

Polly shakes her head. "No. There's a history. On file. She won't get Larissa back right away."

"What history?"

"Don't know."

"Okay. So can I get her?"

"Not without jumping through the hoops."

I think about the number Mrs. Walker gave me. Why hadn't I called the minute I got home? Where is it? I check my pocket. It's there. "Okay. How long will the hoops take me?"

"At very best, three months, maybe six. Her mother could get her back in six months, or not, depending."

"I can't wait that long, Polly. She's so little. She shouldn't be in some strange foster home."

She hesitates, and I know what she's thinking, that my home would be a strange foster home, too. But she doesn't say this. She clasps her hands together, leaning forward. "I'll help any way I can."

I say, "Thanks."

Polly drives me down to the impound lot and I get my car. By the time I get home, it's dark. There are two messages on my answering machine. The first is from the Hearing and Speech Center. I missed an appointment, an evening AA meeting I do once a month on Friday nights. I forgot all about it. Jesus, I've never done that before.

The second message is from Yolanda Walker, letting me know that Larissa is safely in a foster home and that her mother has been found.

I pick up the phone, my fingers itching to press the buttons that would call a number no longer in service. I call my parents instead. Vince would be the wrong person to call anyway. He'd have gone on and on about how fucked up the government is, how I shouldn't trust Yolanda Walker or anyone in Children and Family Services, how Larissa would be scarred for life by the process. He would have gotten so worked up, I wouldn't have been able to sleep all night.

"Hey, Dad," I say when he answers the phone. "How are you?"

"We're doing okay, honey. Is everything all right?" It's ten o'clock on a Friday night. I imagine my mother looking up from a magazine, anxious. She a worrier with her own set of fears: heights, storms, snakes, spiders, botulism, strep infections that eat away at your flesh, and a whole set of fears for her children. During one visit home, in the mid-eighties—I was over thirty years old—she had me swear on her grandfather's Bible that I would always use a seatbelt.

"I'm fine, Dad. Just fine."

"Good. I'm glad to hear that. Your mother wants to talk to you. I'll let her tell you."

"What? Tell me what?" But he's already handed the phone over.

"Alice, is everything all right?"

"I'm fine, Mother," I say. "What do you have to tell me?"

"The boys are coming for Labor Day. Friday through Tuesday. I was going to call you tomorrow. You can come, can't you?"

"Really? She's letting them come?" I haven't seen Vince's kids since his funeral. We thought they were coming for the Fourth of July, but Cindy changed her mind at the last minute, and it really upset my parents. My father actually called her a fool. Fool is the worst thing he ever calls anyone, but when he says *fool*, it sounds as bad as any swear word I ever use.

"We got the tickets the minute she said yes. We had to pay fifty dollars each, just to change those old ones! Your father told her if she changed her mind this time, he was making her pay us the hundred dollars, plus the price of the tickets. Oh, Alice, you'll come, won't you? We haven't all been together since . . ."

"I know, Mom. I'll be there. Absolutely. I'd love to see them."

"It will be wonderful to all be together again," she says sadly. *Wonderful* is relative now. All sorts of words have different meanings since Vince got killed. "Now why are you calling so late at night? Tell me, are you all right? Has something happened?"

I can't tell her. She'll be so upset, I'll never get off the phone, and she'll call me every day for weeks. "I'm fine, Mom. Really. Just thought I'd call. How's Daddy? Is he okay?" Ever since Vince died, my father's been drinking more, berating himself for selling the hardware store instead of letting Vince take it over. But True Hardware paid good money for it, and Vince would have only driven it further into the ground. It was the right decision, but you can't tell him that now. If Vince had been at the hardware store, he wouldn't have been in Akron, walking across that street.

"Yes," she says. "He's doing fine." Her tone says she knows exactly what I'm asking, and I shouldn't be. My father's drinking is not my business. "Now, what's happening with you? Tell me."

We talk about my job, the weather, her arthritis, my dad's podiatry appointment, what we'll cook for Labor Day. We talk for a half an hour. The world is not such a bad place. I'll show Larissa what a wonderful place it really is.

The next morning I call the number Yolanda gave me, and tell them I want to become a foster parent. They say they'll send me some paperwork.

"If I wanted to get started right away," I say, "what should I do?" The woman tells me where to go to for foster parenting classes. "Start there," she says. "I'll let them know you're coming. You'll need to take all eight classes." I thank her. Eight classes, each offered twice a week. The first class I can get to is Tuesday morning. That means it will take me four and a half weeks.

I stay as busy as I can. I go to Pilates class Saturday morning, keep digging in my backyard all afternoon, and go to a play with two of my deaf friends Saturday night. Sunday morning I mix in peat and fertilizer, completely frustrated that I'm supposed to wait a few more days to plant anything, then plant half the perennials anyway. Sunday night I go to my book group and nod as everyone says what they think. I'm having a hard time even remembering the author. Monday I interpret at a seminar on "improving your self-worth through imaging," which takes up half the day and pays really well, then teach a class at the Hearing and Speech Center from seven to nine.

Tuesday morning, I drive to my first foster parenting class.

Chapter Eight

The classes are held in a tiny one-story church in Euclid, right off State Route 2. The building sits like a hatbox surrounded by a large, almost empty parking lot.

Inside, the chapel is modern and light. I sign in at a card table, and the woman sitting behind it hands me a stack of papers and tells me to take a seat down front.

There are nine other people in the chapel, clumped in groups of twos and threes. I sit by myself in the fourth row as more people arrive, no one hurrying much. At the head of the aisle is an easel with a large pad of paper. Printed in capital letters are the words CULTURAL ISSUES IN PLACEMENT.

An extremely thin woman wearing a lavender skirt, a lavender blouse, and matching lavender shoes, walks up to the easel and in a loud, friendly voice introduces herself as Julia. "Hello, and welcome." Some people say hello back. By now there are at least two dozen people in the room, with more still straggling in. Besides me and Julia in her lavender outfit, there are only two other white people.

"What *is* culture?" Julia asks as people take their seats. "What does that word mean to you?" She isn't asking this rhetorically. She looks at us expecting an answer. Not getting one, she points to a man in the front row. "Come on," she says. "Name me one component of culture."

"Music," he says.

"Good!" She points to the person next to him. "You?"

"Religion?"

"Yes, certainly religion. Thank you. Next?"

Her pointing finger is getting closer. I think about what to say. When she gets to me, no one has taken my answer. "Language and dialect."

"Good!" she says. She writes all these words down on the pad. "Now," she says, "we need to talk about these things. They will all have an impact on your foster child."

She forms us into groups of six and gives each group a particular aspect of culture to discuss. Our group gets *family rules and codes of conduct*. For fifteen minutes we are to share our own family stories about how we were disciplined, the standards our parents expected from us, what our own standards of discipline are, and whether these would be appropriate for our foster child.

A woman holding the hand of the man who came in with her says that in her family, children never talked back. "We gave our elders respect. Our parents raised us that way. Not like children today. But I'd expect respect from my foster child. I'd like a little one. Raise him right." One man shares a story about his father using a belt, and a few people nod. Afraid to seem stand-offish,

I tell them that my father never used a belt, but he'd been firm. "I never talked back to him," I say, knowing that I had.

"You can't touch a foster child," says the man who told the story about his father beating him with a belt. "No matter what they do."

I didn't know that. Does that also mean I can't hug her? I know teachers can't hug students anymore. I don't ask, afraid to look stupid.

After this, Julia opens up the discussion to the whole group. We talk about how foster children might have different religions, expect different foods, different family rules. I don't know what religion Larissa is. I was brought up Protestant, but no longer go to church. What if Larissa is a Muslim? Or a Jehovah's Witness? All this talk is making me feel less capable, not more.

After a quick break, Julia hands out clear plastic cups to everyone, then gives one person in each group a container of small colored beads. White beads, black beads, red, yellow, blue, green, and purple beads. She writes on the sheet of white paper which race each color bead represents.

"Okay, listen up, now," she says. "I'm going to ask you a series of questions. For each answer, pick the *one* bead that represents your answer. Ready?" There are some murmurs of yes, and then she begins.

"You are?"

It takes a moment for some of us to understand. One by one each person in our group picks a bead. Five black beads, then I pick out a white bead and drop it in my cup.

"Your immediate family?" Once again, five black beads, and one white: me.

"Your spouse or partner? If you're single, your last relationship." White bead.

"Your co-workers? Pick the bead that represents the majority."
Some interpreters are black, but most are white. White bead.
"Your boss?" White bead.
"Your teachers." White bead.
"Your principal." White bead.
"Your friends."
I want to ask if there is a bead to represent the Deaf culture.
Then I can pick a bead that isn't white. I put a white bead in
my cup.
"Your doctor?" White bead.
"Your dentist? White bead.
"Your hairdresser?" White bead.
"The authors of the books you read?" White bead.
The questions go on. I fill up my cup with white beads.
All the other people in my group have a mixture of colors in
their cups. They look at me and I lower my cup into my lap. I
want to run out of the room.
Julia talks about our cups, how we may need to broaden our
cultural lenses. She speaks about avoiding ethnocentrism, helping children develop a positive racial identity, but as hard as I try
to listen, as much as I need to listen, I'm looking at my cup of
white beads. I can't do this. I can't come back to this class again.

That afternoon, I call Yolanda Walker at work. "How is she?
Can you just tell me if she's okay?"
"You're still applying to be her foster parent, right?"
"I went to a class this morning," I tell her, feeling a tightness
in my chest. I can't do this. I won't be any good at this at all.
"I've finished the paperwork. It's in the mail."

"Okay, I'm talking to you as an interested individual." She isn't whispering, but her voice is low. I listen carefully. She tells me that the judge agreed Larissa needed to be in care of the county. The aunt wanted to get Larissa moved to her care, but couldn't. She'd been in the hospital for diabetes during the time of the "incident of abandonment," and would be off her feet for at least a month, and she only has one bedroom anyway. Larissa's mother had shown up at the hearing, quite angry. "She called me a bitch," Yolanda says. "What, she thinks we should just let her daughter sit there, alone, till she decides to come home? You don't call me a bitch and get my sympathy. There'll be another hearing in a few weeks, concerning temporary custody and Larissa's mother's case plan. Then we'll see what she's made of, if she shows up."

"I'm sorry she said that to you," I offer.

"Yeah, well *she* will be too." She pauses. "I never said that."

"Fine with me."

"Stick with the classes. I'll see what I can do here to speed up your home visit."

"Thank you, Yolanda. Thank you. And please, how is she?"

"She's sad," Yolanda says. "At least she's still got emotions."

I do go back to the foster parenting class a week later, hoping no one will remember me, but they do, smiling and nodding, asking how I am. "Fine," I say. "How are you?" The woman who was holding the man's hand last week tells me she's taking in twin girls next week. This is her last class.

"I'm a twin," I tell her, the words catching in my chest. "That's really great, your taking them in."

"Oh my," she says. "Sit next to me. Tell me all about it. I need to know more about twins. God sent you to me today. Jeffery couldn't come. Sit with me."

By the end of class, she's holding my hand. "That poor Vince," she says. "That poor boy. I know you loved him. I know that. He's with God now. You can be sure of that."

Obviously she didn't listen to a word you said, Vince says.

"I'm sure you're right," I tell her. "Thank you."

"Well, I won't see you next week, but you be good now. You take care of yourself. I'll be praying for you. You'll make a good foster mother, I can see that. I certainly can."

She's very kind to say so. The class was on separation and attachment impact, and the more I learn, the more worried I get. At night, as I fall asleep, I list the reasons I should do this, *could* do this. During the daytime, my life fills in. I agree to jobs, parties, a concert with Polly and her husband, a day hike in the Allegheny Mountains. I can't stop living, waiting for Larissa. The first Sunday in August, I invite three interpreters over for chicken marseilles, risotto, and grilled vegetables. I buy a lemon meringue pie. We laugh and network, talk about movies and books. I never mention Larissa. That night, before I go to bed, I plan my next dinner, whom I'll ask, what I'll make, but I'm making two sets of plans now. I live one life in the daytime, but at night I never go to sleep without imagining Larissa. It is not her face I see, but her hair, and her small feet, her wet wrinkled thumb, her hand in a fist by her side. I am afraid that I have forgotten her face, but I haven't forgotten what it felt like to hold her.

One night Polly calls to tell me that her mother has some kind of viral infection, something no one can diagnose. Polly's going to

Massachusetts to visit her for a few days. "Tell her I said hi," I say. "Call me as soon as you get back."

Thursday, August eighth, almost three weeks after Larissa called my house looking for her aunt, Yolanda calls me.

"Alice, there's a problem. Larissa's not talking. To anyone. She won't talk to me, her mother, her foster mother, or any of the children in the home. This kind of thing happens, but it seldom lasts this long. It's causing some resentment in the home she's placed in. Her foster mother's asking for a transfer. It'll be brought up at the hearing on Tuesday at the magistrate's office."

I think about what she just said. She's telling me this for a reason. "If you're going to move her, can she come here?" I ask. "The home study is in two and a half weeks. I've gone to four classes. I've missed a few."

"It's probably too early for that, but if we know you're interested, we may be able to hold off the transfer until you're ready. Would you consider a visit with Larissa? I'm thinking you might be less threatening than I am, less emotionally disrupting than her mother, and you have experience in communication, right?"

"Yes. I do."

"So you would visit with her?"

"Yolanda, I'd love to see her."

"Thought so. I mentioned you to the foster mother. She said I could give you her home phone number. You call her and make an appointment to come by."

"Oh, God, thank you!" I sit down on my kitchen chair. Outside it's raining. It hasn't rained for weeks.

"Listen, Alice. This is not standard procedure. Even Larissa's mother doesn't go to the foster home. Visitations are at the Metzenbaum Center, not foster homes. This visit is a privilege you need to respect. The foster mother asks you to leave, you leave. She doesn't want you to come again, you never call back. Do I have your word on this?"

"Absolutely."

"If you can get her to talk, it would be great."

"I'll try."

"And, Alice, one more thing. Because we might have to transfer Larissa, I'm going to suggest that you come to the hearing Tuesday as an interested individual. The magistrate might say no, but I think she'll say you can come in. You should be there just in case. We should have your criminal background check done by then. So, next Tuesday. Eight-thirty?"

"Where do I go?"

"The hearing's at Juvenile Court, Twenty-second and Cedar. And Alice, if your visit with Larissa goes well, we could ask her foster mother to speak up on your behalf. But even if the magistrate goes for it, things don't happen right away. Nothing here happens right away. Larissa's in the system now. You understand?"

"Yes. I do. Can I call this woman now?"

She gives me the name and number, then pauses. "I won't be there, Alice. It will be a visit outside the system, just between you and the foster parent. But if it goes badly, I'll get the blame."

"It'll go well," I say. "I promise."

"Then I'll see you Tuesday morning at court."

I sit at the kitchen table, tracing my fingernail along the wood grain. Outside, the ground is so hard that the rain bounces back up like hail. Rainwater runs in a river down my driveway and out to the street, spilling into sewers. Once, after a hard rain like this, I found a wet, frightened rat in my basement. I called the animal warden, but by the time he came, the rat couldn't be found. He said it probably went back down through the toilet in the basement, the way it must have come in. I had the toilet removed and the pipe capped. How far back would they check?

I take a deep breath and call Larissa's foster mother.

Chapter Nine

I go to visit Larissa the next day, following a long morning interpreting for deaf parents of a hearing child who's enrolling in the
Cleveland Heights school system. I make mistakes as I interpret,
and have to apologize several times. This is the school system
Larissa will be in if I get Larissa. It's August ninth. Might I get
her before school begins? What grade will she be going into?

The houses on 116th where Larissa's foster mother lives are
much like those in my own neighborhood, but on a smaller scale,
older homes with front porches and meager lawns, the houses
built close together. Women chat from their porches and children
run across lawns. Like my own, except every face I see is black.

In the late-morning sunlight children play in the street, riding
scooters, tossing a ball. I have to drive carefully, and still I hit a
pothole the size of Kansas. Something in my car clunks loudly.
At least I have an old car, I think, as if that might make me fit in

better. Actually, most of the cars parked on the street are bigger and newer than mine.

I find the address. It's a side-by-side, dark blue with white trim, and a trellis of pink roses across one side of the porch. There's a bright yellow plastic slide on the small front lawn, and a few toy trucks. I think about my upside down frog sprinkler. Maybe Larissa will like that?

On the porch is a black woman holding a baby. She's talking with an elderly man who leans against a post. Walking up the front walk, I clutch my purse under my arm as if someone might run right by and grab it from me.

"Hello," I say, standing at the bottom of the steps. "Mrs. Hunt? I'm Alice Marlowe?"

"Yes. I imagine you are," she says with a chuckle and a glance over at the older man. She has deep wrinkles around her eyes, and a line of small moles across her throat like a necklace. The baby in her arms is no more than a few months old.

"Come on in," she says, opening her front door.

"Good morning, miss," the elderly man says, tipping his hat as I walk by. I say hello, then follow Mrs. Hunt inside.

The front door leads directly into a small living room with dark wood paneling on the walls and heavy drapes over the windows. A fan on a tall stand rotates back and forth slowly, blowing warm air against my face. It takes a moment for my eyes to adjust from the bright light outside. In a corner, a TV flickers, the sound turned down low. In another corner is a playpen with a toddler peeking above the netting. "Up," the child says, raising its chubby arms toward Mrs. Hunt. The room has an odor I can't quite place.

"Just a minute, baby," Mrs. Hunt says. "Larissa, Mrs. Marlowe's here." She turns toward the corner by the door we came through, and before I can tell her it's *Miss,* not *Mrs.,* I see Larissa. She's curled up in a plaid recliner, her knees to her chin, wearing her pink pajamas, no slippers. It's almost noon. *I'd have her dressed by now,* I think. Lucy is in her arms, one soft ear lying against Larissa's cheek. She looks up at me and her eyes widen for just a moment, then she quickly looks down again as if she got caught doing something she shouldn't. Her hair has been unbraided. It's so thick that even tied back with a rubber band, it flies out all over, framing her face like a fuzzy halo.

She looks all right, not harmed in any obvious way. Driving here, I imagined her with a cast on her arm, a black eye, a dazed look, as if the harm of living in a foster home would be physical as well as mental. Not that any of the people I met at foster parenting classes were bad people, but I couldn't help thinking the way I always had about foster homes.

"I told her you were coming," Mrs. Hunt says. "I don't know what she understands. She don't talk to me."

"Up," the toddler says again. "Up."

"Hold on, baby. Let me put this one down." She crosses into the next room, just as dark as this one, and places the baby in a crib. Everywhere there are toys on the floor. It can't be safe to walk around in such a dark house with all those toys on the floor. "Shhh, shhh, now, you go to sleep," she says to the baby, and puts a pacifier in its mouth.

Back in the living room, Mrs. Hunt plucks the toddler out of the playpen with an ease I don't expect from an older woman. Maybe she isn't much older than me. Maybe she just looks a lot older. "I'll leave you be by yourself. I'll be right out here, on the porch. Have a seat."

"Thanks," I say.

"Be nice to the lady." She closes the screen door behind her, leaving the big wooden door open. Outside, I can hear her murmuring to the toddler. The old man says something and Mrs. Hunt laughs, a loud hearty laugh. Are they laughing at me?

The couch is too far away from Larissa, so I pull over a blue-topped stool meant for a child and place it in front of Larissa's chair, just two feet away. When I sit down, my knees come up higher than my waist and I must look foolish. Still, I'm on the same level as Larissa and that's what counts. I put my purse on the floor between my feet, and sign as I speak. This is what I've decided to do on the drive over.

"Hello, Larissa. I told you I'd see you again. I'm sorry it took so long. I missed you, Larissa."

As soon as she catches the movement of my hands, I've got her attention. When I sign her name the second time, the *L* to my chest, she takes in a breath that says *oh!* As an interpreter, I watch people's faces, so even though it's just a small breath, a small *oh*, I see it.

"Are you watching a cartoon?" I ask, nodding my head toward the TV. "What cartoon is it?"

She looks at the TV, then back at me.

"Is it *Sesame Street*?" I'm not even looking at the TV, just at her face. There's a slight frown on her forehead. Maybe *Sesame Street* is no longer on TV these days.

"Mrs. Hunt seems nice. Do you like the other children here? How many are there?" I try to keep the patronizing tone out of my voice. How can she take care of so many children?

Larissa doesn't answer, just watches my hands. "Is she nice?" I whisper. "Does she take good care of you?" Completely inappropriate, but it just slips out. Larissa shrugs.

"You know, Larissa, I came because you're not speaking to anyone. I know how you feel, but it's important you talk. Having a voice is important. You shouldn't hide yours. You're important. The things you say are important."

She only frowns.

"How's Lucy?" I ask. She looks down at her rabbit. A seam is split along the rabbit's neck, a puff of gray stuffing sticking out. "Would you like me to sew her up?" I ask, still signing every word. She shakes her head hard, clutching Lucy tighter. "It wouldn't hurt her," I say. "It would just tickle her to sew her up because stuffed rabbits are special that way. I just don't want her to fall apart. I know how much you love her."

Larissa shakes her head again, but now looks at Lucy with obvious worry. She sticks a finger in the tear, pushing the stuffing back in.

"Would you like to sew her up yourself? I could show you how." I have a small sewing kit in my purse, one of those things that looks like a big pack of matches. My mother gave it to me, telling me to keep it with me at all times.

Larissa glances at me, surprised. Then she nods, just once.

Taking out the sewing kit, I find a needle and thread it with brown thread, making a thick knot at the end because Lucy is made out of a loose-woven material. "Okay, Larissa, you hold the needle like this. Be very careful." Maybe I shouldn't be letting her have a needle, like a prisoner not being allowed to have sharp objects. Could I get in trouble for this?

"Okay, put Lucy on your lap. Get her comfortable. Let's get her head turned this way." Moving Lucy causes the stuffing to tumble out again. Gently I push it back in. "Now, start here, right here, on the inside, so the knot won't show, and push the needle right through." I talk Larissa through the process, not signing now, pointing to each place she needs to put the needle. She does pretty well and I encourage her to give a good tug, to make the stitches tighter, like a good doctor would. She lets me tie the knot when she's done. I stick the needle back in the packet and put it away in my purse, relieved that her foster mother didn't come in and see us. Larissa looks down at her bunny with a smile. It's the first smile I have ever seen on her face, and I know that I want her to smile at me that way; my forty-eight years of life has boiled down to this strong, possibly obsessive need for this child to care for me.

"Oh, I bet Lucy feels so much better now! She must be very thankful you're so good at sewing her up."

Larissa looks up at me, the smile lingering slightly in her eyes.

"Don't you think Lucy looks so much better now?" I ask.

"Do your hands," she says.

I'm so startled, I just stare at her. "Sign?" I finally say. "You want me to keep signing with my hands as I talk?"

She nods once. It's a no-nonsense nod. She knows what she wants.

"Okay." I wipe my hands on my slacks, then rub them together as if I'm about to give a performance. "This is how you say *okay,* and this is how you say *yes.* If I ask you a question, you can sign *yes,* just this way. It's very easy. See?" I repeat the sign for *yes,* elbow bent, a fist held out, flexing my wrist up and down twice.

Those dark straight eyebrows lower down closer to her eyes. She's watching, concentrating.

"Can you say *yes* with your hand?"

Slowly, she lifts her hand up, makes a fist and bobs it, just as I showed her. I grin like all get-out. "Good! Very good. And I bet you'd like to know how to say *no,* because that's an important word too. It's easy, too. Just like this." I make the sign for *no* several times, and then she imitates me. "Good," I say. "That's very good!"

We sit silently for a minute, satisfied. I listen to the whirl of the fan, the mumble of the TV, the sounds of the street outside.

"I have an idea," I say happily. "A game. I'll ask you questions, and you sign *yes* or *no*, okay?" She doesn't answer, or sign, but I go on. "Okay, let's start. Is your name Larissa?"

Those eyebrows lower. It's a tell, like in poker. She's thinking, deciding if she should participate. Finally she signs *yes*. It's working!

"And is your rabbit's name Hermione?"

She looks confused for a moment, then smiles and makes the sign for *no*. She smiled again! Two smiles! I wish I had this on camera. I want to prove to the whole world she smiled twice while I was with her. I ask her more questions, and she signs *yes* or *no*. Three more times, when I ask silly questions, she smiles. I'm up to five smiles when her foster mother opens the screen door.

"You two doin' okay?"

"Yes," I say, signing the word *yes*, glancing over at Larissa. The corners of her mouth turn up, and I count that as the sixth smile.

"We're talking in sign language," I say. "Larissa is a very smart girl. She also said a few words, out loud."

Mrs. Hunt crosses her arms under her chest. "Well, I wish she'd talk to me. It's hard, her not talkin'. I don't know what she wants. The other kids, they tease her, call her names. Truthfully, it gets on my nerves, her not speaking to me."

"Larissa," I say, also signing, "Won't you speak to Mrs. Hunt?"

Larissa shakes her head and makes the sign for *no*. I feel myself start to grin, and stop.

"She only wants to help you, Larissa." I want Mrs. Hunt to know I'm on her side. Sort of.

Larissa sits there stonily. Frowning.

"Well, that's up to her, I guess," Mrs. Hunt says. "You might want to remind her school starts in a week. She'll have to talk there."

Want to bet? I think.

"I got to make lunch. You staying much longer?"

"Oh, I . . . I don't want to interfere with your lunch." I suddenly imagine myself sitting at her kitchen table with however many children she has here.

Wuss, Vince says. *What, they might bite? Rabid maybe?*

Shut up, I spell with my hand.

"Well, how about you stay until lunch is ready. About fifteen minutes more?"

I nod.

"You can come back another day, if she want you to."

"Thanks," I say. "Would you like me to come back again, Larissa?"

Larissa looks at me, then over at Mrs. Hunt. She lifts up her hand and signs *yes*.

"That means yes," I tell Mrs. Hunt.

"Well, so does noddin' a head." She walks off into the kitchen.

I look at Larissa, and lower my voice. "People get mad at you when you don't talk to them. It hurts their feelings and then they get mad so they don't get hurt. Do you want to hurt Mrs. Hunt's feelings?"

Larissa shrugs, indifferent.

"Try just saying yes or no when she asks you questions. Then she won't be so hurt. Just give her that little bit, and she won't get mad."

All of a sudden, tears are running from the corners of her eyes, spilling down her cheeks. Her thumb is back in her mouth, her breathing heavy, just like I heard on the phone that night.

Oh, God, don't cry. I lean forward on the small stool. "I know, Larissa. This has got to be very hard for you. But it's temporary. It's only for a little while. They say maybe you can come stay with me for a little bit. Would you like that?"

"I want my mommy," she says. "I want to go home."

I feel such loss, and anger. *Your mother abandoned you,* I want to say. *She must be an awful mother to have done that. It's good you're no longer with her.* At the same time, I'm talking to myself. *Stupid idiot. God, am I naive. This child smiled at me, and so I think she might want to live with me?* All these thoughts are in my head, *and* the thought that I have to get her to stop crying before Mrs. Hunt comes back in. My hands bunch up, frustrated with words.

"I'm sure your mommy wants you, too, Larissa," I say. "But everything is going to take some time. That's what they told me. I'm new to all this. I just want to help. We got Lucy all sewn up, didn't we? She's better now. You will be too. We all want everyone to be better." I'm thinking about her mother. What *is* wrong with her? Can she get better? "Mrs. Hunt just wants to help you. This is the sign for *want.*" I spread my fingers out, curling them, palms up, then pull my hands toward my chest. "You *want* your mommy," I say, signing the words slowly. "Your mommy *wants* you. Lucy *wants* to be held by you. Mrs. Hunt just *wants* to be able to talk with you. I just *want* to be your friend. This sign, *want,* is one of the first signs I ever learned. Can you do this?" I show her again. Using the arm holding Lucy, she makes the motion with that hand, a small gesture, just the beginning of *want.*

Her face is blotchy, but the tears on her face are beginning to dry off. "Very, very good," I say. And then her foster mother calls her for lunch.

Half an hour later, I walk into my own home and the quiet is unnerving. My cat is nowhere in sight and the place feels so completely empty. It feels as if my house is waiting for people to come home. *I'm* here, aren't I?

I am no longer enough.

I recall the odor of Mrs. Hunt's house and know what it was. People. The smell of people, bodies, in a warm home.

Once, someone told me that I was not a warm, fuzzy person. I shrugged. Who wanted to be warm and fuzzy? What the hell did that mean? I imagine, now, that it means being the kind of person a child might love.

I am a one-trick pony, me and my hands. I am a means for Larissa to communicate, always a means and never the end. I stand between people and interpret what they say, never getting involved. I have been loved by men, and thought I loved them until I had to tell them that, honestly, I didn't; that I was fooled by a love that never quite came full-fledged, unfeared, whole. I am trying to be a foster mother for a child who, if things work out as they are supposed to, will only leave me to go back to her mother. I keep standing in the middle, never making a commitment to anything. I don't know why I am alone. I don't know what I did wrong. I had a normal childhood. What made me a person alone?

Choices, Vince says to me, a common theme in our old talks. He said I was afraid of choices. I said he kept making the wrong ones.

At least I make choices, he'd say.

So you're saying I'd be happier if I were divorced twice?

Better to have loved and lost, he'd say.

Bullshit. You went on a three-month drunk after Cindy left.

So I get emotional. It's a fucking crime?

It was an old argument. I can't help answering him, even now, trying to finish arguments we already had, getting the last word. *Did you choose to walk out in front of a car?* I ask him. It's not the first time I've asked this. How can you not see a car coming at you?

Fuck you, he says.

I deserved that. But I'm still mad at him. Why the hell didn't he look where he was going?

You're always looking, he says to me, *that's why you never go anywhere.*

Fuck you, I say.

I'm talking to a dead man. He's right. I need a life.

I put my purse down and open a can of cat food. Sampson comes running when he hears the sound of the electric can opener. Sitting down on the cool linoleum floor, I watch his quick tongue dart back and forth. I have never sat down on my kitchen floor before. It seems like a very strange thing to do.

Chapter Ten

Tuesday morning, I drive downtown to East Twenty-second and Carnegie, and park in a three-dollar lot near the courthouse. I've never been to Juvenile Court. Interpreting legalese into ASL is a skill I don't have, or want.

One step through the front door and I'm in a line of people. I stand behind a black man wearing a suit two sizes too big for his thin, lanky body. Ahead of him are a couple, side by side, both wearing jean jackets, both with the same exact mullet haircut. Farther up, a bald man with a mustache must have set off the metal detector, and now a policeman waves a thick wand over his body as the mustached man rolls his eyes and mutters. Someone comes in behind me and stands so closely that I shift my weight, almost bumping the skinny black man. Men and women wearing suits duck underneath a strip of black ribbon that holds the rest of us in line, flashing their badges.

When it's my turn, I sign a ledger and place my purse and the book that I brought on a tray. I walk through the metal detector, sure nothing will happen, giving the police officer a quick smile and a nod as if he, too, knows this. Nothing buzzes. The people ahead of me walk up the stairs to the second floor as if they all know where they're going, so I follow them. It's warm outside, but this marble staircase, this whole building, feels dank and cold.

At the top of the steps is a waiting area, filling quickly, with frosted windows at each end of the room. I go to one window and am directed to the other. They tell me to sit and wait. I sit next to a large woman in a long, flowing African dress and head-wrap. She's talking with a woman holding a clipboard. All over sit people, young and old, talking to people with clipboards. I open my book and pretend to read. Which one is Larissa's mother? The woman with the flowery African dress? There wasn't anything very African in Larissa's apartment. Maybe she's the black woman across from me, sitting with a grizzled black man, both in deep conversation with a woman with a clipboard. There are two black women in the row behind me. They have a small boy with them who kicks steadily at the back of the bench with his heel. I try listening to the conversations going on around me, listening for the word *Larissa,* but the drone is low and constant, and I can't make out most of the words. Every time new people walk into the room, I look at them, trying not to be obvious. Maybe Larissa's mother won't come.

Finally Yolanda Walker comes into the waiting room and waves to me. I get up and we move into the area by the stairs. Yolanda's hair is different, higher up on her head with flat curls. She's wearing the same kind of black slacks and jacket, though, and the badge around her neck. "Is she here?" I ask.

Yolanda peers into the waiting room. "Not yet. How'd it go at Mrs. Hunt's?"

"Really well. Larissa said a few words, and I talked to her using sign language and my voice for almost an hour. She likes it when I sign. I think I'd be good for her."

She nods. "I have another case this morning. I'm going into conference for a few minutes. I spoke to Magistrate Lucarelli. She said you could attend the hearing. Someone will call out 'Benton' when it's time for you to come in. You go down this hall." She looks over her shoulder at a closed door with a sign that reads AUTHORIZED PERSONS ONLY. "Four rooms down on your right. I'll be there. It could be a wait."

"I brought a book," I say, wanting her approval.

"Good thinking." She opens the AUTHORIZED PERSONS ONLY door and walks off. When I turn back to the waiting room, all the seats are taken. I stand against a wall and once again pretend to read, checking out each person as they come up the stairs. Eventually I have to use the restroom. When I come out, several people are walking through the AUTHORIZED PERSONS ONLY door, and I think I see Mrs. Hunt. I ask the man behind the window if they called the case for Benton. "Yes, they did," he says.

The fourth door on the right leads into a small office and I peek in. Sitting behind a desk is a woman, maybe forty, with short brown hair, half glasses like Polly's, and a high-necked blouse. Right next to the door, in one of two chairs, is Yolanda. A plump white woman holding a clipboard sits in the chair next to her. They're talking with Mrs. Hunt, who stands there, nodding at something they say. In front of the magistrate's desk are six chairs crammed into two rows. Two people sit in the front row, a blond woman and a young man in a pinstriped suit. Certainly this is not the courtroom, but it doesn't look like anyone's getting up to go somewhere else.

I inch past Mrs. Hunt and move into the back row to sit in the corner against the wall, my purse and book in my lap. Mrs. Hunt finishes talking to Yolanda and sits next to me. We politely nod to each other. I want to ask her how Larissa is, but the room has gotten suddenly quiet, as if in expectation of something about to happen. There are two empty chairs. Larissa's mother must not have come. Without a word from the magistrate, Yolanda reaches out her arm and swings the door closed. The magistrate clicks on a tape recorder on her desk.

"Good morning," she says, studying her papers and lifting up a page. "I'm Magistrate Lucarelli. Let's see who you all are." She looks over her half glasses at Yolanda Walker and the woman sitting next to her. "Yolanda Walker, social worker for Larissa Benton, Leslie Crowley, assistant prosecutor for Family Services." Yolanda and the plump woman both say, "Here," just loud enough for the recorder to pick up.

"Michelle Benton, the child's mother?" The magistrate looks up from her papers at the woman in front of me. The blonde. She has an inch of dark roots showing down the part in the middle of her hair.

"Yes, ma'am. I'm Larissa's mother."

She's white. Larissa's mother is white. It never occurred to me, even though Larissa's skin is not very dark. I'm so confused by this that I hardly hear what the magistrate says next. The man in the suit says something, and Mrs. Hunt next to me, but it's just a muddle of words. I pictured Larissa's mother in so many ways. Heavy, too thin, angry looking, doped up, young. But black, always black.

Now the magistrate is saying my name, with the tone that implies she has said it more than once. "Yes," I say. "Here."

"And you are an interested individual?" she asks.

"Yes. Yes, I am."

The woman with the dyed blond hair—Larissa's mother—turns to stare at me. She has a small oval face, green eyes, a ton of black eyeliner, long flimsy bangs, and is wearing pale, shiny pink lipstick. She looks nothing like Larissa. Has someone made a mistake, like the kind you read about in the paper? *County Gives Child to Wrong Mother?*

"*You* came and took my baby?" she says, her eyes narrowed. "Who do you think you are, coming into my home like someone asked you in? Who the hell are you?"

"Excuse me," Magistrate Lucarelli says firmly, so that Larissa's mother turns back, not without one last nasty look at me. "I won't allow that in here. Do you understand? Everyone in my courtroom will behave properly and will speak only when I ask them to. Once again, Mrs. Benton, do we have an understanding?"

"Yes, ma'am." Her voice is lower now than when she spoke to me, but she certainly doesn't sound timid. She gives me one more evil glance back.

"Now then." The magistrate turns to the assistant prosecutor. "Do we have good service on everyone?"

"Yes, we do, Your Honor."

"All right. This is case number 0292109. Do you all have a copy of the complaint? Mrs. Benton?"

Jesus. Does that mean there have been 292,108 previous cases?

"Excuse me?" Larissa's mother says. "The what?"

"The paperwork we mailed to you along with your appointment for this hearing?"

"Yes, ma'am."

"Good. I want to inform you that as a parent with a child in the custody of the county, you have the right to an attorney, the right to cross-examine your accusers, the right to due process of law, the right to speak on your behalf or remain silent. If you can't afford an attorney, one will be made available to you through the public defender's office. Do you wish to be represented by an attorney, Mrs. Benton?" The words almost lose their meaning in the singsong way she says them, like disclaimers at the end of commercials.

Larissa's mother shakes her head, and even from directly behind her, I can read that head shake. It means she doesn't understand. "I just want Larissa back. She must be scared to death with strangers. I can't stand to think how scared she must be."

"And we would like you to get your daughter back, Mrs. Benton," the magistrate says, "but there is a process to follow. We can stop now, and you can get a lawyer, or we can move on and begin to determine that process. Would you like representation?"

"I just want to do what's right. Get her back soon as I can. You tell me how to do that, and I will."

"Mrs. Benton, once again, would you like a lawyer to represent you?"

"Do I have to?" There's worry in her voice now.

The magistrate sighs. "No. We can proceed right now without a lawyer, if you feel comfortable doing so."

"I just want to do it quickly. Get her back. Let's just get going on that."

"So your answer is no? You don't want an attorney?"

"That's right. Go ahead."

"Then let's get started. Mrs. Walker, will you read from the complaint, please?"

"Larissa Benton was removed from her home on July nineteenth by Children and Family Services due to abandonment," Yolanda says.

"And were you the social worker who removed her?"

"Yes, Your Honor."

"And were there reasonable efforts to prevent removal?"

"Yes, Your Honor. Mom was not on the premises, and had not been for at least three hours."

"And this length of time was determined by?"

"Miss Marlowe, the interested individual, was in the apartment for more than three hours before calling the police. The police arrived at seven twenty-three, and the child was removed at eight-thirty, at which point Mom had still not appeared. At that time we believed she had been absent for forty-eight hours, but Mom now says she was gone only nineteen hours. Please note that amendment to the case. Either way, the time period was substantial. Certainly enough to warrant removal."

Larissa's mother stands up. She's inches from the magistrate's desk, and although she's short, she has presence; her shoulders back, determination in her stance. "I got there right after they took her!"

"You will have your turn to speak in just a moment, Mrs. Benton. Please sit down."

Larissa's mother turns and looks at me before she sits back down. This woman, girl really, despises me. It feels physical, as if she were touching me.

"Is there a history with Children and Family Services, Mrs. Walker?" Magistrate Lucarelli asks when she's certain Larissa's mother will be quiet.

"Not with us, Your Honor, but the mother was arrested twenty-two months ago for driving under the influence of alcohol, and kicked the arresting officer in the shin, along with verbally abusing him. Her driver's licence was revoked, and she was put on a year's probation and was required to attend substance abuse counseling. When she arrived at CFS at eleven A.M. on the morning Larissa was brought to us, Mrs. Benton caused a scene and was verbally abusive to me. One of our security guards had to remove her to a conference room. I am certain I smelled alcohol on her breath at the time of our confrontation."

"Is this last comment in the complaint?"

"No, Your Honor."

"Then put it in or don't mention it."

"I didn't drink nothing for over a year!" Larissa's mother says facing Yolanda. "Nothing until that night. I know I made a mistake. One bad mistake, but you can't take my little girl away for that!" Now she turns back to the magistrate. Her tone changes. "Ma'am, my husband, he was killed two years ago. Shot for no reason 'cept he was black. I couldn't take it—"

"Please, Mrs. Benton. You will have a turn. I promise you."

"I just want you to know—"

The magistrate holds up her hand, and Larissa's mother doesn't say anything else.

"Please finish, Mrs. Walker."

Yolanda reads again from her papers, stating that Larissa was granted emergency temporary custody to the county and placed into a foster home. Temporary custody was granted three days later. Visitation had begun.

"Are there any relatives the child could have been placed with?"

"There is Mom's father, Your Honor, but Mrs. Benton refuses his help."

"No way he's getting my baby," Larissa's mother says. "He's

a nasty son of a . . ." She looks around the room. "We don't talk no more. Enough said."

Yolanda Walker continues as the magistrate keeps her eyes on Larissa's mother. "And there's a set of grandparents on the deceased father's side, but they are out of state and live in a trailer with only one bedroom. Also there is an aunt, who was in the hospital during the time of the incident, and who is unable to take the child at this time due to medical problems."

The magistrate nods and writes on the paper in front of her. I can hear the tick of a clock above my head and Larissa's mother's feet shuffling back and forth on the floor. On the desk are photos of a husband and a dark-haired child.

"Thank you, Mrs. Walker," Magistrate Lucarelli finally says. "*Now,* Mrs. Benton, you may plead to the complaint. Is it true or false?"

"I left to get a job. I was planning on being right back. I thought her auntie was coming to stay with her. I never meant to leave her alone for so long."

"How long were you planing on leaving her alone, Mrs. Benton?" the magistrate says. "Never mind. I apologize for asking that. The complaint, as filed, do you agree to the facts?"

Larissa's mother points at Yolanda. "She only lets me visit my daughter once a week at Metzenbaum, they won't even tell me where she is, and they let this woman who came into my home go see her." Now she turns to me again. I want to move my chair backward, but it's against the wall. "Why's *she* get to see my baby?" She puts one hand over the back of her chair. She has fake nails with little gemstones.

The magistrate turns to Yolanda. "Is this true, Mrs. Walker?"

"Yes, Your Honor. Mom's visits were upsetting to the child. The child would throw fits to the point of physically harming herself a few minutes after Mom showed up, and then become silent and withdrawn. She has not spoken at all since the first visit. Not to her foster mother or the children in the foster home, nothing except for a few words to Miss Marlowe."

"She's just begging me to take her home. Any child would do that! Of course she's upset! But this lady? She shouldn't be allowed to see her!" Larissa's mother slaps the magistrate's desk. "Why should *she* see her?"

Magistrate Lucarelli places both palms down on her desk, slowly lifting herself up from her seat, regarding us with a long, slow, exasperated gaze. "All right. Everyone listen up. First, I am going to recommend Mrs. Benton get a lawyer. Mrs. Benton, I highly suggest you call the public defender's office and make an appointment. I don't see that you are ready to agree to the complaint, and I think you do need some legal advice. Do you agree?"

The blond head bobs up and down. "Fine. I wanna lawyer."

"All right. Now before we make a date to meet again, I want to understand something. Miss Marlowe, how exactly are you involved here?"

I start by describing the phone call and how I went to Larissa's apartment. The magistrate shakes her head from side to side slowly, even sighing several times as if I have just complicated her life tremendously. By the time I get halfway through, she stops writing things down, choosing instead to tap the pen on her desk, which I imagine is not a good sign. Larissa's mother has turned around and is staring at me. It's hard to think. I finish by explaining how I visited Larissa's foster home, how Larissa talked to me, how she seems to like signing. When I'm done, Yolanda clears her throat.

"Your Honor, may I speak?"

"Yes. I would very much like to hear your explanation, Mrs. Walker."

"Miss Marlowe is a trained interpreter for the deaf, and although she did make a choice none of us might have, to go to the apartment rather than calling the police, she did it out of a desire to help the child, and she did end up calling the police. She has made a connection with Larissa, who, by the way, stayed in Miss Marlowe's arms throughout our visit to the hospital and on to the center. Miss Marlowe has applied to be a foster parent, has already attended four foster parenting classes, and has a home visit scheduled in two weeks. She has taken every step necessary to begin this process, and is quite willing to be a foster parent for Larissa while her mother goes through the process of getting her back. I believe she would make a good foster parent for Larissa at this time, and that will be in my recommendation."

Thank you, Yolanda! I'd smile at her, but I don't want to look smug.

Magistrate Lucarelli drops her pen on the desk. "But the child is already in a home, am I right? Mrs. Hunt, you are that foster parent, and you are here because?"

"She's not fittin' in with the other children, Your Honor," Mrs. Hunt says. "It's causing problems. She should go to a home with less children or no children at all."

"And Miss Marlowe came to your house? To visit the child?" She glances over at Yolanda once, letting her know she doesn't really approve of this.

"Yes, ma'am. Larissa talked to her a little. I think she like her some."

"May I speak?" the young man in the suit says. He hasn't opened his mouth yet. I don't know who he is or why he's here, just that he holds a clipboard, his hair is impeccable, and he's thirty at the most. Everyone in this room is younger than I, with the exception of Mrs. Hunt. The place is being run by children.

"Yes, Mr. Phillips?"

"As well motivated as Mrs. Walker would like us to believe Miss Marlowe is, and as much as the foster mother approves of her, I'm not sure I can agree she is the right person for the child to live with."

"And why is that?" the magistrate says, raising her eyebrows.

"As you know, Your Honor, there are people who want to adopt children so badly, they interfere with the family getting back together, then they apply for adoption. There are Web pages with advice on how to do this. How do we know Miss Marlowe doesn't belong to this group? The child is a young, light-skinned African American. She fits the profile of the type of child these people want to adopt."

These people? Who the hell is he calling *these people?* I want to smack him, but I sit still, hands woven tightly together in my lap. I watch *Judge Judy.* I know that the ones who speak out of turn lose the case. The magistrate is already upset with Larissa's mother. I want to show that I can be calm and coolheaded.

"I understand your point, Mr. Phillips. Have you talked with the child?"

"I've visited her once. She wouldn't speak with me."

"So you have no idea how she feels toward Miss Marlowe?"

"No, Your Honor."

"And Miss Marlowe, are you in contact with this group that helps people adopt children through foster care? Is that your plan?"

"No," I say. "I have not been in *contact* with any such group, nor ever heard of such a thing. Look, it was a wrong number that I couldn't ignore. I've never applied for adoption, never tried to find a child to adopt, but I would like to be a foster parent for Larissa, *if* she has to be in foster care." I look over at the man in the suit. "I just want to help Larissa. I can't imagine why you would have a problem with that."

The young man smiles at me, as if he's my friend. "Miss Marlowe has brought up a point, Your Honor. I suggest that Larissa be allowed to go back to her home, under protective supervision, and not be placed in foster care at all. This is Mrs. Benton's first fall from grace, and with protective supervision, and alcohol abuse counseling—"

The magistrate interrupts him, speaking through clenched teeth. "I do not think that is appropriate at this time at all, Mr. Phillips."

He looks back at her for a moment, their eyes locked, then nods. "As long as it's on record."

"It is, Mr. Phillips. Any *more* suggestions?"

"No, Your Honor."

"Then I suggest we make another date to meet, say..." She looks in a small book, turns a few pages. "Three weeks from now, on September third. One-thirty?"

Yolanda Walker, the plump woman next to her, and the young man in his fancy pinstriped suit all look in similar black books and agree.

"In the meantime, Mrs. Benton, I recommend you contact a lawyer. Mrs. Hunt, you will not have to come to the next hearing. We already have your request for removal on record. And Miss Marlowe, I don't think you will need to come, either. I'm sure Mrs. Walker will keep you informed. Thank you all."

We all stand up—except Larissa's mother. She just sits there, arms folded, separating herself from the people who took her daughter from her.

. . .

The hallway is narrow and crowded. Yolanda and I move to an open spot a few doorways down. "Who the hell was that man?" I whisper. "What the hell does he have against me?"

"He's Larissa's guardian ad litem. He's a lawyer, not connected to CFS. He's here to represent Larissa's best interests."

"Isn't that what you do?"

Yolanda laughs, a sad laugh. "Supposedly."

"Does he really think I'm part of some group of people who . . . what? Adopt children? What's so bad about that? I thought children needed to be adopted."

"Not like they're doing it."

Larissa's mother comes out of the office and walks down the hall. Another group of people are filing in. God, the magistrate has to hear stories about abused children all day. "Why did she interrupt him when he mentioned Larissa going back to her mother?"

"A high-profile case in the paper a few weeks ago. In Summit County. A child was returned home on protective supervision. She was killed by her mother a few days later, beaten with a meat tenderizer." Yolanda says this so matter-of-factly. She is like the clothes she wears, her lacquer of makeup, her well-set hair; she wears detachment like a badge, something put on over herself. A child beaten with a meat tenderizer. The thought makes me want to crawl into bed for months.

"That's so awful! But she doesn't think Larissa's mother would do that?"

"The magistrate just has to be careful, Alice."

"How do you do this? Every day?"

She shrugs. "Sometimes it works."

"God, I hope so. So, can I still visit Larissa? At Mrs. Hunt's?"

"That's between you and Mrs. Hunt."

"Thank you, Yolanda. Thanks for everything."

The hallway is mostly clear now except for two men in gray suits talking by the door to the waiting room.

"Yolanda, before you go, can I ask you something?"

"Sure. What?"

"Why are you doing this? Helping me? You said you could get into trouble."

Yolanda looks down the hall at the two men, then at the papers in her hands. She shakes her head. "First, I'm doing it for Larissa. I think you might be good for her. Second, I do my job the best I can. I'm just . . . You got me thinking out of the box. This box." She nods toward the magistrate's room, then tries to smile but shrugs instead.

"I'm a little burnt out," she continues. "I like the kids. Most of them. I just need to . . . trust my instincts for once. My instincts tell me to trust you."

I don't know what to say. I feel a huge responsibility to make everything work out right. "It's got to be a hard job, Yolanda. For what it's worth, I think you're great."

She smiles now, a slight but honest smile. "Thanks." A door slams somewhere. "I better go. You take care. We'll talk."

"Could I take you out for coffee now? Lunch? Are you hungry?" I ask.

"Thanks, but I have to get back to work. Good luck with your home visit." She looks down at her clipboard. She's said too much.

"Thank you for everything," I say.

She turns one way down the hall, I the other way, toward the door out into the waiting room and then down the marble stairs.

I pass by the metal detector and the policeman with the gun. Outside, the sky is still blue.

Playing the whole experience through my head again like a movie, trying to figure out if I said anything wrong, I walk down Twenty-second Street to the corner, where I stand dumbly watching the signal with the flat orange hand that means wait, don't walk. From behind, someone taps me sharply on the shoulder.

"Hey, you."

It's Larissa's mother.

"I wanna talk to you," she says.

The walk signal comes on and for a second I think I'll do just that—walk quickly to my car and drive away. Larissa's mother scares me. But I stay and look at her.

I don't know her first name. I suppose the magistrate said it, but I was so surprised by the fact that she was Larissa's mother that I hadn't caught her name.

She's not only white, but extremely pale, as if she hasn't been out in the sun for a long time. She's short, at the most five-two, and I look down on her dark roots. Through her long bangs I can hardly see her eyes, just the black smear of eyeliner. And she's very young. She must have had Larissa when she was a teenager. She looks a lot like my brother's ex-wife—maybe not exactly, but she has the feel of my brother's ex-wife. Trashy. Vince loved her. I never understood why.

You wouldn't, he says.

"You went *in* my place?" this girl who is Larissa's mother says. "How could you do that? How could you just come into *my* place when you don't know me? Get my child taken from me? Who the hell are *you*? God Almighty? Well, fuck you."

She certainly isn't intimated by my height, or the fact that she left her child alone in the first place. Her hands are balled into fists and she looks as if she wants to use them. Cars drive by, and less than a shout away two policemen stand chatting in front of Juvenile Court. But it isn't a physical threat I fear, it's *her,* the mere fact of her, that throws me off balance.

"Listen," I say, holding up a hand, just like that orange don't walk sign. "I know you're mad at me, but your daughter was frightened and alone. She called my house by mistake. What was I supposed to do? Ignore the fact she was scared and crying? Go back to sleep and hope someone else helped her?"

A look crosses her face that says she's momentarily unsure of her own anger. We stand on the downtown street corner staring at each other.

Finally she speaks again. "My daughter oughta be home with me. I'm a good mother. She loves me, and now she's terrified, doesn't know why people took her away. She thinks she did something bad. I told her it was *me,* not her, but she thinks they took her away 'cause she was a bad little girl. You tell them she should be home with me. You should tell them that, after what you did. Tell them that for me."

Tears are running down her cheeks now, and I want nothing more than to be away from this woman. I don't want to feel sorry for her.

"Look," I say. "That's not my job. They're not asking me something like that."

"I need my daughter. Don't you or no one understand that? *She* needs me."

I can't stand this. "Listen, you left her alone for almost twenty-four hours. That wasn't right. You've got to admit to that. You've got to be sorry you did that, otherwise nobody's going to give your daughter back to you."

She lifts her chin. "You don't know," she says. "You could never know. You got it so good, you don't know nothing."

Without missing a beat I tell her, "I don't have it so good. I'm not rich. I'm not married. And I don't have a little girl who loves me." I can't believe I'm explaining myself to her, saying this to a stranger, standing here on this stupid street corner. Traffic passes by. A pigeon paces back and forth along the sidewalk. Nothing seems real.

She crosses her arms, steps one step closer to me. "So you want mine now?" she says in a low, threatening tone. "Huh? You want her cuz she's a pretty little light-skinned black girl? You wouldn't be doing this if she was dark-skinned, not so pretty. You think you'd be trying to get my daughter, she were shiny black, pudgy, big-lipped? I don't think so. You wouldn't be here today if Larissa weren't a pretty little light-skinned girl."

"Go to hell," I say. "You don't know me." I look at the walk signal. That orange hand says to wait but I hurry across the street. Run to my car. Larissa's mother shouts at me as I run.

"Bitch!" she yells. "Baby stealer!"

Chapter Eleven

I call Polly at work and invite myself over for dinner. Tuesday night is takeout night at her house, as well as Thursdays and Sundays. Tuesdays is Chinese.

"It didn't go well?" she asks.

"No."

"Anything you want to tell me now?"

"Not yet."

"Okay. We'll talk tonight. You okay?"

"You tell me," I ask. "I'm okay, right? I'm not so bad, am I?"

"You're the best."

"Tell that to the guy in the suit. And her mother."

"She showed up?"

"She sure did."

I can hear someone call Polly's name, phones ringing.

"I'll be there at six. Thanks." I hang up. It's only a little after noon. I have a job at the library at three. It seems like years since I left my house this morning.

I bring a bottle of white wine and a dozen large chocolate chip cookies. Fortune cookies are not going to do it for me. I want something without a proverb.

Polly's husband, Patrick, takes the wine from me, winks at the cookies, and kisses me on the cheek. He's a good man who teaches high school English and coaches tennis. His hands always smell of the old tennis balls he tosses to their dog, Max.

In the dining room, I stick large spoons into the containers of Chinese food as Polly carries plates to the table and Patrick sets out the wineglasses. All of us have to maneuver around the piles of books and paperwork that practically line the perimeter of the dining room. Max follows us back and forth, wagging his tail. When we finally sit down, Max slips his large head onto Patrick's lap. I smile and take a breath that feels like the first good breath I've taken all day. We've done this so many times over the years— with their kids drinking Kool-Aid, then Cokes, then beer. Polly's daughter, Rachel, and I would sign quickly in ASL, food in our mouths, a bit smug that Polly and Patrick couldn't keep up. We shared a lot of laughter at this table.

Now we talk about the cost of college, property taxes, and the falling stock market. "Let's sell our houses and buy a place in the Ozarks," Patrick says. "Fill the cellar with food and line the walls with books. Your parents could come live with us, too, Alice. Your dad could fix anything that went wrong. What do you think?"

I smile. "My mom could spin wool from sheep and make all our clothes. Hell, she could sew us a cozy to go over the house and we wouldn't have to heat it."

"It'd be a long trip for good takeout Chinese," Polly says.

Patrick makes a show of thinking it over, then laughs. "Point taken." Lowering his plate to the floor for Max to clean, he adds, "Well, it was a nice idea. Guess I'll just go watch some TV now. Let you two talk." He takes a cookie with him, tipping his head with a nod of thanks.

"You didn't tell him I went to court today?" I ask.

"Yeah, I did. I just told him not to mention it. So tell me. Was it awful?"

"Pretty much. Did you know the hearing is held in this little office?"

Polly nods. "Yeah. They're cramped for space."

"Anyway, her mother's white."

Polly lifts her chin, studies me. "Interesting. You weren't expecting that?"

"No. And she's so young. Trashy looking, but there was this . . ." I stall. I can't think of the word. "I don't know. Energy? Once you look at her, you can't look away. She's tough. She's not afraid of anything." I pick up the wine goblet, twirl the stem between my fingers. "I've been misjudging people for weeks now. I thought the social worker was too young, but she's great, really great. Yolanda Walker. I told you about her?" Polly nods. "And then there's the woman who taught the foster parenting classes, and she wore this awful lavender outfit and lavender shoes. I thought she was a fool until I heard her talk. She knew her stuff. And I was sure Larissa's mother was black because black women marry black men, right? Jesus, Polly, what the hell's the matter with me?" I look at her, wanting to see the truth in her face.

"Look, Alice," she says, looking right back at me. "Don't worry so much. We're getting older. People under twenty-five

look too young to know jack shit. And the woman in the lavender, we all do that, judge people by the clothes they wear. Maybe
she does that on purpose, if she's so smart. Part of the plan. And
Larissa's mother, I figured she was black, too." She leans back in
her chair, crossing her arms. "Let me ask you this: How does
that change things? That she's white."

"I can relate to her better, that's how it changes things," I say
without thinking, but then know it's true, as much as I don't like
it. "I was stereotyping the mom. Dismissing her because she was
black. All of a sudden all my expectations were gone and I had
to start all over again. She's so young. Jesus, she could be my
daughter. I'm not saying I *like* her, but I saw something . . . not
like something of myself, I'm way too responsible to be where
she is today, but something of *her*. Does that make any sense? If
she were black, would I have seen that? I don't think so. Jesus
Christ, I'm prejudiced. All these Goddamn classes, people telling
me stuff I don't want to hear . . ." I push my plate away. "There
was this lawyer, this young kid lawyer in a spiffy suit and polished shoes who accused me of wanting to foster parent Larissa
so I could adopt her, because she was light-skinned and pretty,
and then Larissa's mother said the same thing, shouted it at me
on the street corner. Really, am I judgmental? Prejudiced?"

Polly breaks a cookie in half, hesitating. "Yeah, you get a little judgmental sometimes, but I would never call you prejudiced.
It's not like you're shrugging this off. You're a good person, if
that's what you're asking. That's why you're my best friend."
She smiles at me and takes a bite of the cookie.

"Thanks. But you know what's strange? If Larissa's mother
had been black, I never would have been so stunned. I wouldn't
have thought twice about it, I never would have understood what
my expectations had been, how I'd judged her before I met her.

It took a white woman to show me how prejudiced I really am. Isn't that weird?"

"Come on," she says. "You're not. Really."

I don't know what more to say. It feels weird, trying to convince her that I am. I put down the goblet, squint my eyes, and tilt my head. "So . . . how *am* I judgmental?" I say it lightly, trying to get rid of the somber mood.

"Well," she says, raising an eyebrow. "Like those last two guys I fixed you up with. They weren't so bad."

"So, I'm supposed to want to live the rest of my life with someone you characterize as *not so bad*?" I say with a laugh.

"I'm just answering your question."

"Okay. But I have something else to ask."

"All right." She feigns a heavy sigh. "What now?"

"I want to ask the mayor to write me a recommendation. I'll ask her myself. I just want you to know I'm going to, unless you say no."

I did the mayor a favor last year, going to her daughter's school, visiting several classrooms, explaining my job. She asked me to do that at this very table, over a dinner, one Polly actually cooked. It's not like I'm asking a stranger.

"I don't know," she says. "She likes you, but she doesn't really know what kind of person you are, to write a recommendation." From the living room, Patrick laughs loud and quick at some show, as if the joke is hysterical but quickly over.

"She thanked me a million times for the school thing. And she knows I'm your best friend. Being your best friend makes me a good person, right?"

She smiles, knowing I'm using her own words to win this argument. "Okay. But let me ask her." She shrugs. "It can't hurt to try."

"Thanks."

As I help Polly clear the table, I look around at the cluttered dining room—Patrick's paperwork and books, a box of files from Polly's office, the dinner plate on the floor for the dog, paper bags filled with stuff for Goodwill, and in every nook and cranny there are family pictures, so many it feels like a family of countless children rather than two. I think about the home study woman coming next week, how neat my house is. I'm willing to bet this is the house they would prefer.

The next day is the six-month anniversary of Vince's death. I drive down to see him, what is left of him: a place. My parents keep their half of him in a brass container on the mantelpiece. A month after he was killed I brought my half to the park where we used to walk when I went to visit him in Akron. There's a large swamp that covers some twenty acres, and Vince would stop at a certain spot on the path, propping his workman's hands on the wooden railing, and stare out over the murky land. We'd stand there, watch patiently for a blue heron to land, point to large snapping turtles sunning themselves on old logs, hope to catch sight of one of the eagles they said lived nearby, which we never did. We hardly had to talk. Once I put my hand on his as we stood there, just for a moment. We hugged occasionally, but seldom touched. My hand on his felt right at that moment. It is from that spot that I threw his ashes into the swamp.

I went steady with a boy in tenth grade. He was an artist, and I loved the beautiful things he drew and the words he used, like *chartreuse* and *magenta*. I wanted to be like him, so I signed up for Saturday classes at the art museum and bought creamy pastels and expensive books with thick paper. He thought it was great that I was trying to be an artist, and that word *trying* sat between us like a rock. He moved away at the end of the year.

In eleventh grade, I went steady with two boys. The first was on the chess team and played drums in a makeshift rock band. We broke up because we broke up; it was what you did when there were other possibilities. The next boy was the opposite of the chess player. A jock, blond, and as cute as a button, as my mother would say. One night he coaxed me into a closet at a party and kissed me too hard, his tongue in my mouth. As I tried to stop him, he pushed me against the coats and we stumbled on boots against the back of the closet, dark and hot and crowded with us and all that clothing. He put his hand on my breast and kissed harder, held me there as he rummaged his other hand down my low-slung bell-bottom jeans. I tried to kick him, but kicked an empty boot. I couldn't even yell with his tongue in my mouth. I bit him. He slapped me. My hand went to my face, and his hand cupped my crotch. "Say a word," he said, "and I'll tell them we did it plenty before." He was cute as a button and one of the most popular guys around.

That night I cried in my bed and Vince came into my room. He sat on my bed and asked me why I was crying. His concern made me cry harder. I told him about the boy and the closet. Two days later the cute-as-a-button ex-boyfriend came to school with a black eye and a limp.

There were boyfriends at college. None of them lasted. I gave up easily, or found men who would give up easily. We were usually well matched in that way. Hardly ever bitter. Then when I was almost twenty-eight, I moved to Cleveland, following the man who didn't really love me. And then he moved away.

Vince never went to college. He was planning on owning the hardware store one day. The store hadn't broken even in years, yet Vince believed that when it was finally handed over to him—there being no other relatives remotely interested—that he would turn it around. He had big plans. When my father sold it to True Hardware, Vince was furious. My father felt so bad that he tried to give Vince some of the money. Vince wouldn't take it.

He moved to Akron, took up house painting, and wouldn't visit our parents until he had his first son and Cindy was pregnant with the second. Then he called our mother and told her that he was coming back and everybody better be damn polite. We were. We were always nothing if not polite.

A few years later, just after Cindy left him, Vince brought along a buddy to our family's Thanksgiving dinner in Columbus, a man named Jimmy Bain, with whom Vince painted houses. Everyone loved Jimmy; he was that kind of guy, friendly and talkative, humble, no ego. When I first met him he told me how his last car, a real clunker, had run out of oil on I-77. The car began to smoke, made a loud crackling noise, then stopped running. He walked away and never looked back. He was one of those people who abandoned their cars on the highways, then laughed about it. He had an easy smile that I liked, and that annoyed me to no end. What did he have to smile about so much? Vince's kids thought he was cool because he was six feet four and lifted weights. My parents thought he was sweet. Everyone loved Jimmy but me. I just liked him.

After that Thanksgiving, Vince would come up to Cleveland once or twice a month for the weekend, bringing his kids and Jimmy. We'd hike in the Chagrin Reservation, go to the museums, eat at cheap restaurants. Jimmy flattered me in such a friendly way that I never knew quite how to take it. He flattered everyone: waitresses, clerks, my mother. Then one Saturday, Vince took his kids to an afternoon movie, some cartoon Jimmy and

I didn't want to see, and we decided to go get lunch. Over lunch, Jimmy said, "I've kind of developed a crush on you, Alice. Is that okay with you?"

I was unsure, but my head nodded, my body wanting this. We slept together three weekends later. He always came up to Cleveland, so affable about making the drive. He'd bought an eighteen-year-old Chevy just to get here. Then one night, after making love, he told me he wanted to move to Cleveland. "You'll marry me someday, Alice," he whispered to me in the dark. "Won't you?"

I was so touched by this intimate whisper, I said yes.

He moved to Cleveland, moved in with me. He found a job painting houses. We lived together for almost two years, his belief that we were happy carrying me along. I don't know why I wasn't. I don't know why it took me so long to see that. When he asked me to marry him, one knee on the floor in the light of day, I said no.

It was the only time I ever saw him angry. He moved out that day. He was the only man who ever asked me to marry him.

Vince asked me why the hell I didn't marry Jimmy. "He's not good enough for you, right? That's it?" Vince said.

"No, I'm just not in love with him."

"Right. Because he isn't good enough for you."

But Vince was wrong. That wasn't why I didn't fall in love with Jimmy. I didn't fall in love with Jimmy because he was too happy-go-lucky. I needed someone I could argue with, then love again. I needed someone that seemed as tough as me.

Once, after the man I thought loved me moved away, and before Jimmy Bain, I went to a gay bar. I was terrified and incredibly turned on. I knew that with my short-cropped hair, the way I wore it spiked up, that I looked a bit butch. I went home with a woman, to her house, not mine. I was so nervous the whole time that I never did it again.

I want someone in my life, but I am afraid I will never find him. It gets harder and harder. Maybe I wasn't meant to live the rest of my life with a man, or a woman.

Maybe it wasn't a wrong number, after all.

At the marsh, I watch for a blue heron to arrive, no longer hopeful for the sight of an eagle. It was Vince beside me that made me believe we might see eagles. I wait a long time, and then I leave. I drive home with the radio off.

Chapter Twelve

A few days later I call Mrs. Hunt and ask if I can come by and visit Larissa again. She tells me it's not a good time; one of the children has the measles.

"Has Larissa had the measles yet?" I ask.

"Your guess is as good as mine, honey. She still ain't speaking to me. Call next week. Should be better by then." I call next Tuesday. "Not a good day," she tells me. "Maybe Friday. You call me on Friday."

I call Friday morning at ten. "Can I come today?" I ask. "Would that be all right? Is everything okay?"

"She ain't here right now. My neighbor walked her down to school. She gonna meet her new teacher and have a tour of the place. You can come later today if you like."

"How is she?" I ask.

"She seems fine, but she don't talk. She waves her hands

around, like you do, when she playing with her stuffed animal. That's about all she does. I take her to the park with the others, but she just sits there and won't play. I hope they find her a new place soon. It's not like I haven't tried."

"I have a job at two. Can I come after that, around four?"

"That'll be just fine," she says.

Then I call Polly. "Is she in?" I mean the mayor.

"I asked already. She said she'd have the letter done by this afternoon. She really does like you. She said good luck."

I can hardly talk. "Thanks. You're the best." And she is. I may not have a man in my life, but I have one hell of a best friend.

Around four, I drive to Mrs. Hunt's house, coming from my job downtown—interpreting a rally for a group of people who are going to Washington for the antiwar protest. It's a warm sunny summer day and at the house next door a half dozen children run through a sprinkler, shrieking at the top of their lungs. I feel a great energy invade me, a feeling of decency and joy. I want to come here, play with Larissa, sit down and talk to Mrs. Hunt on her front porch. This feeling began as I interpreted for the large crowd of people at the square downtown, the speaker's passion so impelling. I signed with his enthusiasm, getting caught up in the rhetoric. I almost signed up for the trip.

Mrs. Hunt comes out her front door, shaking her head widely, lips pressed together. I know right away whatever she is about to say isn't good. "She ain't here. She took off. The police are looking for her."

I stop walking. "What?"

Her chest heaves with indignation, as if she's been running.

"She took off when my neighbor, Mr. Klewer, be showing her the school. He can't walk that fast. He was just trying to be kind, taking her there. I can't believe she ran off on him. He's a good man, and now he has to be talking with the police, giving them his name. They got up by the school, and he bent down to pick up a quarter off the sidewalk. She took off running. It wasn't his fault. No one should go blaming him."

"I'm not," I say, blaming him, blaming her. "How long has she been gone?" A child running through the sprinkler hollers, and I want to shout at him.

"This morning, when we talked. Right about then. The police been looking for her." Mrs. Hunt kneads her hands together, looks back at her house.

"Maybe she went home? It isn't that far away."

"I don't know. They don't tell me anything. They gonna bring her back here when they find her, but this has got me so upset, I don't know I want her back. Too much drama, that child. Mr. Klewer, he's got a bad heart. This coulda killed him, he run after her."

"Okay," I say. "I'll go looking for her. Will you call me, please, if they find her? I'll write down my cell phone number."

She sighs. "I will. But I just don't know—"

"It wasn't your fault, Mrs. Hunt. These things happen with foster children." Here I am, an expert after a few foster parenting classes.

"I appreciate your saying that. I've never had this kind of trouble before."

I walk quickly to my car. One of those kids is going to run too fast through that sprinkler, run right into the street between all the parked cars and get hit.

I drive to Larissa's apartment, parking in the lot behind it off a narrow side street. Sitting in the car, I turn my head slowly, looking for movement. From where I sit, I can see into the back-yards of the nearby homes. Garage doors are open. Some drive-ways have three cars parked tight together. She could be hiding anywhere. I remember hiding behind the McHughs' house so long ago, sitting between the bush and the porch steps. No one would have been able to see me there.

After a while, I get out of the car and walk up the back metal steps to the third floor, and peek through the window on her back door. A half-filled cup of milk sits on the kitchen counter. I listen carefully. No sounds. Finally I knock. I don't really expect her to come to the door, and she doesn't, but I bet anything Larissa was here, that that was her cup of milk.

I drive home slowly, looking around for the shape of her, spelling *Larissa* with my hand, as if my hand is calling her name out the open window.

There's a message on my machine when I get home. Yolanda. She says to call her. They put me on hold for almost ten minutes be-fore someone finds her. She starts to tell me about Larissa run-ning off, and I interrupt, saying I already know.

"Well, we found her," she says. "Mom took her to Burger King, says she was going to bring her back to us right after din-ner, but a policeman noticed them first. Just happened to be one of the few policemen actually looking for her."

"Larissa *did* go back home?"

"Yes, she did, and Mom should have called us right away, it would have looked good on her record if she had, but she didn't." She pauses. "And, Alice, they're taking me off Larissa's case."

I don't understand. "Because she ran away?"

"No, it's standard to switch to a permanent social worker. I just thought they'd let me stay with her if I wanted. I was wrong. They . . ." She pauses, on the verge of saying something more, but doesn't. "They're still considering you, Alice. If they move her, which they probably will, they'll move her farther away from her own neighborhood this time. We can't get her to promise she won't go back home. We can't get her to talk at all."

"They're really thinking about me?"

"Yes, but the person you have to influence now is her GAL."

"The guy in the suit?"

"His name is Larry Phillips." She tells me where I can reach him.

"I should call him?"

"I would. It's too late now. Try him Monday morning."

"I will. God, I'm so sorry. I really hope it wasn't because of me."

Yolanda ignores my apology. "Listen, Alice, Larry's got a bit of mud on his face right now, suggesting Larissa go home, putting it on record, then Mom not calling the police this time. He's going to be very careful what he suggests next. He might recommend you, he might not."

"Okay. I'll try. My home study visit is Monday. Any suggestions?"

"No. Be yourself. She's a nice woman. Erin. Oh, by the way, your fingerprints came back clean."

I knew they would, but it's still a relief. "How is she? Is she okay?"

"After being dragged screaming out of Mom's arms? Physically, she's fine. It's what we're doing to her right now that's causing the damage."

"Do you think she should be back with her mother?" I ask.

"I've seen worse, but she left her all alone, Alice. She lost her right to be a mother. She has to earn that back, and she's not doing a very good job of it. I don't like her personally, but that doesn't matter. She has a right to be Larissa's mother, if she gets her act together."

"I meant what I said about taking you out for lunch."

"Thanks."

"I'll call this Larry guy. Thank you, again."

I hang up, and call Polly, ask her if the mayor wrote the recommendation yet.

"Yeah. It's pretty powerful. When she writes something like that she could sell snow to Eskimos."

"Could it be delivered there Monday morning? To this guy?" I read her the name and tell her where to send it.

"Yeah. I'll have the service take it over. You owe me, Alice."

"I win the lottery, I'll give the whole thing to you."

"You have to play it first, Alice."

"Now you sound like Vince."

"He wasn't always wrong, you know."

"Well, how about ice cream at Hershey's then? The works?"

"That'll do it," she says.

"Let me know when," I say.

"I will," she says. "Oh, I will."

I decide to wait until Tuesday morning to call Larry Phillips, make sure he gets the mayor's letter first, and the home study visit will be done by then. I can even fit in another foster parenting class on Saturday morning, before my lunch meeting with Ed, a college student who's been a client for two years. Saturday

I wake up feeling positive, energetic, hopeful, until, of course, halfway through the foster parenting class. *Working with Sexually Abused Children.* Now I have to worry about what her uncle might have done, if she has an uncle. Or a neighbor. Everyone has neighbors.

These classes are making me crazy.

I meet Ed for lunch at Jillian's, a billiard hall that serves great hamburgers, or so Ed says. He's a student at John Carroll University, working on a BS in psychology with a minor in philosophy. He's already at a table when I get there, drinking a Coke.

Hi! I wave. *Finish-you food order?* I sign, lifting my eyebrows and making it a question. He signs *Wait you come. Nice guy me.*

A young girl comes over to take our order, and Ed writes on my pad what he wants. *Hamburger, no lettuce, American cheese, grilled onions.* I get a chicken sandwich. It's been years since I ate a hamburger. When the waitress leaves, I sign, *Books?* Ed volunteered to pick up the textbooks the school gives me for his classes, since parking anywhere near the bookstore is impossible. He points to the floor, where a large canvas bag sits by his feet. The top book in the bag is a collection of Shakespeare's plays, and I laugh, finger-spelling *Ha-ha.* Ed was born deaf and is fluent in ASL, but has some trouble with the English language. Last year, in jest, I suggested he try reading Shakespeare, that the syntax might be a little more to his liking. I can't believe he really did it. Then again, I can.

I slap the side of my head then spread out my hands, palms up, moving them slightly in round, jerky motions. *What were you thinking?* Not ASL, but after two years together, we've come up with a few of our own favorite English phrases.

He grins. *Shakespeare class and theater class. Both. Actor, maybe, me. Who knows?*

I shake my head. What will the acting teacher think about having a deaf student?

The waitress brings over our lunch. "Everything okay?" she asks, forming the words carefully in case Ed lip-reads, which he can; he'd just prefer not to have to.

Ed nods.

"Good. Have a nice meal." She says this slowly, with a flirty look on her face. Ed's got a head of blond hair and muscles everywhere. She hardly glances at me.

He smiles at her shyly, then bends his blond head over his food. "Thanks," I say, signing it also. She looks back at us as she walks away.

She likes you, I sign. *Ask her out+date.*

He shakes his head.

Too damn shy, I sign. Then I look down at the books on the floor. Too damn smart, too. The pile is two feet high. Shake-speare. Jesus.

Just behind us, someone breaks the balls on a billiard table. Someone else laughs loudly. Ed never even looks up.

Have schedule? I ask. I love interpreting for Ed, and another deaf student, Shaun. Shaun has some hearing and can read lips, but still misses a lot and uses an interpreter. He's a goof and cool at the same time; he would have asked the waitress out, then we'd never be able to come back after he broke up with her a month later.

Ed shifts his weight and digs a folded-up piece of paper out of his back pocket, handing it over. His philosophy class is at night, seven-thirty to nine on Tuesdays and Thursdays.

Night? Have to? I ask. He nods. I smile and shrug, but he catches the tightness of my smile.

What?

Problem, maybe. Maybe not. Wait see.

He raises his eyebrows.

I tell him I'm thinking about adopting a child. I don't mention Larissa, or how we met. Ed is a friend, but we are limited in some ways by the student/interpreter relationship. I don't want to get too personal. Still, he sees the hope in my eyes, how much this means to me. He signs *Wow! You? Really?* I nod, smile a little.

Good luck, he signs with a big smile.

Thanks, I sign. He's got a great smile. The waitress comes back and asks if there's anything else we need.

Polly calls me around eight. "Alice, I'm in Massachusetts," she says. "My mom's in the hospital." She stops talking for a moment. "She had a brain embolism. It's not good. Patrick's here with me."

The quaver in her voice makes my eyes well up. I swallow. "Oh God, Polly. I'm sorry. How is she?"

"She's alive and breathing on her own. It was touch and go for a while. It was a big one. Now we just wait."

"Can you talk to her?"

"Not yet."

"Are your sisters there?" I need to know if there's someone there for her to turn to. Then again, she has a husband.

"Bev just got here. Janice was here before me."

"Should I come?"

She pauses, and I imagine her trying not to cry, getting it together. "No. Not now. Not yet. Thanks for asking."

"You're sure? I'll come, really." I *could* leave Monday, after the home study.

"No. It's crazy here. Patrick just went to find us a hotel room.

Bev and Janice are sleeping at Mom's. I just wanted you to know."

"I'll be thinking of you, Polly, every minute. I'm so sorry."

I can hear people talking in the background. It occurs to me that almost every time I talk to Polly on the phone, I hear people in the background.

We say good-bye. "Love you," I add, but she has already hung up.

Chapter Thirteen

The home visit woman turns out to be a man. He apologizes as I stand gaping through the screen door. "Hi, my name's Adam Harris. Erin slipped in the shower this morning and broke her wrist."

"Ouch," I say, opening the door.

"Yeah, sounds nasty to me, too. I've never broken a bone in my body, not yet." He knocks three times against the wood frame of the doorway. He's short and his nose is flattened as if it's been broken more than once. His hair is black, but he has a gray goatee. He looks like a boxer trying to be a poet, and yet he's carrying a thick black briefcase, with, I imagine, a clipboard inside, just like everyone else from Children and Family Services.

"Come on in." I lead him into the living room.

"Can I put this down somewhere?" he asks, lifting the brief-case.

"Anywhere is fine," I say casually, trying to sound as if I'm not too finicky. I was up until two last night arranging my house so it would look clean, but not fussy. I organized my interpreting manuals at pleasing angles on the coffee table, then whisked them off and piled them on a bookcase, then put them on the couch as if I'd just been reading them, then finally put them back on the table by the couch, but not so neatly. He places his briefcase next to them.

"You're an interpreter?" he says.

"Yep," I say, nodding once with my fist.

"That's a sign?" he asks.

I do it again. "Yes, it is." I'm trying to be friendly, but now I worry I'm coming off as a know-it-all. I put my hands behind me, tell them to behave.

He takes a clipboard out of his briefcase and fills in my name and address on the top sheet. It's beginning to bother me how many people want my name and address.

"I'd like to look around the house first, if you don't mind. Okay?"

I give him the tour. He bends down to check electrical sockets, looks up to check smoke detectors—even climbs up on a chair to make sure the batteries work, which I replaced yesterday. He asks which room I sleep in, although it has to be obvious, and what room a foster child would sleep in. He inspects my furnace, notes the temperature of my hot water tank, asks if I have an escape plan in case of a fire. I almost say *Jump out the nearest window,* but admit that I don't. He says I need one, in writing. I will also need two fire extinguishers and a carbon monoxide detector. In the kitchen, he asks where I keep cleaning chemicals. He uses a friendly, pleasant tone of voice, trying to make me feel comfortable as he pries into my house like a doctor checking out a patient for lumps. I smile and thank him when he says everything seems okay.

"Now we have to sit and talk a while."

I offer him coffee and we sit at my kitchen table, which I scrubbed to the bone the night before. There's a plant on the table, and salt and pepper shakers. All my vitamins are on a high shelf, as if I do that all the time. I'm hoping a salt and pepper shaker are okay. Anything in my house might betray me.

He asks standard questions: my age, working hours, what neighbors I know, if I smoke cigarettes. Then he puts down his pen and says, "So tell me, why do you want to do this, be a foster parent?"

I'm not expecting this. I thought he was just going to check out my house. I tell him the story about the phone call, the police, the trip to the hospital, going down to Children and Family Services, my visit to Mrs. Hunt's. He never shakes his head or rolls his eyes. He lets me tell the story without interruptions. No one has ever done that. I find myself looking in his eyes and glance away.

"That's quite a story," he says when I'm done.

I nod. Take a sip of my coffee. I wonder what he thinks of me.

"Okay," he says. "Now for the really tough questions. I apologize up front if they offend you." He picks up the pen again. At least he didn't bring a tape recorder.

Folding my arms, I lean against the back of the chair. "Okay. Shoot."

"Well now, how about that, to begin with. Any guns in your home?"

"No. None."

"Does anyone come into your home who owns or carries guns?"

"No."

"Does anyone who comes into your home do drugs?"

Not anymore, I think. *He got hit by a car.* I shake my head no.

"Who does come over?" He says it simply, but we both know it isn't a simple question.

I pause. "My friends."

"Do people sleep here overnight?"

I feel my face get hot. "Not for a while."

"Sorry," he says. "For asking, I mean." Now he blushes. "I need to ask this though. When was the last time someone spent the night?"

"I really have to answer that?"

"You don't really have to answer anything, but these are the questions I have to ask. You can plead the fifth, but it doesn't look so good." He smiles apologetically. I like him, which makes this all the more difficult.

"Over a year ago. Is that good enough?"

"Good enough." We're quiet for a moment. This is worse than a blind date. He's going to leave knowing how old I am, what's under my kitchen sink, and when the last time was that I had sex, and I don't even know if he's married.

There are more questions. How I plan on finding day care. How I would discipline my foster child. The distance to the school. Transportation to school. Am I on prescription drugs. Have I ever been clinically depressed. Sampson comes wandering in from a nap, and Adam asks if he's up on his shots. I wonder if he thought of that on the spot, if he gets to ask any question he wants to. Do I pick my nose? Date short men? What is the limit here? I feel compelled to answer the most intimate questions. I've almost forgotten why he's asking me all this when he hands me a stack of papers. "Your homework," he says.

I look at the papers with dozens more questions. How much further can I go before I hate myself in the morning? I laugh. It just escapes.

"They're pretty simple questions," he says. "Some about your childhood, a few essays. Please answer them as fully as you can. I'll pick them up next week when I come back to check off the missing items, the fire escape plan, extinguishers, and the carbon monoxide detector."

The first essay question is, *Explain one event growing up that had a profound effect on your life*. I look back at him with obvious confusion.

"I know. But it's for the best that we know who you are. You've been very frank so far. I think you'll be a very good foster parent." He puts his papers back into his briefcase, combs his hair back with his fingers. "Thanks for the coffee." His hands are wide, his nails trimmed. There's black hairs on the back of his fingers. I like his hands. I like the way he's made me feel comfortable. He's the opposite of the foster parenting classes. He makes this seem possible.

"You really think that? I'd be good at this?"

He stands. "Yes. I do."

"Thanks." I stand up, too. "That means a lot to me. After all, you go around interrogating people all the time. You should know." I say it with a smile.

He laughs. He has a nice laugh, as if he's having fun. "Get those fire extinguishers," he says. He lowers his voice. "I'll be back." We both roll our eyes.

I watch him walk to his car. He as much as said I passed the test. *And* he has to come back.

I want to call Polly and tell her how well the visit went, but then I remember that she's with her mother. At two o'clock I have a meeting with Shaun, the other student I interpret for. On the way home from that, I buy fire extinguishers, and a carbon monoxide detector, and some board games for kids. I get the ones I used to play. It's amazing, the life of a board game. Love should last so long.

After dinner, I sit down to do my homework. I draw up a fire escape plan, crumpling up the one with the stick figure jumping out the window yelling "Help!" Then I tackle the questions. For one of the essays, I write about being a twin, how as a child I always thought everyone had a twin, and when I found out that wasn't true, I felt some great loss for the world, a terrible sadness— then I began to worry that twinless kids would steal my brother in the middle of the night. I tear that up, thinking about the psychiatrist that will probably be reading it. I write instead about having a deaf boy live on my street, and try to tie it all together with my desire to be an interpreter even though it isn't true.

I think about Adam reading all this. I want to tell him things he didn't ask.

Polly calls me again late at night. Her mother is able to talk, but her voice is slurred and her left side isn't working well. The doctors are talking about sending her into a nursing home for rehab sometime next week. Polly's going to stay there for a while. Once again I offer to come. Once again, she refuses. When I hang up, I wonder if my offer to come isn't something like the offer to pay for the pizza she brought to my house. What if she said yes? Would I walk away from all that's happening?

· · ·

Tuesday morning I interpret at a PTA meeting in Mentor. From there, I go to the bank and to the grocery store. When I get home, there's a message on the machine. It's Larry Phillips. I was just going to call him. He says to call back as soon as possible.

Cradling the portable phone between my shoulder and my ear, I begin to put the groceries away as I wait for someone to find him. Then, as he speaks, I have to sit down.

I'm not sure if I'm hearing him right. He tells me they will bring Larissa over tomorrow if I can get validation of day care, and bring that and a few other things down to Children and Family Services by four o'clock today. He reads me a list of the paperwork I need. He sounds formal, not friendly. He sounds serious. I say, "Yes," and "Of course," and "I will." Then he hangs up.

I'm getting Larissa. It's so huge I can't really believe it, can't get my mind to think about what this means. I just go into action. I call the day care place that I talked to last week and ask if they still have a spot. I'll need them only during school vacations. They say they do and that I can come over and get it in writing. I run upstairs, get my birth certificate and social security card out of my safe, grab my phone book, find my canceled checks for rent and utilities, check that I have the receipt for the fire extinguishers and carbon monoxide detector, pick up my fire escape plan and homework, run out of the house, and drive off. Only as I park my car behind Children and Family Services at two-thirty do I remember that I left the groceries out on the counter at home.

I ask for Larissa's social worker when I check in, but it's Yolanda who comes to the waiting room to get me. She's smiling.

"They haven't transferred me off the case yet," she says. "Not till tomorrow."

"So you did this?" I ask. "Like some last-minute presidential reprieve?"

"No," she says with a laugh, leading me down the hallway. "It was a group decision, and Larissa's guardian was all for it."

"You're kidding?"

"I think the letter from the mayor persuaded him." She looks at me with amusement. "Determined, weren't you?"

We turn into a large area with cubicles. Each cubicle has a computer and a small desk piled high with papers. Yolanda waves me to a chair. For half an hour, it's all business. I fill out forms and sign my name at the X a few dozen times. Yolanda makes copies of everything that I brought with me and gives me pamphlets, names of people who will help me, and a pink copy of everything I sign. I don't chat or ask her any unnecessary questions. I don't even allow myself to get excited; I'm sure there will be some bump in the road. Some paperwork I've forgotten. Then Yolanda says, "That's it."

When it sinks in, I say, "Thank you," on a breath of held-in air.

Yolanda nods in acceptance. She's done so much to help me, but she doesn't seem to need me to tell her that. Every time I see her, I like her more. "Larissa will need to go to Metzenbaum at least once a week to visit her mother. You'll need to make sure she's available at those times." She looks at me carefully, letting me know that even though she's all for me getting Larissa, I still have to pay strict attention to the rules.

I nod. "What is her mother's name?" I don't mention our encounter on the street corner.

"Michelle."

"Will she know I have Larissa? Will she know where I live?"

"Not unless you tell her. I wouldn't suggest her coming to your house until we know she's following her case plan. And remember, she was verbally abusive to me. Be careful."

"Okay."

"Listen, Alice. The best advice I can give you is to have patience. Keep going to the foster parenting classes. Call us if you have problems. If Larissa starts talking and wants to call Mom, set up definite times for phone communication, set time limits, but let her have those calls. I'm going to stress this again. The goal is reunification."

I nod solemnly. I understand—but my heart doesn't. Then I think of something. "I'm going to my parents' in Columbus for Labor Day weekend. My nephews will be there. Can I take her? Should I?"

"You have to let us know, but you can take her."

"But should I?"

"I don't know. Are they good people?"

"Yes," I say. "They're good people."

"Then you should. But see how she's doing first."

"All right. I will." I pause. "So, they're bringing her tomorrow?"

"Around one, after lunch."

"I'm scared," I say.

Yolanda looks up at me from something she was typing. "You'll do fine. Just give her plenty of love." She clicks the mouse and the computer screen brings up her wallpaper: a deep blue ocean and a sandy beach. A dolphin arches across the water. It must be a place she wants to go, away from these cubicles, these unending tragedies. And yet, I am exactly where I want to be, sitting here, being told it's all official. Larissa is coming to stay with me.

"Oh," I say. "I will."

As soon as I get back home, I phone Elaine at the Hearing and Speech Center and tell her I'm not available until next Wednesday. That will give Larissa and me six days together before she starts school. Then I call Ed on my TTY. I tell him that I can't do any night classes, and why. He's very sweet and says he will find another time for his philosophy class. I get teary, and thank him profusely.

In a week, I'll be sending a first-grader off to school.

I throw away the meat and the milk that had been left in the hot kitchen for hours, and rush back out to the grocery store to buy peanut butter, jelly, white bread, and everything a little girl might like. No pop, but I get six different kinds of fruit juice. I tell the checkout girl Laura that I'm foster parenting a little girl. She smiles widely. "Oh, that's wonderful!" she says, and I want to hug her.

Back home again, I call my parents. "Mom," I say, "I might be bringing someone with me." My left hand spells *Larissa*.

"Oh?" Her tone means: *Is he nice? Am I in love? Do I think I should be bringing him along already?* All that in her *oh*.

"No, Mother," I say to her unasked questions, "It's a little girl. Her name is Larissa and I'm going to be her foster mother for a while."

"Oh?" This time she means, *Oh, that's interesting,* and, *Oh, that might be trouble, do you really want to do this?,* and *Oh, why am I just now hearing this?*

"It'll be fine, Mother. It's a long story, and I'll tell you the whole thing when I get there. Don't we have that cot? Could you set it up in my old room for her? She's not allowed to sleep in a bed with me. She's six." I almost add that she's black, but I don't want another *oh* right now.

"We have the cot," my mother says slowly. "A little girl?"

"Yes, Mother, and she's a bit traumatized. She may not speak much, but I want you to meet her."

"All right. We'll, this is all very interesting. I look forward to meeting her and hearing your story."

"Thanks. See you soon."

It isn't the phone call that I wanted; I wanted the same reaction as Laura the grocery store clerk gave me: happiness for me, no questions.

I stay up late, playing the *1812 Overture* and fixing up the room for Larissa, filling it with the things I bought: a Mickey Mouse lamp, the ceramic unicorns, a music box, Beanie Babies, posters, a pink quilt. Then I check the whole house for hidden dangers that the home study guy might have missed. I could fail here, big-time. I need to be careful.

Somewhere around three in the morning, I sit on the couch with Sampson in my lap. I tell him that Larissa will be coming tomorrow. I warn him that we can love her, but we can't keep her.

You're going to try to, though, Vince says.

Her mother abandoned her, I say.

She's not a kitten.

And you're not really here. I'm just talking to myself.

Sounds to me like you were talking to a cat.

Don't you ever sleep up there? I ask.

You're the one up at three in the morning.

I'm getting a foster child tomorrow, I tell him. And I can feel his smile. I can feel his hand on mine.

Go to bed, he says, or I say. *Tomorrow will be a big day.*

I don't fall asleep for a long time.

Chapter Fourteen

A stranger brings Larissa to me. She's Larissa's new social worker, Crystal somebody, and she's carrying that damn canvas bag. I sign some papers, and in fifteen minutes she's gone. Larissa stands in the center of my living room as if my furniture might attack her, the canvas bag by her feet. Her thumb is in her mouth, Lucy in her arms.

She's wearing jean shorts, a red T-shirt, and white tennis shoes. Her knees are rougher and darker than the rest of her skin, and her arms and legs are ropy, muscular for such a little girl. I can imagine her running away from Mr. Klewer at the school, running with all her might toward home. She stands up straight, almost leaning backward; the stance of someone feigning indifference. Her curly hair hangs down in her face and I want to tie it back so she can see better, so I can see *her* better. How long will it be before I feel comfortable touching her, doing her hair?

Larissa looks around the room with her eyes, but doesn't move her head. I said hello to her at the door, but she didn't answer me. My hands are sweaty and I rub them against my pants.

Instinct drives me. I sign *Hi, Larissa,* keeping my mouth closed and my face blank. When signing to a deaf person I use facial expressions, but I think that might be a bit too much for her right now. Larissa isn't deaf; she has just decided not to talk. I'll go along with the program for the time being, in my own way.

She doesn't move, but her eyes are listening, interested in what I might do next. I'm not like other adults because I talk with my hands, and not being like other adults is a big plus right now. I sign *Hi, Lucy,* looking at her bunny, and she looks down at Lucy, then back up at me. I point to the couch and sign *couch.* Point to the TV and sign *TV.* Point to the table and sign *table.* I don't say a word. Then I sign *Follow me,* the way anyone would. She follows, probably because she doesn't want to be left alone standing in a strange room. In the kitchen, Sampson hops down from his napping spot on my kitchen chair, and I sign *cat* and spell his name. The sign for *cat* is somewhat iconic so she knows what I mean, and Larissa smiles a tiny, quickly withdrawn smile. Once again, I begin counting smiles.

Back in the living room, I pick up her bag and head upstairs, signing *Follow me* again. There's no music playing, no TV, just the sound of our footsteps. I show her the room that I prepared for her. I sign *your room,* and put the canvas bag down next to the dresser. I point to the bed and sign *bed.* Point to the pillow and sign *pillow.* Then sign *yours.*

Opening the drawers in the dresser, I show her that they're empty, for her clothes. I don't know if she understands, but it doesn't matter right now. We'll unpack her bag later.

Next I show her my office with the computer, fax, and TTY, holding my hand up and shaking my head, meaning she should stay out of that room. I don't want to be rude, but I can't have her fussing around in there. The bathroom's next to it, then my bedroom. Her eyes widen slightly when I sign *my bed*. She saw me sign *bed* before. The sign for *my* seems just as obvious as the word *cat*. She understood what I said. I allow myself one small smile.

I want her to think it's just a game right now. She's had enough reality for a while.

I sign *You bed?* meaning *Are you tired?*, knowing she will understand the sign for *bed*. She stares at me then shakes her head no, her thumb still in her mouth. I sign *You me eat?*, putting my fingers to my mouth as if about to eat something. She shrugs. I decide a shrug isn't a no, and if we eat, she'll at least have to take her thumb out of her mouth. I wave for her to follow me.

In the kitchen, I take out the bread, the peanut butter, the jelly, a box of raisins, baby carrots, apple juice, potato chips, and a cut-up cantaloupe, and put it all on the kitchen table. I hand her a carrot and point to Lucy, then pull out a chair for her. It has two pillows on it. A pink one and an orange one. No mere phone books for this place. I have enough pillows from my mother to cover all the chairs, and then some. There's no way for me to explain in sign how my mother made all these pillows, but I want to. I want to tell her everything, but instead I make peanut butter and jelly sandwiches. As I open the bag of chips, we both notice the loud crinkling of the chip bag and our eyes meet for a moment. I pour her a glass of grape juice, and we listen to the slosh of liquid. I sign *Eat,* and she waits a minute, then picks up the half of a sandwich, and I hear myself take a breath of relief. What if she wouldn't eat? Would I have to call someone and let them know?

What should we do next? Take a walk, show her around the neighborhood? There are so many reasons I might need to speak outside. People might say hello. We should stay inside. And do what? I can't read her a book if I'm not speaking. What could we do without talking? Then I know.

I clean up the food and she sits at the table, taking in everything with her eyes, thumb back in her mouth. Finally I sign *Follow me* and go into the living room. I point to the couch and sign *Sit, please*. She may not know what I'm signing, but pointing to the couch seems to do it. She sits down on the far end. I turn on the TV and immediately hit MUTE. Then I find a cartoon station and sit down on the other end of the couch. Larissa looks at the TV, crosses her legs underneath her, and settles in.

We watch TV, and just as I knew would happen, Sampson comes in and sits on my lap. Even without the sound of the TV, he assumes I'm sitting down for a while. I look at Larissa and sign *Silly fat cat*. The corners of her mouth turn up.

I know that if I move Sampson over to Larissa's lap, he'll lie there until she gets up. I point to Sampson, then to her lap. She nods. I put Sampson in her lap and he seems to melt, his whole body adjusting to her small shape by sagging off the sides of her legs. Larissa touches his head, and he begins to purr. She smiles. Three!

A half hour later, Larissa's eyes close and her head leans sideways against the couch. I don't move. I breathe slowly, noticing that my heart, which has been beating hard since the doorbell rang, has slowed down. I watch Larissa sleep, my cat in her lap. She has a small scar near her chin, like a tiny crescent moon.

I sat on a couch while she slept once before, and I try not to think about that night in her apartment. I try not to think what I've taken her from. It's not my fault, I tell myself. I'm the good guy.

I'm reading one of Ed's philosophy books when I notice movement out of the corner of my eye. Larissa is waking up, and I turn just in time to catch an expression on her face that says, *Where am I?,* then one of understanding. I don't see fear, or anger, just a look that is much too adult: resignation.

I wish I could ask her if she loves her mother, if she's forgiven her so easily. I wish I could speak and say *Do you like me at all?*

I stick to the plan: Let her speak first.

Using a lot of pantomime mixed in with sign, we play Chutes and Ladders sitting on the rug on the floor. The rug is a good one, one of those gifts I bought myself, wool with colorful stripes to match my southwestern theme. Now I wish it were soft, plush. Maybe she's allergic to wool.

When I sign *Drink?* she nods, and I get apple juice and ginger snaps, putting them on a tray, then the tray on the floor. We can hear each other chewing. After the third game, I take her outside into the backyard and show her the garden I'm digging and the gnome statue my parents gave me as a birthday present. I want to tell her I will buy her a swing set. Maybe it is for the best that we're not speaking. What else might I promise her?

Back inside, Larissa points to my cat, then walks over to the couch and sits down. I put Sampson in her lap again, and she pets him, gently brushing her fingers along his head. He probably can't believe his good luck. I point to the TV, and she shrugs, so I don't turn it on. I sign that I'm going to make dinner, and she looks at me curiously, not quite understanding. Still, she looks content to sit and pet Sampson, so I leave her there and go into the kitchen. In the kitchen, I lean my back against the cool refrigerator door and close my eyes. Silence is exhausting me.

I make grilled cheese sandwiches and a salad, set the table, and put out a bowl of chips. Sampson comes into the kitchen when he hears me using the electric can opener to open a can of cling peaches. Larissa follows him in.

We sit at the kitchen table again. Larissa leaves the crusts of the grilled cheese sandwich, eats only the carrots out of the salad, finishes all the potato chips, and just glances at the bowl of cling peaches. I put one on her plate and she looks at me with one eye squinted. *They good,* I sign, and rub my stomach, closing my eyes and making my face look happy and satisfied. She just stares at the peach quarter. I cut it into little pieces for her. After a lot of thought, she picks up her fork and prods a piece of peach, then puts it in her mouth. She chews a moment, making a face that says she's not quite sure, then shrugs. She doesn't eat any more.

Dinner is over and it's only six. What time should I put her to bed? Eight? How will we get through two more hours without talking? What if the phone rings? The idea of the phone ringing bothers me, and I take it off the hook. We play Chutes and Ladders two more times, crayon in a coloring book, do a small wooden puzzle that's obviously too easy for her, then watch an *Everybody Loves Raymond* rerun with the sound turned off. In its own way, everything is going very well, I tell myself. My shoulders, though, are so tense I can hardly turn my neck.

Finally I point to her, then make the sign for *bed.* She shrugs and looks down at Sampson, who has happily made his home in her lap again. She points to him, then upstairs, and I nod. She smiles. I pick up Sampson and we all go upstairs.

Four.

In her bedroom, I point to the canvas bag and then to the dresser, and she just shrugs, so I put away her clothes without her help as she watches, leaving the pink pajamas on the bed. I think maybe I should smell them, see if they're washed. I pick them up and carry them to the bathroom, and Larissa follows. I show her the new toothbrush I bought, and open the package for her. It's a child-size toothbrush, thick-handled and bright purple with soft bristles. I stopped myself from buying more. One toothbrush at a time.

Pulling out the small step stool I found at a garage sale, I motion for her to climb up and brush her teeth. I point to the folded washcloth on the sink and sign *yours,* and leave the bathroom, closing the door behind me so she can have her privacy. Outside the door, I stand listening to every sound. My razor is on the high shelf. Certainly she can't reach that.

Anything could happen, things I never considered in fortyeight years. How the hell am I ever going to sleep again?

Because of our silence, I can't read her a bedtime story, so we look at a picture book about African wild animals and I sign the names of the animals. About three pages in I begin to worry that the pictures of tigers and lions might give her nightmares. What a dumb choice of bedtime books.

Finally I place Sampson on the middle of the bed, by her feet. She holds Lucy tight in her arms, just as she has done all day. The thumb has been in her mouth also, unless pulled out to move a Chutes and Ladders piece, or hold a crayon, or pet Sampson, and at these times her thumb looked like a puckered raisin. Did she wash her hands in the bathroom? Should I have told her to? I turn on the night light, cover her up, and sign *Good night.* She nods. I walk out, leaving the door halfway open. In my bedroom, I sit on the bed and put my head in my hands. Should I have brushed her hair? Given her a bath? Made her talk? Is all this signing going to make her never want to talk again? How am I ever going to give her a bath? Can I leave her alone in the bathtub? Might she get up in the middle of the night and walk out?

Still, she smiled. She likes Sampson. She ate dinner, went to bed without a fuss. Not too bad, right? It could have been worse. I did okay. She's not going to walk out in the middle of the night.

But then I hear a sound almost like the gurgling in my radiator pipes, but nothing like that at all. I have to strain to listen, and then I know what it is. She's crying.

I get up quietly and sneak over to her door, standing there a full minute, hoping she'll stop. She sniffles. Her nose must be running. Now there's a gasping sound, as if she can't quite breathe. I go into the bathroom and get the box of Kleenex.

Larissa turns sharply toward me as I enter the room, tears streaming down her cheeks, her nose running just as I thought. In the dim light, what stands out are the reddish-whiteness of her eyes, the shape of them now not wide but angry, furious, and forlorn all at once. I hand her the box of Kleenex and she grabs it out of my hand, then, bottom lip stuck out, she motions me away as you would a fly or a bug. I back out of the room, close the door halfway again, then close it even further. I back down the hallway, keeping my eye on her door, listening in case she calls out to me. I sit on my bed.

What should I have done? Knelt by her bed, spoken softly to her, told her everything would be all right, lies she would have known and hated me for? There hadn't even been time to think. Her waving me away was quick and sure. Her look said that I had seen something I wasn't supposed to, that she thought she had some privacy at last, and I came when I wasn't wanted. In her look was the girl who had told the police officer to fuck off. In her look was the reality we have been avoiding all day: that she's not really a happy child. That she could so easily hate me. So much in a look, but that's what I'm good at, reading faces. Right now I wish I were blind.

I sit on my bed for a long time, numb, just breathing. Then I get up and go downstairs, double-check the doors and windows.

Chapter Fifteen

My alarm rings at six-thirty in the morning, a god-awful time of morning, but I'm afraid Larissa might get up before me. I peek in her room as if I am doing something wrong. Larissa's sound asleep, the blanket crumpled around her. Sampson looks at me lazily, then closes his eyes again.

I make coffee and read through the stack of paperwork the social worker handed me. Larissa's religion is listed as Baptist, nonpracticing. Her father's name was Charles. Her birthday is June sixteenth. Just ten days after my birthday. She has only been six for a little while. She's not allergic to anything.

Larissa comes downstairs around eight, her eyes puffy and red, and we nod to each other like strangers warily acknowledging each other on the street. I wave to the table, and she eats. After that, she walks to the couch and I turn on the TV, automatically muting it, and she slips her thumb in her mouth. Surely I am doing something terrible by not talking, but I don't know what else to do. Sampson comes downstairs, eats, then hops up onto Larissa's lap, content to live so simply.

I go upstairs and clean up all the used Kleenex in her room, telling myself this is my right, to come into this room. As I make her bed, I smell urine and pull the covers back farther. There's a yellow stain drying on the white sheets. She's wet her bed. I pull off the sheets and pile them in the hall. The mattress is still slightly damp. How do I clean this up? I go downstairs, get paper towels and dish soap. Larissa looks at me from the couch, seeing the towels, the soap. She turns her head quickly away. I go upstairs, scrub at the mattress, dry it with the hair dryer. Only as I'm doing this do I realize she still has on her pajamas, which must be soaked in urine too. And she's sitting on my couch.

She'll need more pajamas, and I'll have to get one of those plastic mattress covers. Where do I get those? I've never seen them displayed in Dillard's. I make the bed up with clean sheets, pull up the quilt. The room looks so clean, just as it did before Larissa came, as if she had never been here.

I take the sheets down to the basement, but leave them on the floor. I should wash her pajamas too, and give her a bath. And I need a shower myself. Already I see the day half gone.

I could talk. I could tell her that she needs to take off her pajamas and take a bath, but when I walk up to her as she sits on the couch, she looks so peaceful. We have a truce, a way to live with each other, and it is in this silence. It won't be forever, but I'm not ready to break it yet. I kneel in front of her. I don't use sign, but pantomime. I pinch at the material of her pajama bottoms, noticing now the smell of urine, and pretend to throw them off her body. Then I scrub myself, and point to her. Turning off the TV, I motion for her to follow me. She doesn't move right away. Yesterday she didn't want to be stranded in an unfamiliar room, but now she has Sampson in her lap and she knows the layout. She's more in control. I clap two times, my signal for Sampson to get down from whatever he's up on. He too does not move, which pisses me off. I clap two more times, and he gets up and hops off the couch. He looks at me, wondering what my problem is. Make up my mind. Didn't I want him with the little girl? I walk over to the bottom of the steps and turn and look at her. *Come on,* is on the tip of my tongue. There must be something in my look, because she gets up, follows me.

In the bathroom, she watches me as I wash out the tub, begin to fill it up. She grabs my shirt and gives a tug. I almost say *What?*

Larissa points to the shower head. I make a face that says, *Really?* She nods vigorously. I make all sorts of motions, pointing to her, pointing to the tub, pointing to the shower head again, use my fingers to mime water coming down on her head. She makes a fist and signs *yes* so firmly that I laugh. Okay. She wants a shower. How do I wash her hair then? She goes out of the bathroom, and this time I follow her. She gets clothes out of her drawers, so adeptly switching Lucy around in her arms that the bunny never has to be put down. Then we go back to the bathroom and she puts her clothes down on the hamper. I place a towel on top of the clothes. Larissa brushes her teeth, and I watch as she does a perfect job, like a commercial for brushing teeth, and I think about her mother, how she must have taught Larissa this. I shake my head. I do not want to think about that woman. I turn on the shower and adjust the temperature, and Larissa motions for me to leave.

Can I leave her alone? What if she slips? Does she know which is the shampoo? The conditioner? She motions for me to leave again, not like last night, but with an assuredness that strikes me as both funny and frightening; I don't know her at all. She likes my cat, and that is the only thing I can be sure of.

I pick up the shampoo, pretend to wash my hair, pick up the conditioner, do the same, put them on the ledge of the shower. She rolls her eyes, nods. I leave the bathroom. I feel worn out, ready to go back to bed. I lean against the wall and wait. Will I hear the thunk of her head hitting the bathtub over the sound of the running water? At what age do kids start taking showers these days? Larissa seems like an old pro. What else can she do? Maybe she knows how to get my computer to stop freezing up whenever I try to download something. I know I'm giddy. I'm living a silent movie, Charlie Chaplin or something. There is such sadness in his old movies, a sadness in his humor that would have been ruined by voice.

I time her. Twelve minutes until she turns off the shower. Ten minutes later, she comes out, dressed, a towel around her head. Who taught her to wrap a towel around her head like that? Oh yes, she has a mother.

We sit on her bed, and I carefully comb out her hair. I am very, very gentle. It takes a very long time to comb out her hair.

I take my shower. Put everything in the washer, then decide not to take her shopping for pajamas today. Maybe tomorrow. How can you shop without talking? I could pretend to be deaf, I've done it before, but just the thought exhausts me.

I decide to take her to the nature center. I don't know how to tell her, but I try, signing *drive-to,* holding an imaginary wheel and moving it outward. Then I mime us walking, mime trees, mime breathing in fresh air. She may not understand a thing, but she follows me to the car. She will be good and follow me along; maybe if she's good, they'll let her go home.

In the parking lot, Larissa steps out of my car, but just stands there. When I offer her my hand, she keeps her thumb in her mouth, but shifts Lucy into the crook of that arm, gives me the Lucy hand. This is new. Usually I get her hand with the wet thumb when we walk. It's cooler out today, and feels like rain. Maybe she's afraid of the rain.

Everything is so dry that our footsteps on the pebbles sound loud and crinkly, like the potato chip bag. She holds my hand tightly and stays so close to me that I'm afraid I'll trip on her. A chipmunk scurries by and she flinches. I want to tell her she's safe, that the animals are more afraid of her than she is of them, but how the hell am I going to mime that? When a bluejay cries out and flies across the path, she stiffens and refuses to go on. We turn back.

At home again, we have lunch: peanut butter and jelly sandwiches. We color and play several games of Chutes and Ladders, all in silence. I become aware of a humming in my ear that I never noticed before, the *click* of my water heater turning on, the *scritch* of crayons, the slight *plunk* of the game pieces on the Chutes and Ladders board. I have lived here in the silence of just me, and the silence of deaf friends, but this is different. Experiencing the sounds of us, together, without the words we *could* speak, is in some way curiously beautiful, as if the two of us are discovering a whole new world.

A little before five, the sky turns dark and we hear thunder rolling in. The thumb that came out of her mouth for Chutes and Ladders is back in her mouth with the first crack of lightning. The game is up. She goes over to the couch and sits down, legs crossed underneath, Lucy to her chest. Then she looks around the room. A worried look crosses her face and she looks up at me.

I sign *What?*, tilting my head, holding my palms out, shrug. She points to her lap. She wants Sampson. I nod. He doesn't like storms much either and is probably under a bed. He'll come if we call, though. He always comes if called, curious as cats are, wanting to know why we might want them.

I shrug, meaning *I don't know where he is.* Her bottom lip quivers and she looks at me pleadingly. I sign *Wait a minute,* in the way anyone would, one finger up, and walk around the house, go upstairs, come back down. I'm right, Sampson is under my bed. But I don't bring him down with me.

I shrug again, shaking my head. Lightning cracks and thunder rumbles, and her bottom lip quivers again. Using the best pantomime I can, I say *We have to call him,* then silently mouth the word *Sampson* a few times, showing the words coming out of my mouth with my fingers. She understands, I can see that in her eyes. Another crack of lightning, and the rain begins to beat down against the windows, coming sideways with a great deal of force. She looks down at her empty lap, then back up at me, nods, her eyes big. She wants me to call for Sampson, but I want her to. The problem is, I've never said Sampson's name out loud except for that night I went to her house, and I'm sure she doesn't remember his name. As I stand thinking about this, she points to me. I shake my head, point to myself, then back to her, then back to myself, so she knows I mean the both of us. She stares at me, then nods. I wave her over to me, by the bottom of the stairs. "Sampson," I call softly, not wanting him to come yet. I wait. No sign of him. I turn to her, nod. She looks up the stairs. Finally, she says it.

"Sampson."

She calls his name as softly as I did. I call again, a little louder. She waits a second, then calls him again. On her third call, he comes slowly down the stairs, knowing he's wanted but not wishing to look too needy. I pick him up and we go back to the couch. I place him in her lap.

"Good kitty," I say softly, and rub his head. Then we sit and listen to the rain, watching *Everybody Loves Raymond* again with no sound. Larissa flinches with each crack of lightning. Finally it's bedtime. I'm so tired I feel twitchy.

After the bedtime routine, she gets into bed and I cover her up. I have lined the space between the mattress and the bottom sheet with plastic garbage bags. Next to her, on the little table by her bed, is the box of Kleenex.

Larissa looks at the space where Sampson slept last night, and I know what she wants. I sign *say,* a circular movement of one finger by my mouth, and she understands. She points to me, then to herself. I'm to go first again. I call him, softly, adding, "Here kitty," then look at her.

"Sampson," she calls. "Here kitty." Her voice sounds so sweet. After a few tries, Sampson comes into the room, hopping up on the bed and lying down right where he slept last night, knowing now that this girl is his new best friend. Larissa takes her thumb out of her mouth and gently strokes his head between his ears. Her little fingers must feel like moth's wings. He purrs, the purr growing louder until it's a warm rumble. I sit on the edge of the bed, holding the book *Goodnight Moon.* When she looks up from Sampson, I point to myself, then the book, and make the sign for *say* again. After a moment of thought, she nods. In a quiet, almost reverent voice, I read *Goodnight Moon.* It's just the right voice for reading this book.

When I'm done, I stand up and turn off the light, leaving her night light on. "Good night," I say, in the same soft voice I used for reading the book. She just looks at me.

Standing in the doorway, I make a very sad face, a clown's sad face. I point to her, then to myself. I sign *say,* point to myself again, and repeat the sad clown face. She watches me for a minute, then softly says, "Good night." I smile widely and leave, closing the door halfway. I make it as far as my room before my legs give out and I sit on my bed. The effort it will take to wash my face is beyond me.

Tomorrow we're supposed to go to Columbus for three days and nights to stay with my parents. Can she handle that? Can I?

I hear a sniffle from her room, a small, soft sob, then nothing. I'm listening so hard I think I can still hear Sampson purring. I wait.

Not hearing any more signs of Larissa crying, I begin to think of other things. I haven't heard from Polly. The phone is off the hook and although I checked for messages several times whenever I could without Larissa noticing, there was nothing from Polly at all. She doesn't even know I have Larissa.

I go downstairs and call Polly's mother's house in Massachusetts. No answer. I leave a message. "Hi, this is Alice, calling to see how Constance is. I hope she's doing better. My love to all."

The next morning, Larissa comes downstairs in her pajamas, holding Lucy. I'm sitting at the kitchen table looking at Ed's philosophy book, hoping I'll find the answer to all my problems; I need some wise, thoughtful insights, but it seems philosophers don't have the answers, just the questions.

"Good morning, Larissa," I say, not in a whisper, but as softly as I can, as if my voice might break things.

Larissa comes straight up to the table, stands in front of me, arms crossed, Lucy tucked to her chest. "I want to go home. Now."

She doesn't say it as if she hates me, just as if I might actually do this for her. Apparently she has decided that I'm on her side; she could try, once again, to ask for what she wants most. I know whatever I say will silence her again, and I'll become just another bad guy, just like Mrs. Hunt, and Yolanda, and whatever social worker they assign her.

All my pretending we're getting along fine is fool's gold.

Larissa waits patiently as I think about what to say. I could blame everything on the government, like Vince would. Say the county took her away from her mother and there's nothing I can do but keep her until they let her go back home. Or I could blame it on her mother, remind Larissa how she had been abandoned—which I think she has forgotten, put away into some place deep inside where it can't bother her. All of these things are true, but I can't say any of them.

"Your mommy's trying very hard to find a job right now. She's out looking for one and she can't take care of you right now, until she gets the job she needs to support you both. There are a lot of people trying to help her. Sometimes we all need a little help. I'm helping by keeping you at my house so that you are taken care of while your mommy looks for a job. It must be very hard for you because you miss her, and she must miss you very much, too. There's a whole bunch of rules in this world, and the rules right now say you have to stay someplace else while your mommy . . . gets some things together."

She looks at me with her chin up, eyes narrowed, thinking, trying to understand, then she just gives up. "I want my mommy! Take me to my mommy now!"

"She needs to get a job first, and—"

"Get her a job!"

"I can't. I'm an interpreter—"

"I want to go home! I want my mommy!" She stomps one bare foot on the floor, glaring at me.

I lean forward in my chair. "Larissa, I can't take you home. They won't let me." There, I resort to blaming the government. How easy that was.

She kicks the cupboard, smashing her bare foot into the wood frame.

"Larissa—" I reach out to touch her arm, and she turns to me, mad as hell, with tears in her eyes from hurting her foot and every-thing else in the world. She reels back from my touch, falling as she steps back. She doesn't even try to stop herself from falling.

"I want my mommy! I want my mommy!" She thumps the linoleum floor with her heels so hard that I hear glasses tinkling in the cupboards. "I want my mommy! I want my mommy! I want my mommy!" she screams. The windows are open, and I wonder if the neighbors can hear her. She strikes out with her hands, thrashing around in the tight space, pounding on the wall and cupboard, howling. Her fist makes a dent in the wall; the plaster underneath is old, but it still has to hurt her hand. Lucy gets flung from her arms, landing in a jumble of legs and arms, looking nothing at all like a bunny. Larissa doesn't even notice. I lower myself to the floor, saying her name over and over again, gently, softly, the sound of tears in my throat. She just kicks and hits anything near her, screaming, "I want my mommy!" I can't restrain her. It's one of the rules. I can hug her, but I can't re-strain her. Can I put my arms around her and call it a hug? Can a word change the meaning of what I do?

I wait. She's wearing down. After a minute or two, she

slumps against the wall, into the corner, weeping harder now that she's not in a fury of movement, settling into a full-fledged cry. "I . . . want . . . my . . . mommy!" She can hardly get the words out now; they are more gasps for air than words. She can't even get her thumb into her mouth because then she won't be able to breathe. I crawl over to where Lucy lies heaped on the floor, and with my arm stretched out, not moving any closer to Larissa, hand her the bunny. She tugs it to her chest as if I stole it from her in the first place. With Lucy now back in her arms, she stiffens, holding herself so still she looks like someone determined never to move again, as well as never speak again. I want to scream: at Yolanda, at the magistrate, at the whole system. Why did they give her to me? Are they all so stupid not to know that a woman with no children wouldn't know what to do with this child? I feel tears running down the outside corners of my eyes and rub hard at them with my thumbs. I'm tough, but not this tough. I feel useless, less help than a stuffed rabbit.

"Would you like to call her?" I whisper. "Would you like to call your mother on the phone?"

Abruptly, she looks up at me and nods once.

"Fine, then. You can. You can call your mother."

She just sits there, snot running out of her nose. I'm worried it will get on Lucy. I don't think Lucy can stand a washing, even if Larissa would let me do such a thing. "We need to get your face washed, get you dressed, and have you eat a little breakfast, and then you can call her. I promise."

She nods again, warily, but nods. Well, I can get her to do things if I let her call her mother.

I hate being a foster mother.

. . .

After getting her changed—her pajamas and the sheets are once again wet—and getting her to eat seven spoonfuls of Cheerios, I give her the portable phone, dialing the number for her so she won't get it wrong. "You can take it up to your bedroom."

As she walks up the stairs, I hear her say, "Mommy," and then, crying again, "I want to come home." Then she closes her door.

I gave Larissa the phone hoping her mother wouldn't be there, that she would be out looking for a job. What is she doing home at nine in the morning on a Friday? Why isn't she looking for a job? How long might they talk on the phone? Should I make Larissa hang up after a half hour, an hour? I give myself ten minutes, then creep up the stairs.

I can hear murmuring, a sob, a long pause, then Larissa talking again, then another long pause. I can't hear what she's saying, just the sound of her voice. I go into my office and shuffle through papers. After fifteen minutes, I go back. This time, through the closed door, I don't hear any sound at all. I count to sixty, then knock.

Nothing. I knock again. Finally I just open the door. Larissa is curled up in a ball on the bed.

"Larissa? Is everything all right?" What a stupid question. I close my eyes and take a breath. "Did you talk to your mommy?"

She doesn't move. Jesus, I'm back to square one, a silent, injured child. God damn her mother. What did that woman tell her daughter?

I sit on the end of the bed. Larissa's loose hair completely hides her face. "Larissa. Is there anything I can do?"

Nothing: It's her answer, and exactly what I can do. My jaw grinds back and forth and I feel the pressure on my old teeth. I get up and go downstairs. I call my mother.

"We can't make it today," I say. "I'm sorry. Maybe tomor-row."

She can tell I'm not in the mood for questions. Real mothers know stuff like that. She says to come whenever I can. I have a quick vision of me driving Larissa back to Children and Family Services, giving her back, driving down to Columbus and sob-bing in my mother's arms.

I sit on the couch, turn on the TV. It's set on the cartoon sta-tion. The sound comes on—a braying laugh—and startles me. I hit MUTE. I stay there, on the couch, staring at the TV, seeing myself around the age of five, sitting on my parents' couch next to Vince. My five-year-old self is content with this, so I just sit here. Sometime later, much later, Larissa comes down the stairs.

I think it helps that I'm watching the TV with the sound off. She sits down on the couch and stares straight ahead, just like me.

I'm angry at her, and it frightens me.

At a commercial, I ask if she talked to her mother. She nods.

"Do you feel a little better now?"

She shrugs.

"We have to go to the grocery store," I say. "Can I fix your hair first?"

She waits a few seconds, then shrugs. I get her comb and brush. The brush is cheap plastic, and I want to get her a nice brush, one of those good wooden ones. There's a CVS near the grocery store. Then I remember her mother's prescription bot-tles. We'll go someplace else.

I braid Larissa's hair in one loose braid, using a beaded rub-ber band I found in her bag. I put two pink plastic clips shaped like butterflies near her temples, to keep some of the flyaway hair out of her face. Bringing over a warm, wet washcloth, I wash her face again. She sits there without expression, and I'm angry again. *See how hard I'm trying?* I think. *Can't you see that?* I put out my hand, and she takes it. We walk to my car. I fasten her seatbelt securely.

In the grocery store, not Tops, I feel people giving us second looks, checking out the white woman with the little black girl. I feel the second looks inside my chest. I wonder what Larissa feels.

We get a brush at a drugstore, a nice sturdy wooden one with pads at the tips of the bristles. Larissa doesn't seem to even understand the brush is for her. She looks like someone who just doesn't care about anything. And then it hits me. Her thumb is in her mouth, but there is no Lucy clutched to her chest. I'm anxious, seeing her without Lucy. Something is very wrong.

Chapter Sixteen

There's a woman sitting on my porch steps when we get back from our errands. Larissa's mother. My heart starts beating hard, and my hand spells *Shit*. I think seriously about driving right by my house, heading straight to Columbus.

"Mommy!" Larissa cries out.

I pull up to the garage, park, and bound out of the car, my keys in my hand, point out. Larissa's mother is walking up the drive, and I walk quickly to intercept her. "What are you doing here?" I hiss. I actually hiss.

Larissa jumps out of the car and runs to her mother. *Michelle,* I remind myself. That's her name. Does she know mine? How did she find us? Fuck, she's *here*. What the hell am I supposed to do now?

She's wearing a tight black T-shirt with TRY ME in white letters across her chest, and her hair still has that dark stripe down the middle. She doesn't look like a mother. She looks like the babysitter from hell. I can't imagine her cooking soup, wearing an apron. She looks like someone who *needs* a mother.

Michelle kneels down on my drive and Larissa runs into her arms. I have groceries in my car. Milk. Frozen mac and cheese. Peppermint ice cream.

I can't yell at this woman in front of Larissa. "I don't think you're supposed to be here," I say as calmly as I can. My voice trembles, and it makes me madder. "I have groceries that need to be put away." I almost say *food for* your *daughter.*

"I gotta see my girl," she says to me over the top of Larissa's head. "I just got to see her." She cups Larissa's head in her hands, kisses her forehead several times. Then she looks back up at me. "I know I shouldn't be here. Please don't call no one. Please. I just had to see my baby. I miss her so bad. You don't know how bad I miss her. It's awful. She's all I got." She presses her head down against Larissa's hair that I just braided. "Oh, sweetie pie, I miss you so bad I just had to come see you. They told me I can't, but I just had to. I just hope this nice lady won't get mad and report me. I just hope she understands how bad I miss you."

So now I'm a nice lady. "I have to put the groceries away before the ice cream melts."

"I don't mean to cause no trouble. I just wanna see my little girl."

I'm afraid to move. If I go into the house, might they run off? "Will you stay right there?" I ask. "Promise me you'll stay right there while I put my groceries away?"

"I promise," she says. "We're gonna stay right here, won't we, honey?" She looks right at me and adds, "We could help, if you want."

She sees the look on my face—the fear of her in my home—and she smiles. She knew exactly how I would react. "No thank you," I say. "Just stay there."

Inside, I think about calling the police, but Larissa would never forgive me for doing that twice. I think about calling Children and Family Services, but it always takes forever to get someone on the phone. I unpack the groceries, putting away only the things that need to be refrigerated. When I go back out for the rest of the bags, Larissa and her mother are whispering to each other. I feel plotted against. I want to throw a bag of groceries against my house and scream.

They're all wrapped up together, Michelle sitting on the ground, Larissa in her lap. Right in the middle of my driveway. "Why don't you sit on the chairs on my front porch," I say.

"Thank you," Michelle says. "Thank you kindly." She gets up and, holding hands, they walk down the drive, turning across my lawn to the porch. As soon as they're out of sight, I wonder if they've even gone to the porch. Maybe they're walking off right now. *Larissa,* my hand spells, and I hate my hand, myself, Larissa's mother, and the whole system. Maybe even Larissa.

I go back into my house, and from in here I can see the shape of them on my porch. I put the rest of the groceries away. I'll give them ten minutes. This is *my* house. I'm the adult in charge of Larissa. I have responsibilities. And what the hell else can I do? Sit and read a book?

Exactly ten minutes later, I walk out my front door. Larissa's sitting in her mother's lap, her small head resting against the words TRY ME. They both look up as I come out, Michelle's fingers woven into her daughter's hair, Larissa's arms around her mother's neck, both their eyes red from crying. Michelle's wary tenseness, that fighting look, is gone. She seems completely worn down, collapsed into her daughter. It's like finding a strange wounded animal on my front porch. In my wicker chair. I want to go back inside.

I sit on the cement steps, their cool hardness just what I need right now. "Larissa, I have to talk to your mother for a few minutes. I left the crayons and the coloring book on the table inside. Could you go color for a little, while I talk to your mother?"

Larissa stares at me, showing nothing on her face. I'm no one now.

Michelle eases Larissa off her lap. "You go color, sweet pea. I'm gonna talk to Mrs. Marlowe for a little bit. Then you can come back out. I won't go nowhere without saying good-bye. I promise."

Larissa rubs her head against her mother's chest. Her mother nods once, and Larissa gets up and goes inside my house. Michelle and I both begin to talk at the same time.

"It's not *Mrs.*," I say, finding the only thing I'm sure of to say.

"I know I shouldn'ta come," she says. She actually sounds as if she means it.

"No, you shouldn't have. How did you know where to find me?"

She brushes the bangs out of her eyes, tucking stray hair behind her ears. "Larissa told me on the phone she was with the white-haired lady. I remembered your name from court. You're in the book."

"Well, it's *Miss*," I say. "*Miss* Marlowe."

"I'm Michelle." She smiles a small, fragile smile. She can't be more than twenty-two, if that.

"I know. Look, you really can't just come here. You know that."

"I'm sorry I hollered at you that day. It was a bad day. They all been bad days lately. I'm scared they might take her away for good. I can't find a job, except at fast-food places. I'll take one, next week, I guess. I need the money."

Part of me starts to feel bad for her; the other part of me knows I'm being played.

"Well, maybe you should be out looking right now?" I imagine her in this T-shirt asking for a job. Maybe she's a prostitute. "Do you have clothes for job interviews? Maybe that's why no one's saying yes."

She nods. "I have a real nice suit, but it's bad luck, that suit. I won't wear it again. I need to get something else."

"A suit's not bad luck. You make your own luck." Jesus, what am I doing? Trying to teach her about life? I just want her off my porch.

She shakes her head, her bangs falling back into her eyes. "This one is. I never shoulda brought it with me in the first place. This move . . . It was supposed to be a new life but it's just the same old shit. Same bad luck. I'm not putting it back on. I'm going to take it to a thrift shop. Maybe they'll trade me?"

I almost get pulled into this conversation about thrift shops. It's got something to do with the way she looks right into my eyes. "Well, you need something decent to wear. Some outfit or something."

"I got that suit for my husband's funeral," she says, touching her chest, rubbing her fingers along some imaginary fabric. "He was shot dead by the police, just taking his wallet out. Some other black man shot a policeman, and Charlie was black, so they fucking shot him. Fucking Goddamn police. Maybe you saw it on TV, some two years ago? My husband was just in the wrong place at the wrong time. A lawyer called me said that. He said we should sue them, but nothing happened. I miss him. I really miss him."

Her eyes are welling up. I look away. Mrs. Myerson across the street is watching us from her lily bed, holding a bunch of lilies in her hands. "I'm sorry," I say. I almost tell Michelle about my brother getting killed; I feel this urge to share my story with her, let her know I'm human, too. I keep my mouth shut. My hands are killing me.

Michelle is absently twisting the ring on her finger. A gold wedding band. There's no engagement ring. "His name was Charlie Benton," she says, talking quietly. "He hadn't done nothing wrong at all. They just shot him dead and then they said they was sorry. Everybody said they was sorry, but what good does *that* do?

"That day I left her alone, it was the second anniversary of him getting shot dead. The day I went for that interview and wore that suit? It was the suit I wore to his funeral. I went to Kristen's, that fancy shop sells expensive clothes. I was supposed to be there at four o'clock, and so I had to leave our place at three to get there. Charlie's sister Teya was supposed to come over right after work, at five. She's a lot older than Charlie was, but she's real good with Larissa. I told Larissa to be a good girl until her auntie got there. She watches TV that time anyway, maybe you know that? But her auntie got sick and taken to the hospital. I thought her auntie was there. Honest, I did."

"What happened? Why didn't you come home?" I ask. If she had been mugged or something, it wouldn't have been her fault. They wouldn't have taken Larissa away if she had a damn good excuse. But Yolanda said Michelle had been drinking.

Michelle looks down, shuffling her feet. They make a rasping noise against the porch. "They didn't want me. These two women, they looked at each other, then the one said, 'Oh, we don't have any openings. You must of made a mistake. When you called, we thought you were a rep.' They lied right to my face. I looked good in that suit, my hair done, but they didn't even give me a chance to hardly say my name. They wanted me out of that store so bad they nearly pissed their pants trying to sweet-talk me and move me along like I was stupid." She pulls her legs up, wraps her arms around them. The temperature's dropping and she's just wearing that stupid T-shirt. "I called her a bitch. Well, she *was*. I said, 'Why do you have to be such a bitch? What's the matter with you? Why won't you give me a chance? I woulda been a good worker for you. You don't know what you're passing up.' She said she'd call the police if I didn't go." She pauses. I imagine her in that shop, talking back to those women. I'm embarrassed for her.

She rests her head on her knees, looking at me. Her eyes are green, her lashes pale, and her eyeliner is smudged under her eyes like a raccoon, and yet she's mesmerizing. She's so thin and small, like the kids who were in those ads some years ago, the heroin ads they were called. But she doesn't look drugged; she radiates this intensity that compels me to look right back at her and listen. She has this need, she says with her eyes, to talk to me, just me, like I'm important to her, like she's never told anyone this before. "I was walking to the bus and I never wanted to stop walking. I walked right past the bus stop, thinking maybe I'll just walk home since I don't have no money anyway to be spending on buses. I thought Teya was with Larissa. I needed to be alone anyway, so I wouldn't be so mad. Then I saw this bar. I didn't drink nothing for eighteen months, but I sat down and ordered a beer. This man came over, bought me two more, with shots. I wasn't with no man since Charlie, and it was so nice. God it felt good, someone talking nice to me like that. I went to his place with him." She stops, lifts her head up. "I'm a good mom. I love Larissa and she loves me. I did a bad thing, a really bad, stupid thing, and I'm sorry, but they shouldn't of taken her away. I'll never do nothing like that again. It wasn't even good. It was awful."

The sky is darkening and the wind picking up. Mrs. Myerson has gone inside. It's going to be a bad storm, I can tell. *Please don't rain,* I think. *Not yet.* I want this woman to leave, but I want to know what happened to her first.

"You went to his place?"

She nods. "Yeah. Stupid." She rubs her lips with her fingers. Her nails are a bright garish orange. One fake nail is missing.

"I got real drunk and passed out. In the morning when I woke up, he wanted to start all over again, but I knew I had to get out of there. He kept playing with me, not letting me get to the phone, teasing me mean, you know, like we was playing a game. Finally I called home, but no one answered. I figured her Auntie Teya took her to her place. I had to get the bus home. He wouldn't take me. I don't know why I did what I did. I was just low. I needed a job and they made me feel like shit. I'll never do that again. I promise. You gotta give her back to me."

I stiffen. So that's where this was leading. I'm such a sap. "It's not up to me." I feel a raindrop and get up from my step, move under the porch. My butt hurts from the concrete.

Michelle leans forward, pressing her hands together as if she's about to pray. "You could say good things about me. Tell them I'm a good mom. I can't stand this, being without her. It's wrong. She's scared. She doesn't know what's happening."

Thunder rumbles, and Larissa opens the front door, her face peering out from behind the screen. "Mommy?"

"It's okay, sweetie pie," Michelle says to Larissa, then turns to me. Once again she has that look on her face, as if she is opening up for the first time in her life, as if she needs me. "It's all my fault she's scared of thunderstorms. I told her that's what a gun sounds like, that lightning sound. I shoulda kept my mouth shut. I got a bad habit of saying things out loud I should just be thinking. That's why I yelled at you. Really, I'm sorry. Can I hold her again?"

Jesus. How the hell can I say no to that now? I nod.

Larissa goes over to Michelle and puts her arms around her mother's drawn-up legs. They lean together, becoming one thing with four arms, four legs. They have the same contour, thin but sinewy. Michelle kisses Larissa's head and they hold still like that for a moment, Michelle's lips against Larissa's hair. I move over to the door.

Slowly, Michelle shifts her weight and rises, Larissa still hanging on to her mom's legs. "Can I come back? Just see her now and then?"

"Call first," I say.

"I will."

Larissa pulls her arms away, crosses them across her chest. Her lips are tight, her eyes narrowed, eyebrows drawn down. Her body language says, *If you're not taking me home, I'm not hugging you good-bye.*

"I got to go," Michelle says to Larissa. "I can't take you. I want to, but I can't. You be good with this lady. I'll come back soon as I can." She kneels down on one knee, holds out her arms. Larissa doesn't budge.

"I love you, baby. Mommy's going to get you back." She looks up at me. "You'll take good care of her, won't you?"

I nod.

"I love you, honey. Don't ever forget that." She stands and leans over to kiss Larissa on her forehead one last time, but Larissa twists away and runs inside.

"Well, then, I guess I better go," Michelle says, looking at the closed door. But she doesn't move, just chews at her bottom lip. "Listen, don't take this wrong. I'm sure you're doing a good job, but she should be in the backseat in a car, 'cause of her weight. She shouldn't be in the front seat till she's fifty pounds."

"Oh. Okay." My face is hot. Jesus, what else am I doing wrong? For a second, I want to ask a girl with a T-shirt that says TRY ME what else I should know.

Michelle walks down the steps, into the rain and down the sidewalk to the corner. I could give her a ride to the bus stop, but I'm afraid of the urge to do so.

Chapter Seventeen

Larissa won't speak again. For the rest of the day as the rain beats hard against my house, we play Chutes and Ladders, color, watch TV shows without the sound, look at picture books, eat. I'm just as quiet inside myself as she is, and oddly we fit together perfectly this way, our timing in unison as we silently, with only a slight movement of our eyes, agree this will be our last game of Chutes and Ladders. Only a tilt of the head is needed to turn on the TV. When Larissa falls asleep on the couch around four, I go upstairs and call Yolanda.

"I'm not her social worker anymore," she reminds me.

"Okay. Can I talk to you as a friend then? I don't know anyone who could understand what I'm feeling. I'm lost."

There's a moment while she pauses, and I wish I hadn't called. "Sure," she says. "What's going on?"

I let my breath out. "Her mother came," I say. "She just

showed up." I tell her how we talked on my front porch, the story about her husband getting killed.

"Yeah," Yolanda says. "If you can believe her."

"What?" I don't know what she means.

"Alice, Alice, you're so innocent. The story about her husband, it's such a setup. Poor Michelle."

"You mean he wasn't killed?"

"Oh, he's dead. But the details . . . Who the hell knows? I don't trust her as far as I could throw her. Alice, hasn't anyone ever lied to you?"

No, I think, dismissing every lie ever told me. But this? Lying about her husband getting killed by police? I close my eyes. What an idiot I am to think she was confiding in me. But then I remember her face when she told me. I'm an interpreter. I can tell when someone lies just by watching their face.

"Well, it could be true. And she sounds like she's really sorry. I think she's learned her lesson. She'd never do that again, leave Larissa alone. Couldn't Larissa go back with her now?"

Yolanda laughs, quick and hard, and for a moment I don't like her at all. "Alice, you bought it? The story? Come on. She's desperate, what do you expect her to say? 'I went out drinking and forgot my kid'? Alice, Aunt Teya can hardly walk. She's three hundred and some pounds and uses a walker, has been in and out of the hospital for the last year. You really think Mom thought she was coming over? Come on. And let's pretend her story was even close to the truth; no, Larissa's in the system now. Mom has to do all those things I told you before she gets her daughter back. There's no shortcuts. You have Larissa now. You're responsible. Mom is not to come over unannounced. You need to report this."

The way she says *Mom* instead of using Michelle's name

bothers me. It didn't before, but now it does. "I don't want to re-port her, Yolanda. If she does it again, I will. I promise. I told Michelle to call first, next time."

"Next time? You know, Alice, when I met you, I thought you were so tough. I'm beginning to wonder . . ." She laughs again, but it's a friendly laugh this time, I think. "Look, it's nice of you, not reporting her, telling her she can come back, calling me and asking if Larissa can go home now, but you're doing all this 'cause you feel inadequate. It's natural for a first-time foster par-ent. You're doing fine. Any problems with Larissa herself you want to tell me? We can handle her mother."

I think about her not talking, the frightening scene in my kitchen. "She wets the bed," I offer.

"That's your biggest problem? Get a plastic mattress cover. Is she talking?"

"A little," I say. "She likes my cat, too."

"Good. You're doing fine. It could be a lot worse. But with Mom showing up like that, I think Larissa's going to need coun-seling. I'll have them set up an appointment for Wednesday, the same day she visits her mother at Metzenbaum. Hold on while I check and see if that'll work."

I wait. Five minutes later, she gets back to me. "Okay, it's set," she says. "Can you get Larissa to Metzenbaum by four?"

I have a job at that time, but I think I can move it around. "Yeah, I can do that."

"Just keep doing what you're doing, Alice, but watch out for Mom. I think she's trouble."

"Yeah, okay. But I'm going to take Larissa to my parents' in Columbus tomorrow. I have to get out of this house. Who do I tell?"

"Give me their address and phone number, and I'll pass it on.

And listen, hang in there. We went through a lot of trouble to place her with you."

We means Yolanda, and I know that. "Okay," I say. "I will."

After I hang up I think about Yolanda saying there are no shortcuts. There are, though. I got Larissa in six weeks. All Michelle needs is a letter from the mayor.

That night, Larissa tucked in, I sit on her bed and clear my throat; I want to signal to her I'm about to speak. "Larissa, we're going on a special trip tomorrow. We're going to go visit my parents for Labor Day weekend. My brother's sons will be there. They're twelve and fourteen. Their names are Bruce and Dylan, and I think you'll like them." I don't mention my brother is dead. "We'll have a good time."

Larissa doesn't nod, shrug, or blink. This *nothing* hurts. I want to go to bed and curl up, sleep for a week.

Sampson saunters into the room, and Larissa pats the bed. He jumps right up and settles in.

Stupid cat. Doesn't he know I need him too?

In the morning, while Larissa takes a shower, I tear off her wet sheets, throw them in the basement, then pack her things into a suitcase while she takes a shower. I'm not traveling with that canvas bag.

It takes so long to dry and brush her hair, but she's going to have to take a shower every morning because of the bed-wetting. I'll have to remember to put a plastic bag on the cot she sleeps on at my parents'. Before we leave, I show Larissa where I keep Sampson's dry food, and ask her to pour him a big bowlful, and another of fresh water. I tell her this will be her job from now on, and pleasure shows on her face. She still isn't speaking, though. I am, but not much. I say everything quietly, with the fewest words possible. Sometimes I sign the words, sometimes not. The quiet inside me is growing; I'm in an in-between place, partly who I was before I met this child, partly someone new I don't know yet.

As I drive to Columbus we listen to children's songs on tapes. We don't sing along. Now and then I say something, like *This is the highway to Columbus,* or *Those are turkey buzzards up there.* She's in the backseat. I have to look at her in the mirror.

Driving by Akron I think about Vince. *Miss you,* I think.

Ditto, he says. *Remember when we didn't speak for five months?*

I remember.

After I broke up with Jimmy Bain, Vince stopped coming to visit me, and we stopped speaking for almost five months, neither one of us wanting to give in and make the first call. I knew, though, that it would have to be me, that I was tough, but Vince was just plain stubborn. I told myself there was a difference. On the day of our fortieth birthday, I drove down to Akron.

Bruce and Dylan ran to meet me as I got out of my car. "We knew you were coming!" Bruce shouted, hopping up and down, slapping his brother across the head. "Told you she would!"

"Dad said you aren't talking to each other," Dylan said, younger than Bruce by two years, and quieter.

"Where is he?" I asked. It was early June, a Friday. Sun sparkled through the green leaves, the feel of summer on the light breeze.

"At work," Bruce said, shrugging almost apologetically. "Dad says you aren't talking 'cause him and Jimmy are too low-rent for you."

Why the hell did Vince go around telling them this stuff?

"He's not talking to me because he's made all sorts of assumptions that are not true. You got the card I sent you?"

"Yeah," Bruce said. "Thanks for the money for my birthday."

"He was supposed to send it back," Dylan said. "He told Dad he did, but he didn't."

"He made me give him half not to tell," Bruce said, looking at his brother, raising a fist. "Don't tell I didn't," he said to me. "Please?"

It was just like my brother to tell a seven-year-old kid to mail back money, not wonder if a kid could address an envelope and put on a stamp. Then again, most likely Vince knew Bruce wouldn't send it back, allowed him this unspoken bit of rebellion. Vince appreciated a bit of rebellion.

"Don't worry," I said. "I won't tell. It'll be our secret. And I'll make up for that half you had to give Dylan." Dylan and Bruce looked at each other. It was okay now, now that more money was coming.

"Thanks," Bruce said, then looked down at the ground and kicked a stone. "Did you bring Dad a present?" he asked, pretending it really didn't mean much to him if I did or not.

"And why would I do that?"

"Because it's his birthday!" Dylan said, coming around and standing right in front of me. "And yours!"

"That's why I knew you were coming," Bruce said. He stood right next to his brother, spreading his fingers out over the top of Dylan's head. They were seven and five, and perfect, their skin just beginning to pink from the summer sun. They'd both have freckles in a week that would spread across their face like days across the summer.

"Who's watching you?" I asked.

"She is," Dylan said, nodding his head to their neighbor's house, where a Mrs. Hathaway lived, sixty and hard of hearing.

"She even know where you are?" I asked. Bruce shrugged.

"Well, I'll go tell her I'm here, and she's off duty. Then you can help me unpack."

"Did you bring him a present?" Dylan asked this time. Presents were big things in their lives. They meant you were loved.

"Yeah, I brought him something," I said. "It's in the trunk. Did he get me anything?"

They both nodded, smiling. Goodness filled my throat, and I smiled back. Vince and I enjoyed the weekend just as if the last few months of not speaking hadn't happened. But when I got into my car Sunday evening, he leaned over and looked at me through the open window.

"Remember that time you got drunk with me?" he asked with a chuckle.

"Yeah, why?" Usually I got his drift before it needed to be explained, but not this time.

"You threw up in my hands," he said.

"Yeah, I did." And then I knew.

"I'd do it again," he said. "Anytime." We were both silent for a minute. "You need someone to fix that dick mower of yours? Have you even tried it this year?"

"I pay a kid to mow," I said.

"Damn. We'll come up next weekend. I'll fix it."

"Thanks," I said.

When he was killed, I wasn't worried that I'd ever forget him, but that I couldn't, not even for a moment.

. . .

Almost to Columbus, I turn into a rest stop. It's a holiday week-end and the place is overflowing. The sky is a vibrant blue, not a cloud in sight, as if it has forgotten the storm of just yesterday—or maybe the storm was never here. Maybe it was only over my house.

We park all the way at the end of a line of cars, a good distance from the bathrooms. A man walks a golden retriever by us, its tail wagging, nose to the ground as if he's discovered a whole new country. I almost got a dog once, but I thought a dog might get in the way of the things I do. I can't even imagine now what I thought I did.

I hold Larissa's hand as we walk into the building. I want to tell her to not sit on the seat, but she's too little to stand over a toilet. "Don't touch anything," I whisper as we stand in line.

I open a stall door for her and she looks up at me, worried. "I'll stand right outside the door," I say. I wait a good two minutes before I hear a tinkle, then flush. When she comes out, I realize how badly I need to go.

"Here" I say, placing her by a sink. "Wash your hands until I come out." I squirt a handful of liquid soap into her hands. "Look, it's pink!" I say, as if this is miraculous, and now she will be happy.

Afterward, we use the hot air blower. Her hand is warm and soft as we walk back to the car. My mother will love this child.

Over the past eighteen years, I have brought four different men with me down to a holiday dinner at my parents'. My mother liked every one of them. Two made it down for a second visit, one for a third, but we broke up soon after.

One of the reasons I don't date anymore is because I can't do that again, make the drive down to my parents' with my new man, the hope that goes into those rides—telling family stories, hearing theirs, the way my mother looks at these men as if they might save me. It's her look that makes the car ride back so uncomfortable.

I no longer want to *find* love. I want to have *had* love, the history of love, not the possibility.

I pull into the driveway. Vince painted their garage a few months before he got killed, and it still looks fresh and bright. I bet my father washes the garage monthly. "They're nice people, Larissa," I say. "I know they'll like you very much. You don't have to speak if you don't want to, but they are going to talk to you. It's friendly to talk to people, and they're going to want to be friendly. Do you understand?"

Larissa nods, her face showing concern. My mother walks out the back door and waves, a hand up high. Even from here I can see the sag of skin beneath her arm.

"That's my mother."

My mother moves slowly down the steps; she has arthritis and is a bit bent over. Her hair is short and gray, with one of those perms that older people get. She looks like so many other women her age that even in Cleveland I sometimes imagine that I see her in a store or parking lot. Sometimes I help those women who look like my mother. I open doors, help them load their cars. I hope someone might do the same for her.

I get out of the car and wave back in the same way. "Hello, Mother! We're here!" We tend to say the most obvious things in my family. Well, Vince didn't, but I've always stuck to the program. Without him, the three of us are so white Protestant.

Not anymore. I walk around the car to Larissa's side and unbuckle her. She takes my hand and we meet my mother halfway.

"Hello, Mother," I say again. "This is Larissa, the little girl who I'm taking care of for a while. Larissa, this is my mother, Mrs. Marlowe."

"Hello, Larissa," my mother says, bending over even farther. My hand reaches out, in case she falls over.

Larissa looks down at her feet.

"Would you two like to come in?"

"No, Mother," I say. "We drove all the way here to stand outside on the driveway."

She laughs. It's just the kind of joke she loves.

As we walk in, my father comes into the kitchen. "Well, look who's here," he says. "Hello, Alice." He looks down at Larissa. "And who is this little girl?"

My father has gotten so thin that his cheekbones poke out from under his skin. His ears are large and his earlobes get droopier every time I see him. He has a Band-Aid on his chin.

"This is Larissa, Dad. I'm going to take care of her for a little while. Where are the boys?"

"They've gone down to the drugstore. Seems we don't have the right kind of pop. We do have Pepsi, though, if you're thirsty. The boys should be back soon with the better stuff, according to them. Pepsi's just fine with me. Are you thirsty, Larissa? Would you like some pop? Can I get you some?"

Larissa looks at me.

"Would you like some pop?" I ask.

She shrugs.

"Okay, Dad. One for both of us. Thanks."

The next fifteen minutes is spent getting the tour of the house from my mother. It's a very slow tour. I play my part and help narrate. "My mother sewed all the curtains, and she slipcovered the couch and those chairs." She still sews, even with the arthritis.

The toaster has a handmade cozy with bread appliques. The teapot has a tea cozy with teacup appliques. There are pillows of every shape and size on the couches, chairs, and window seats, and in the corner of every room. There are no plants in the house; there is no room for them. You have to move pillows just to sit on the couch. I get a pillow every year for Christmas. I inherited Vince's pillows when he died.

Upstairs, my mother shows Larissa the bathroom. The bathroom gets softer each year, as if it's growing orange fur. This year my mother found shaggy orange material that matches the shaggy orange rug and toilet seat cover. She made a cover for the Kleenex box, a cover for the waste can, and a curtain for outside the shower. Larissa looks around in wonder, and I smile at her, rolling my eyes. My mother has already moved on to my room.

"This is the cot we set up for you, Larissa. I hope it'll be comfortable enough." It has three pink pillows, and a pink-and-white quilt that was mine when I was little.

We go back out to the car and get our things, my mother following, my father insisting he carry our bags, the both of them leading us back up the stairs to my old bedroom as if I might have forgotten the way. I tell them I need a moment alone with Larissa.

"Certainly, certainly," they say. My mother shoots me a questioning look over her shoulder as she leaves the room.

"Okay, Larissa," I say, moving pillows so I can sit on my bed. "I want to explain something to you before we go back out."

Larissa stands, looking at me, thumb in her mouth. I don't expect to see that thumb again while we're here, except at meals. But her eyes seem alert and curious, the dull gaze of yesterday gone. There is a pink color to her cheeks, a healthy glow, not the blotchy look of rubbed-in tears. She stands there patiently waiting for whatever I might tell her, becoming used to being told all sorts of strange things. When very young, I used to pretend that I was Alice in Wonderland. My father had bought that book for me on the day I was born. My mother would read it adding warnings as if they were written into the text. "And so you should never wander far from home," she'd say. "Or speak to strangers." But Larissa, she must really feel like Alice in Wonderland, and I imagine now it's not fun at all. To be lost in someone else's world, wanting only to go home.

She's so little, I think. *So brave.* And it occurs to me right now that this brave, good kid is how she came to me, not someone I have created with my magic finger-spelling, my Cheshire cat. She was a brave little girl, a tough little girl, and polite except when driven to anger and frustration. She's a six-year-old girl who was left for too long by a mother who raised her to be a cool little kid. I look at Larissa and think about Michelle, how she's a child too, who will someday be older, maybe wiser. Then I see Larissa again, the baby fat still in her face, her thumb in her mouth, her small hands, and I can't imagine her growing up, getting taller, her face thinning, dating boys, becoming a woman. My bedroom makes me think all this. What must it be like for my mother, my coming home to sleep in my own room at almost fifty years old? Knowing, too, that her son will never come home again? I am sure, as I watch Larissa watching me, that I will never forget exactly how she looks right now. She will always be standing here, in my bedroom, a few feet away.

I shake off my thoughts and tell her what I need to. "My nephews, who are staying here this weekend, who I told you about, Bruce and Dylan? They're my brother's sons. My brother Vince and I were twins. He died six months ago. I just want you to know that. Their mom won't be here with them. They flew in from Arizona by themselves, where she lives. They were living with my brother when he died, and now they're living with their mother. They haven't been here since their dad died. This place has memories for them, of their dad, coming here with him. It has memories for me, too. This was my bedroom, and the bedroom next door was Vince's. My dad and mother are still very sad about Vince dying." I don't say getting killed. "Everyone wants to be happy, and they'll act happy most the time, but if they're quiet, or looking sad, I want you to know why. I just wanted you to know how people here are feeling. Not that we won't have a good time." I stop. Saying all this makes me wonder why we even came.

"Okay?"

She nods seriously. I so like that serious nod.

"Okay. You ready to go out there? Have ourselves some fun?"

She shrugs. I take it for a yes.

As we walk downstairs, I hear voices at the back door, the sound of bags being put on the counter, my father saying that Aunt Alice is here with the little girl. Larissa stops walking. "It's okay," I say, and take her hand, easing her down the steps. We walk into the kitchen together. The boys turn and look at us.

"Bruce! Dylan!" I let go of Larissa's hand and hug them both. They're taller, I can feel that in my arms. They hug me back like they mean it, and it takes me a minute to let go of each of them, a minute to blink back tears. They both look so much like Vince; scraggly and thin, high cheekbones, green eyes.

Vince's kids are gorgeous, but goofy looking. "Hey, what did you do to your hair?" I ask with a laugh. The hair on the top of their heads is combed up, meeting in the center like a miniature

Mohawk. Then I notice Bruce's ear. "Oh, my God, you got your ear pierced!"

Bruce grins sheepishly. Both of them are always more quiet at my parents' house than they ever were at mine.

"This is Larissa," I say. She's standing behind me and I step back so they can see her. Bruce and Dylan say hello. Larissa stares at them.

"Are you getting your ear pierced, too?" I ask Dylan.

"Not till I'm fourteen," he says.

"Oh well," my dad says. "Too bad about that."

"Larissa, you have your ears pierced," my mother says. "Didn't that hurt?"

Larissa slowly shakes her head no.

"No tattoos you're hiding?" I ask Bruce.

He smiles, showing a flash of white crooked teeth. "Not yet."

"Thank goodness for small miracles," my mother says.

"You gonna drink that pop you bought or let it sit on the counter all day?" my father asks, rubbing his hand across the top of Bruce's head. The hair bends over, then stands right back up.

"You want some Coke, too, Larissa?" my father says, not lowering his voice to talk to her as my mother does.

She shakes her head up and down quickly as if he might change his mind, and hands me her empty pop can.

"Okey dokey," he says. When the hell did he start saying *okey dokey*?

Once everyone has a Coke in their hands, my father clears his throat. Now, that throat clearing, that I remember. "The boys and I are making a doghouse in the basement. They got a dog back home named Bruiser. You want to come down and help us out, Larissa? We have a whole lot of work left to do."

Everyone looks at her. She shrugs. This shrug means she's

afraid to do this, but afraid to say no. I'm getting good at reading her shrugs.

"I'll come down, too," I say, as if she has agreed.

"I think I'll stay up here and make some egg salad," my mother says.

"I'll be back up to help in a bit," I offer, tilting my head toward Larissa, meaning, *when I can*. My mother doesn't need my help, but I'm expected to offer.

My mother smiles tightly. "Thank you." I ignore whatever's bothering her and take Larissa's hand, walk her down the basement stairs.

Chapter Eighteen

The basement is the exact opposite of the rest of the house. There are no pillows, and although I do remember my mother sewing some sort of quilted cover for my father's table saw, I see no sign of it now. The basement is all tools—True Hardware did not get its hands on all of the merchandise from my father's hardware store. Larissa's eyes dart everywhere. I don't know much about her life, but I figure it's not filled with furry orange bathrooms and a basement that has the feel of a torture chamber for wood. This is the culture of *my* life.

There is no doghouse, and I look at my father.

"It's in bits and pieces," my father says, as if reading my mind. "We've cut the walls and floor and roof. Now we're going to mark the holes for the screws, drill the holes, then take all the parts outside, put her together, then take her apart. I don't see any way we can fly a doghouse back to Arizona, so what we're going to do is make sure the boys know how to put it together, then ship the pieces, and the screws, and a few tools they'll need. I think I have enough to spare," he says with a wink. "Ever use a drill, Larissa?" He reaches over to the workbench and picks up a pencil and a right angle.

I'm not sure I'm supposed to let a six-year-old foster child play with power tools. "Ahh, Dad, I don't know about that—"

"If she don't want to, I will," Bruce offers.

My father turns to Bruce and silently looks at him, then looks at me. "It will be perfectly safe, Alice. I know what I'm doing."

Does he? I look for a tremor in his hands, but he seems fine.

"We need to do some measuring first. Bruce, get that floor board we cut and bring it here. Dylan, you get the piece marked *left wall*. We're going to hold them together and mark where to drill the holes. Larissa, can you come here and hold this pencil for me? Then I'll show you right where to make a mark."

She looks at me.

"We could really use your help," my dad says.

"Why don't you help, Larissa?" I say. I move us a few steps closer to my dad.

"Can we put this rabbit fellow someplace safe?" he says, looking at Larissa's stuffed bunny clamped firmly under her arm. "We don't want him to get hurt while we work. He can see us fine from here." He nods to a shelf nearby.

I hold my breath. Larissa looks at me, at the boys, back at my dad.

"Do you want to put him over there yourself?" my dad says.

She nods, and goes over to the shelf. Carefully and with obvious doubt, she sits Lucy down, balancing the rabbit against a paint can and adjusting the long legs to hang over the edge of the shelf. Lucy is so loose and floppy, she sags like a deflating balloon, but she stays there.

"Okay," my dad says. "I'll show you just what to do." I see myself in him, the way he just accepts what he wants to believe, the way he goes forward with only the slightest bit of encouragement.

He hands her the pencil. It has a sharp point. He hands it to her point down, but I still shudder.

It takes quite a while to get the boards lined up. My father makes numerous measurements before he finally says, "Right here, honey. Make a little X. That's good. That's perfect. Thank you." He looks up at me and smiles. *See,* he says with his smile. "Okay, Dylan, now hold that wall steady." He makes a few more measurements, and Larissa makes a few more marks. "We'll drill the holes when we've marked the whole thing. Dylan, put this wall back and get the back wall, please." As they mark the second piece of plywood, Larissa looks over at Lucy every few seconds, but each time my father tells her that she did a good job, the corners of her lips turn up, along with the corners of her eyes.

My father is meticulous and exact, and they're going so slowly I can tell it will take forever before they use the drill. Maybe not until after dinner.

"I'm going to go help Mother make that egg salad," I say. "Is that okay, Larissa? I'll be back down soon."

My father keeps measuring as if this question is no big deal, but Bruce and Dylan stop what they're doing and look at Larissa. They somehow understand what a big step this will be. I love them even more.

Larissa holds perfectly still for a moment, then shrugs. Not a real firm okay, but an okay all the same.

"I'll be right upstairs in the kitchen."

"All righty, put an X right here, Larissa," my father says, and I go upstairs, my left hand spelling *careful*.

My mother sits in the living room, reading a catalog. The egg salad is in the refrigerator, tightly covered with plastic wrap.

"Thought I'd rest for a moment, while everyone was occupied," she says. "Everything okay down there?"

"Shouldn't it be?" I ask, wondering if there's something I missed.

She meets my eyes. "Yes, it should be just fine, *Alice*." She emphasizes my name, making me feel like a little child. A mother's trick. I won't do that to Larissa.

I sit across from her in a chair covered with a summer blue slipcover that matches the slipcover for the couch. She'll switch to her fall-colored slipcovers after Labor Day, like a woman putting away her white shoes.

"So, do you want to tell me about Larissa now?" she says.

"Okay. Yeah. I do."

She puts the catalog down on the table. "So tell me."

I tell her about getting the first phone call from Larissa. Before I can get much further, she interrupts me. "You didn't *go* there in the middle of the night, did you?"

"Yeah, I did. But listen first."

She shakes her head and huffs. By the time I get to describing the walk up to Larissa's apartment, her jaw is set. As I tell her about looking around the apartment for the phone, she has picked up the catalog and rolled it tightly in her hands. She smacks it on her knee.

"God in Heaven, Alice," she says. "You could have been killed!"

"By a six-year-old?"

"You know exactly what I mean. You should never have gone to that girl's apartment."

"You know what? I know that. But look, nothing bad happened to me. I can't be afraid all the time. You know, I'm scared of heights, too. Because of you."

She sits up straight, holding the curled catalog in one hand, looking as stunned as I feel for saying that to her. "Excuse me?"

Tears come to my eyes. "I'm sorry. Look. I just want to tell you my story without you condemning me. Or Larissa. Can't I just tell it? I did something brave, Mother. I guess that's what I was hoping you'd see. Be proud of me."

Her chest heaves with each breath. She just stares at me.

"I'm sorry," I say. I don't know what I'm sorry for, it's just an automatic response.

"I can't take any more pain, Alice," she says. "I just want you to be more careful. And I'm not condemning that little girl. I don't know why you say that."

"Because you're assuming that because she's black and was abandoned, that she lived in some awful place full of drug dealers with guns who might have killed me in the middle of the night."

She looks away from me. "I never said that. I'm not prejudiced."

"I thought not. Can I just tell it, now? Will you listen?"

"Yes, I'll listen. I won't say a word, if that's what you want."

The last time I saw my mother this mad was at the trial for the man who'd hit Vince. And I knew she was just as mad at Vince for jaywalking.

Yeah, well, look what happens when you're too careful. The woman lives in a house with padding. And you're fuckin' worried about a little girl holding a pencil.

I roll my eyes, angry at Vince's quips, and angry at myself. *I* had thought Larissa's apartment building would be some awful place. I love my mother, but I want to blame her for who I am.

I pick up a pillow to keep my hand from swearing, and bunch it in my lap.

"I don't want you *not* to say anything, Mother," I tell her. "But listen. It turns out well. She's a beautiful little girl. She's very sweet."

"Go on," she says with an indifferent shrug. "Tell it."

So I do. My mother never really unlocks her jaw. I tell her about looking in the medicine cabinet, the scene going down the stairs. But I don't tell her Michelle Benton showed up on my doorstep. My mother would never sleep again.

"So she's living with you for a few months, and then her mother will get her back?" my mother says, very matter-of-factly.

I close my eyes and answer her. "If she follows her case plan."

"And do you think she will?"

I open my eyes and look directly at her. "I don't know, Mother."

"Then what? If she doesn't?"

"I'd like to adopt her." I know I say it like a threat, and I'm ashamed.

My mother sighs through her nose and closes her eyes. With the both of us closing and opening our eyes, it's like we're talking in Morse code.

"Why are you mad at me?" I ask, leaning forward. "Why be mad at me?"

"Alice, this girl . . . she's lovely and sweet, but she's scarred, she must be, from all this." She waves her arm around. She doesn't mean this house, she means everything outside this house. "And if you adopt her, she's going to keep growing up. She's going to be a teenager and . . . a troubled teenager, no matter how good a parent you are. You're so attached to this little girl already. I worry about you." She pauses, glances at the picture of Vince on the mantelpiece. "I worry all the time something's going to happen to you. That's all. You adopt Larissa, and you'll see what I mean. You'll never stop worrying."

What can I say to that? She's played the *Vince is dead* card. In the quiet that follows, I hear the high whine of the drill and realize I've been hearing it for a while now. I tense, but don't run right down to the basement. "What are we having for dinner?" I ask. I'm worried it might be something Larissa won't like.

"Pizza," my mother says. "Not even homemade."

"Thanks. That's a great idea. All kids like pizza, right?"

"I believe so." She still isn't over being mad at me.

"Well, I guess I'll see how they're doing down there."

I walk down the basement stairs slowly, careful not to distract anyone who might be holding a drill. My dad kneels behind Larissa with his arms reaching around her shoulders. She's wearing plastic goggles that are huge on her small face. My dad holds his hands over Larissa's hands, and they're drilling a hole in the wood. The board is clamped vertically to some contraption my father has rigged up. I sit down on the steps and watch. They drill three holes before he stops and looks up at me. Larissa turns her head up, too. Her eyes, even behind the goggles, show delight and pride.

"We're almost done here," my dad says. "This girl's a champ. How many holes did we drill? Sixteen, right?"

Larissa nods.

"Or was it just fifteen?" my dad asks her.

She shakes her head no.

"Sixteen, yes, you're right. And the boys each did sixteen. Does it look like rain out there, Alice?"

"No, it looks just fine," I say.

"Okay then. Larissa and I will finish up the last side here, then we have to move all these boards upstairs. See where else we have to drill, Larissa?" My dad tilts his head and looks at her. No two faces were ever more different, I think; her round, brown, young face, her closed and silent mouth; my father's pale, white, wrinkled skin, his large ears, his bony cheeks, his grandfatherly grin and yellowing teeth. I've known one my whole life, and the other a little more than a month. My chest hurts. My mother would know why.

Larissa points to a penciled X.

"Okay, let's get this turned around then. Bruce, would you remove the clamp, and Dylan, turn the board so we can get those last few holes? You boys won't mind if Larissa finishes this up, right?"

Bruce and Dylan say, "No problem," almost in unison, just like Vince and I used to do. My father stays on his knees, directing the boys until they get it just right. "Ready?" he says, and Larissa nods. They drill three more holes.

"Okay, that does it," my dad says. "Will you unplug that drill there, Dylan?" It takes him a bit of time to straighten back up, waving away Bruce's offer of help. "Okay, let's move these boards outside. You going to help us put it together, Larissa?"

She nods. A firm nod.

"Okey dokey," my father says.

My father, Larissa, Bruce, and Dylan spend the afternoon putting together the doghouse and drinking Cokes. Lucy gets moved to a new place, this time on top of the bird feeder, for the best view of the action. I hardly know what to do with myself. While my mother takes a nap, I do the same, lying down on top of my bed, cradling my head in a cluster of pillows. One of them smells of lilac.

When I awaken, the clock reads four thirty-eight; I've slept more than an hour. As I come downstairs, I hear voices out in the backyard. My father's in the kitchen, drinking a glass of milk. "Five thousand, six thousand, seven thousand!" I hear someone yell.

"What's going on?" I rub at my face, waking it up.

"They're playing hide-and-seek," my father says. "The doghouse is home base. Dylan wants to sleep in it tonight, but I think he'll chicken out."

"Hide-and-seek?" I say dumbly. "Larissa's playing hide-and-seek?"

"Apparently. You used to, too, you know."

"I know, but . . ." I shrug. I just can't imagine Larissa playing hide-and-seek. "What are the boundaries?" I ask, trying not to sound worried.

"Just our house and the Fischers' next door."

"Okay." I move over to the back door. Dylan stands with one hand on the doghouse. I can't find Larissa. "Ready or not, here I come!" Dylan shouts, and runs off.

"Nice doghouse," I say.

He chuckles. "Grandma's making a big pillow to go inside. Then Dylan will really want to sleep there. Larissa wants to make one for your cat. Sampson, she said."

I freeze, one hand on the back door screen. "What?"

"Oh, don't worry, she asked nicely. Actually she didn't ask. I suggested it, when I remembered you had a cat. That little girl, she does love that cat."

I feel dizzy and hot. "What are you talking about? Larissa told you about my cat?"

My father nods slowly. He's enjoying himself. "Yes, she did."

"Dad, she doesn't talk. I mean, she hasn't been talking hardly at all, for weeks and weeks. She told you about my cat?"

"Well, yes, she doesn't talk much, that's true. But when I asked if she had a dog, she shook her head no, and then I asked if she had a cat, she shook her head no again, then shrugged, which I guess meant maybe. 'Maybe you have a cat?' I asked, and she nodded. Then I asked if it was your cat, and she nodded again, and then I asked if your cat would like a cat house with a pillow inside. Hah! I thought her eyes were going to pop out of her head. I took that moment to ask her what the cat's name was, and she said 'Sampson,' plain as day. I didn't make a big deal about it, but later I told her we had to ask you if you wanted a cat house, and would she help me do that, and she nodded. I said, 'What was that cat's name again?' because we could carve it over the doorway, and she said 'Sampson,' just like she did before. I told her a cat house is a whole lot smaller than a doghouse, and we can probably get it done by Monday, if she could stay that long, and then you two could take it home with you. Were you staying till Monday? Did I make a mistake there?"

"Dad! I don't believe it! She talked to you!"

"She even said 'you're welcome' right now when I thanked her for helping with the doghouse. I won't expect a lot more from her. Don't worry. I won't push it."

I hug him. I feel just like a little girl hugging her daddy, even though I'm just as tall as him now. "Thank you. Thank you for being such a good grandpa and father."

"You're welcome," he says. When he steps back from our hug he looks at me, and I know, just from that look, he's going to say something I might not want to hear. I'll be so pissed if he tells me I'm going to get hurt. It will ruin this whole visit, them both telling me that.

"You know, she's quite a beauty," he says. "I imagine she's just as pretty as any daughter you might have had. I'm sorry that didn't work out for you. I hope this does."

I tilt my chin up, turn my head away, and blink back tears.

"Tag! You're it, Larissa!" Dylan shouts.

I look out the back door. Larissa is a few feet from the doghouse, Bruce already there, a hand on the roof.

"You have to keep one hand on the doghouse and close your eyes and count to ten," Dylan explains to Larissa. "And remember, we'll be only in this yard or that one. Got it?"

Larissa nods and walks over to the doghouse. She puts one hand on it, closes her eyes and starts counting. She counts softly, but I can hear her. "One, two, three . . ." The boys take off running. I look at my dad, and he smiles at me.

"She's okay, that little girl," he says. Once again, I have to look away.

Before dinner, I check my messages. There's one about an interpreting job, and one from Michelle Benton. She wants to talk to Larissa. I save the message about the job.

That night, we eat pizza around the picnic table in the backyard. Larissa doesn't join in on the conversation, but when Bruce sticks a piece of pepperoni on the back of Dylan's head while Dylan is seriously answering some question my mother asked, she starts giggling. When Dylan discovers the pepperoni on his head, he puts it into Bruce's milk, and she giggles harder. My parents exchange looks—these are not the kind of shenanigans

Vince and I would have been able to get away with, but what are they going to say to two boys who have just lost their father, and a silent foster child?

I love the sound of Larissa's giggle; it comes in short bursts, as if she can't quite control it, then comes back again unbidden. I want to blow milk out of my straw, stand on my head, anything to get her to giggle again.

Larissa likes pizza as much as she likes pop, and she listens intently as Bruce and Dylan answer my parents' questions about their school. My father doesn't ask Larissa anything she can't answer without a head movement. My mother is almost as silent as Larissa. After dinner, we walk up to my old elementary school at the end of the block, each house we pass a boxed memory. I remember who gave out homemade candy apples at Halloween—the Shepards' who decorated their lawn for *every* holiday, the brick house where Henry the deaf boy lived.

The playground is different now. In the center is one of those bright plastic mazes with tubes and slides and rope walks all connected togther. Larissa hands me her bunny, an honor I take seriously, holding Lucy gently in the crook of my arm as I would a baby. All three children run off, even though I would have thought Bruce was too old for a playground. He climbs around with Dylan and Larissa, showing off by hanging upside down anywhere he can. At one point he whispers in Larissa's ear, and they dash off to stalk Dylan, chasing him into one of the big orange chutes. In seconds, they all pile out at the bottom in a clump of feet and arms and laughter. The sound of children's laughter, which has always meant to me *someone else's children,* is a whole new sound now.

Back at my parents' house, we watch TV. After watching silent TV with Larissa for days, I now find the laugh track so ridiculous that it makes me laugh out loud. Larissa looks over at me, and I smile at her, pretending she knows why I'm laughing.

By nine, Larissa is half asleep, and I tell her it's bedtime.

"We'll start on that cat house in the morning, all right, Larissa?" my father says, giving me a wink for his play on words. I roll my eyes at him. Larissa nods.

"And," my mother says, "we'll have to pick out the material for the cat's pillow. I have a bunch of fabric in the attic. Is it a boy cat or a girl cat?"

Larissa looks at me.

"A boy cat," I say.

"Well, good night, Larissa," my mother says.

"Good night, Larissa," my father says. The boys chip in a *good night,* too.

"Good night," Larissa says shyly, and bobs her head.

In my parents' orange bathroom, I give her a washcloth and tell her to wash up real good, brush her teeth, and get into her pajamas. She climbs into the cot and pulls up the blanket. She fits the cot perfectly, as if it has always been hers.

I read a few poems from a Mother Goose book. I don't mention her mother's phone call. We've had such a lovely day.

Chapter Nineteen

Sunday morning, my parents go off to church. I stay home with Larissa and Vince's boys, who have been brought up agnostic. Vince used to say that they were *pedestrians,* funny in its own way, right up to the moment Vince got hit by a car.

Yeah, ha-ha, he says.

We sit on pillows on the lush carpet and watch cartoons, eating sugary cereal. Larissa's taken the band out of her hair and it hangs in her face, curling up wherever it damn well pleases. Bruce and Dylan's hair has remolded itself during the night and now sticks out at errant angles all over the place. My short spiky hair has done the same thing and I haven't bothered to comb or style it yet. I imagine my parents are more than happy to go off to church by themselves.

"We look pretty goofy," I say to Larissa, pointing to the

boys' hair. Dylan sticks his tongue out at me. I cross my eyes and make a goofy face at him. Larissa covers her mouth and giggles.

Maybe we will never go back to Cleveland.

Once again, I have nothing much to do all day. My father keeps Larissa busy in the basement except when my mother keeps her busy in the attic, sewing. Outside, Bruce and Dylan take apart the doghouse and put it back together, even though that means they have to take it apart again tomorrow. I tell my mother I'll go with her to the grocery store to get the stuff for a cookout. When I ask Larissa if she wants me to get plain potato chips or barbecued, she says, "Plain." When I ask if she likes mustard or ketchup on her hamburgers, she says, "Ketchup." When I ask her if she will stay with my dad and the boys while I go to the store with my mother, she thinks for a minute, then shrugs. I take her shrug to mean she will stay.

"She's talking," I tell my mother in the car. "Just a few words, but I think she's over the silent thing."

"She must be very traumatized," my mother says. "Is her mother white?"

I blink. "Yes. Why?"

"Oh, I just thought so," she says.

She drives in silence for a while. "Your father's quite taken with her, you can tell. He was humming last night." She says this with an air of sadness, as if it's not necessarily a good thing.

"I'm glad he likes her," I say. "He seems to be in a pretty good mood. I only saw him with one drink last night."

She's driving—insisting on driving just to show me that she still can and I'd better not think otherwise—but now she looks at me a little longer than I think she should while going forty down a two-lane road. I am not to judge my father, her look says. It's not my place. I point my chin to the road ahead. *Look where you're going,* I imply.

"He'll be let down when you leave," she says. "I imagine it will be a hard time for him, then." She's insinuating that my visit with Larissa will make him drink more. I'm almost fifty years old and only now realize my mother is passive-aggressive.

The yellow jackets come out as we eat dinner. One crawls along the side of my plate, circling my food. My mother absently waves her hand above Dylan's plate as he eats. "Next year I'm going to build us a tent, one of those netted things, so we can eat in peace," my father says, and winks at Larissa. My mother and I exchange a look, both wondering what next year will bring. Bruce, Dylan, and Larissa draw faces on their hamburgers with ketchup.

After dinner, while my mother sews something and my father watches CNN, the boys get ready to take apart the doghouse for the last time. "Gonna help?" Dylan asks Larissa, and she nods. As they head out to the backyard, Dylan turns and winks at me. I see Vince in that wink, and my dad. I never wink at people. I didn't get that gene.

A little while later, as I stand drying a pan in the kitchen, Bruce comes into the house for something to store the screws in. He's got them loaded into his pockets, and I hold open a plastic bag as he drops them in. "So, are you gonna keep her?" he asks.

I stiffen. It's the way he says it, as if she's something I can keep or give back, like an expensive present. "Yeah, I'd like to, Bruce, but she might have to go back to her mom."

He nods, solemnly, as if he understands. And then I realize he does. He had to go back to his mom. *Had* to. That's got to be a hard word to put together with the idea of being with your mom. At least Michelle wants her daughter.

"Well, I like her," Bruce says. "Dad would have liked her, right?"

"Yeah, he would have." We stand there silently for a minute. I've still got the bag of screws open. I close it up. "You doing okay, Bruce?" I ask. "Everything okay with you and your mom?"

"Yeah, she's okay," he says. I think he might say more, but he doesn't. I hand him the bag of screws. He runs back outside.

That night, I sit on the floor next to the cot and read Larissa more Mother Goose poems. Before I turn off the light, I ask her if she's comfortable in the cot. She nods. "Did he make it?" she asks.

I smile, knowing who she means. "No, but he could have."

"He's nice," she says. I can't answer her. I'm stunned, and feeling too much for words. I nod and make the sign for *yes*, my hand accomplishing what my mouth can't. I swallow, shake it off. "He is," I say. "Now time for bed. Good night. Sleep tight."

She makes the sign for *yes*, then puts her thumb in her mouth. The well worn-out Lucy is tucked under the covers. *Good night, Lucy*, I say in sign. Larissa smiles at me, then looks down at Lucy and gives her bunny a kiss.

I close the door halfway. I have to stand there for a while before I can move again. The world feels too full of something, and it scares me.

Downstairs, my parents and the boys are still watching TV. I go into the kitchen and get my phone from my purse so I don't put charges on my parents' phone. I call home for messages. There are seven. The first is a phone solicitor. Then a message from Beth in my book group, inviting me, last minute, to a Labor Day picnic. She does this, now and then—remembers I am without "male companionship," and invites me, last minute, to holiday get-togethers. Someone has canceled on her. Next there's a message from Michelle. "Please, could Larissa call me? I just want to say hi. Thank you." Then another phone solicitor. Then Larissa's mom again. "Hi, this is Michelle Benton, and it's eight-thirty, so I figure you're home 'cause I know you want to put Larissa to bed on time and all that, so could she call me now, before she goes to bed? It'd be nice to talk to my daughter for a little." She leaves her number this time, as if I don't know it. The next message, at eight-forty, is her again. "Why you avoiding me?" she says. "She's my daughter, you know. I want to talk to her." She hangs up. I only have a second to worry what she might do—like go to my empty house and break windows—before I hear the last message. It's from Polly.

"Alice. I just wanted you to know that my mom died. About an hour ago. We were all there with her. I'm calling from the hospital. We're taking a few moments to make some phone calls, then we have to meet with someone from the funeral home. It's the same place that did Dad's funeral. I'm okay. We had some warning, so we were all in her room. You can try reaching me on my cell phone if you want." She pauses. "Well, that's it. Good-bye."

I push 3 and hold it down, my preset for Polly's cell phone. I get the busy signal. I try again every five minutes for over a half hour, pacing back and forth from the living room to the kitchen. My mother gets up and asks what I'm doing.

"Oh, that's terrible," she says when I explain. "I know you liked her. Didn't you go there with Polly that time?"

"Twice. And every time she came to Cleveland, we went to dinner together. I can't believe she's dead."

"At least she went before her children," my mother says.

I don't know what to say to that; I don't even know why it makes me angry, but it does. "I'm going to just keep trying her, okay?" I say. She goes back to the living room.

This time, Polly answers. She whispers a hello.

"God, Polly, I'm so sorry. I've been trying to reach you, but your phone's been busy. Was it another stroke?"

"A blood clot," Polly whispers. "Listen, we're in this meeting. There's so much to do. The funeral will be Wednesday, that's all I know. Can I call you back later? Maybe I'll call tomorrow. I don't know . . ."

"I'm in Columbus, at my parents'. We'll be leaving tomorrow sometime. I have Larissa."

She doesn't say anything, and I think we've lost contact, then she says. "You have her? You mean she's with you, now? In Columbus?"

"Yes, it happened quickly."

"Wow," she says. "Listen, I better go. I'll call you tomorrow night, when things settle down."

"How are you doing?" I ask.

"I'm okay," she says, but her voice hitches. "A little numb. I'll call you," she says. "Tomorrow."

"I'm sorry, Polly. I liked her so much."

"She liked you too. Bye."

I stand in the kitchen, staring at nothing. The funeral's Wednesday. There's no way I can make it. Not with Larissa. If it weren't for Larissa, I'd be making plane reservations right now.

· · ·

It takes most of the day Monday to finish building the cat house, and then we have to take it apart so I can get it into my trunk. It's large enough for a small dog, and the pillow's made out of pink satin. Larissa's entranced. She wanders into the dining room several times, where the pink pillow lies on the table, just to touch it. I notice her thumb is hardly ever in her mouth. When I mention this to my mother—Larissa outside playing a final game of hide-and-seek with Bruce and Dylan—my mother tells me that she casually mentioned to Larissa that wet things, like water, pop, or a wet thumb, would stain the pink satin. I smile; how many ways did she manipulate me when I was a child?

"Any chance we can get the boys for Thanksgiving?" I ask, spreading peanut butter on Wonder bread for a snack in the car.

My mother presses her lips together and shakes her head no. "We'd like to fly them in sometime during their Christmas break, but I don't think she'll let us. We get the minor holidays, like Labor Day. Your father and I are thinking about driving out there this spring."

"That's a long drive," I say.

"Yes, it is." She takes the sandwiches I've made and wraps them like presents in wax paper, using paper tape to keep them closed, just as she packed my sandwiches when I went to school. "Take some pops, too," she says.

"Maybe we can come back soon," I offer.

"That would be nice." She folds the top of the brown paper bag over three times, creasing the folds with her fingertips. "You will call us, and let us know what happens," she says, as if now that I have Larissa, I might ignore them.

. . .

Bruce and Dylan will fly back early tomorrow morning. Their school doesn't start until Wednesday, either. Standing out in the backyard, our car packed, I hug Bruce good-bye and tousle his hair with my hand. When I bend down to hug Dylan, he reaches up and tousles my hair first. Maybe Larissa and I can drive to Arizona for Christmas break.

My father shakes Larissa's hand. "It's been mighty nice meeting you, Larissa. You did some very good work on that cat house. You should be quite proud of yourself there. If Alice needs something fixed at home, she should ask you first. Here. You take this with you, just in case." He hands her a wrench.

"Thank you," she says softly with her head tilted down to the ground, then looks up at him with those big wide eyes, and I know tonight will be a bad night for him. He wanted a granddaughter. I'm too old to provide one now, and Vince too dead. Larissa will be it, if I get to "keep" her. He hasn't asked me about any of the details; he's enjoying the pretense that Larissa will be coming back with me next time, until tonight, when he'll ask my mother for the details.

My mother, holding a small brightly colored gift bag, gets down on her knees on the grass, which is not easy for her and makes me nervous. Crooking a finger, she beckons Larissa over. "I have something to give you, too," she says.

Larissa goes over to my mother and stands just out of arm's reach. This morning I braided Larissa's hair and tied it with a red velvet ribbon that I found in my mother's collection of ribbons. The late-afternoon sunlight comes through the leaves, dappling their faces with gold. I wish I had brought a camera. Next time I will.

"Here," my mother says, handing Larissa the bag. "I made an extra cover for the pillow out of flannel, for the winter."

As Larissa stands there, Lucy in one arm, the bag in the other, my mother leans over and gives her a quick hug.

It takes both the boys to help my mother back to her feet. Bruce and Dylan say good-bye to Larissa when she gets into the car. Larissa waves to them. I give the boys one last big hug.

As we drive off, I ask Larissa if she liked our visit, and she nods slowly, thoughtfully. I ask if she liked Bruce and Dylan, and she nods with a smile. "What color is the new pillow?" I ask, and she opens up the bag and peeks inside.

"Red," she said.

My mother has taught me well. "Yeah, she probably would make it red, for Christmas," I say, then wish I hadn't. Ten minutes of silence later, Larissa asks if she can call her mommy.

"Can it wait till we get home?" I ask. "My cell phone's running pretty low."

She nods sadly. Halfway home, Larissa falls asleep in the car. We never eat the peanut butter and jelly sandwiches.

I leave Larissa sleeping in the car when we get home and walk around the house, looking for broken windows. I can't help it. Inside, I check the messages. One phone solicitor, and Michelle. "I called the police on you," she says. "I told them you kidnapped my daughter. How's that feel, huh? Having the police called on you? You better call me back."

I erase the message. My hand spells *shit*.

I take the phone outside and check on Larissa. She's still sleeping. I sit on my back porch, the sun just setting, and call this woman I want to kill.

"Listen," I say, as soon as she answers. "We went to my parents' house in Columbus. Family Services knew about it. It's perfectly legal. Larissa had a very nice time. Don't you dare ruin it. She's talking again. Don't fuck that up. She's sleeping in the car right now. I'll have her call you when she wakes up. Do not upset her, do you hear me? You *do* want her talking, so she can go to school, don't you?"

"You can't just be taking my child to Columbus and tell me—"

"Yes, I can. I certainly can. The police had better not show up here, Goddamn it, and terrify her all over again. Call them right now, and get the story straight. They probably already called Family Services and know you're full of shit, but you call them now. Can you imagine what it would do to her, if the police came?"

"Hey, you called them first, bitch. You should know."

"Call them now," I say, and hang up the phone.

She called me a bitch. If I knew Yolanda Walker's home number, I'd call and report the little dyed-blond cunt.

I can't believe I even *thought* that word. Thank God I'm sitting down on the steps or my legs would give out. Every brain cell in my head is shouting at me to get into the car and drive back to Columbus. I don't feel safe in my house. I think to call Polly, then remember where she is.

I bow my head. *Polly, I'm so sorry,* I think. *I'm so sorry.*

I know I can't leave Larissa in the car much longer. I open her door and softly call her name.

"Mommy?" she says sleepily. Then she rubs her eyes, sees me. "Can I call my mommy now?"

"Sure, honey," I say. "Come on inside and we'll try her."

I honestly think about misdialing the number, saying she isn't there.

I hand her the phone. She's old enough to dial it herself. She'll probably get it right. "You can go up to your room," I say. "If you want." She heads toward the stairs. At the bottom of the steps, she stops and presses the buttons. I can hear the faint melody from where I stand. Then she walks up the steps. "Mommy! Hi, it's me! We went away. We went to visit her mom and dad and these boys. The boys were Dylan and Bruce and I liked Bruce best because he . . ." Her door shuts.

She can talk when she wants to. I didn't miss, either, that she called me *her,* no name. I sit on the couch and breathe. It's harder than I thought.

I put Larissa to bed at nine. Sampson jumps up and curls at her feet, so glad we're home. I left the cat house in the trunk. It's been a long day.

"We never went shopping for school clothes," I say. "You were too busy building things and playing with Dylan and Bruce, but tomorrow we'll go shopping and get some new clothes, okay?"

She nods.

"Good night, sweetie," I say.

She nods. I don't press it.

Back downstairs, I call Polly's mom's house. Her sister Bev answers, and I tell her how sorry I am. "Thanks," she says. "Do you want to talk to Polly?"

"Please," I say, although I'm dreading this phone call.

"How are you?" I ask Polly when she comes to the phone.

"Not so good," she says, her voice hoarse, on the verge of tears.

"You've been crying?" I say. I'm saying everything softly, trying so hard to be comforting with my voice since I'm not there to hug her.

"Yeah. Guess so. Just had a bad spell there, sorry."

"Oh, God, don't be sorry. You should be crying. This sucks, Polly. It's just not fair."

"Yeah, it sucks," she says.

"You know I'd be there if I could. I just can't. God, I'm so sorry. Larissa starts school Wednesday. I just can't come there right now."

She says she knows, that it's okay, Patrick's there, and Rachel and Nora are flying in tomorrow. All her sisters' kids are already there. "It's a big family. I'm lucky," she says.

She's crying now. This is so hard. I think I'll just go—drive there with Larissa, be there for the funeral, do what a best friend should do. I wonder if they'd take Larissa away from me if I didn't get her to school the first week. "I'm sorry," I say again.

"I know," Polly says. "Look, I gotta go. I'm sorry. It's just a bad time. I'll call you tomorrow."

"Okay," I say. "Please do. Love you, Polly."

"Thanks," she says, and hangs up.

No sooner do I put the phone down, than it rings. I think it's her calling me back, begging me to come, telling me she needs me to come. It's Michelle Benton.

"So, you're doing all this fancy stuff with my daughter? Take her on trips? Give her a cat? Teach her stuff? Buy her clothes? What you think you're doing? I'm going to get her back, you know."

The first thing I think to say is *I didn't give her a cat. Sampson's mine,* but I don't. Next I want to defend myself, tell her off. But I'm too exhausted. I hang up the phone. The phone rings again. I'm so stupid, I actually think it might be Polly again.

"Hey, lady," Michelle says. I hang up on her. Then I take it off the hook. I sit there and listen to the high-pitched wail, telling me my phone is off the hook.

Tomorrow I'll call Yolanda Walker, see what she thinks I should do.

Tomorrow seems like a day too full to even consider. I have to take Larissa shopping, take her to the day care place for a visit so she'll be familiar with it when she really has to go, and we have an appointment at her school to meet her teacher, who's going to give us a tour. We need groceries. I need to get to the bank. And I need to sit by the phone in case Polly calls. And I need to leave the phone off the hook.

Wednesday, if it ever comes, I have to take Larissa to school and start working again. I have two college classes to interpret and a meeting at a bank for a deaf man who wants to buy a house, but I have to get Larissa down to the Metzenbaum Center at the same time as the job at the bank, which I never changed. Maybe I can drop Larissa off at Metzenbaum and still make the meeting? Maybe if I tell Family Services what Michelle Benton's been doing, they'll cut off her visits, and I won't have to take Larissa after all—but, still, I have to take Larissa there for her counseling. Maybe she doesn't need counseling now because she had such a great time at my parents'. Maybe I need counseling if I think she doesn't need counseling.

Then I remember I need to get back to the foster parenting classes.

When I finally fall asleep, I dream I'm stuck in a building of hallways with no doors, the nightmare of my teenage years. My heart pounding, I'm awakened at seven A.M. by someone ringing my doorbell.

It's a policeman. I'm almost relieved it isn't Michelle Benton.

I interrupt him as soon as he begins speaking.

"Look, I'm her foster mother. It's all legal. Children and Family Services knew we were going to Columbus."

"Excuse me, ma'am," he says, holding up one hand. He's young, pale-eyed, and smooth skinned. I'm tired of everyone in charge being younger than me. Jesus, I'm only forty-eight.

"They don't have you on record as the foster mother, ma'am. The Benton child is on record as living with a Mrs. Hunt."

"What? No. *I'm* her foster mother. I have all the paperwork. There's a ton of paperwork. I'll show you."

"I'd appreciate that."

"Could you wait out here?" I'm still standing in the doorway. I haven't invited him in. "Larissa's sleeping. I don't want her to wake up. This would be very scary to her."

"I'll wait here, ma'am," he says, but he still regards me suspiciously, as if I might lock the door and run out the back with my stolen child.

"Please don't call me ma'am," I say a little too tersely, and go into the house. *God damn Michelle Benton.* I want to kill her. Only metaphorically, I tell myself. Metaphorically with a long sharp knife.

"Look," I say, when I come back, shaking a sheaf of papers in the police officer's face. "Here it is. It's all official. Her mother called you because she's crazy. I don't know why Family Services told you what they did. I have a new social worker, just switched to my case. Maybe because of the holiday she didn't get it in the computer?"

"Possibly," the cop says, reading a sheet of paper and then another. "This does look valid." He points to something near the bottom of a page. "Here's the transfer from Mrs. Hunt's."

"Thank God. Look, this woman, this girl's mother is driving me crazy. Maybe you should be—" I feel something soft and furry slip by my bare ankle. "Shit!" I've been holding the door open, not wanting to stand outside on my front porch in my bathrobe. The policeman looks up at me.

"My cat got out," I explain. "He's an indoor cat. Goddamn it, now I have to go find him." Then I blush. "Sorry."

"That's all right, ma'am," he says, handing me back my papers.

"Please don't call me ma'am," I say again. My voice has that pre-weepy sound, and he apologizes, tipping his hat. Do they train them to do that?

"I'll check with County again later today, see if they've caught up on their paperwork. You should too."

"Oh, I will," I say.

"Good day."

I nod. I don't feel like saying *good day* to anyone.

Sampson went off to the right of the house and I can't see him anywhere. I call his name a few times, then realize I have to get dressed and go search for him. What a lousy day, and it's only seven-fifteen in the morning.

Larissa comes out of her room as I walk down the hall to my bedroom.

"Is someone here?" she says. "My mommy? Is she here?"

"Sampson got out, that's all. I need to get dressed and go look for him."

Larissa's eyes widen. "I'll come," she says. Then, "Who was here?"

"Just the paper boy," I say, running my fingers through my hair. I need a shower. So does Larissa. I can smell urine. She didn't wet the sheets at my parents'. It must be me, I must be doing something wrong.

"Will Sampson come back?"

Now she's talking, and I'm wishing she weren't. I close my eyes and take a deep breath. "I'm sure he will."

The last time, years ago, that Sampson got out, he was gone three days. I walked around the neighborhood for hours, calling out his name, hung photos on trees and utility poles. Finally I heard him mewing, locked in a neighbor's garage, and I couldn't get him out until they came home from work. But I'm not as worried this time. I have bigger fish to fry, as my mother would say. I need to take kung fu lessons so I can beat the crap out of Michelle Benton.

I take a quick shower, barely three minutes, to save water for Larissa. Then she takes a shower while I get dressed. I don't stand outside the bathroom door to hear if she hollers for me. I just get dressed and mousse my hair up, thinking that I need to get it cut. There is absolutely no time I can imagine doing that.

It takes a half hour just to comb out Larissa's wet hair and I wonder if I'm allowed to get her hair cut. Do I need permission to do that? I didn't get to that foster parenting class yet. How could they let me do this? The entire time I comb and brush and braid her hair, she asks me questions about Sampson. *Could he be hit by a car? Could someone steal him? Would you get another cat if he didn't come back? Maybe he'll come back if we put his house together and put food in it?* I'm stunned by the fluidity of her words, and realize three things. One, that she has been holding back so much it must have been painful for her to keep quiet; two, that means she's even tougher than I thought;

and three, if she ever stops talking again, all I have to do is let the cat out. I answer all her questions as best as I can with no coffee. She doesn't seem to notice that I'm not as pleasant as I might be. Maybe she thinks I'm worried about Sampson. Really, all I can think about right now is why I didn't make coffee when I had a chance. Then I think back, trying to figure out when I did have a chance.

She tugs on my hand as we walk down the stairs. "Come on, come on," she says. She pulls me through the kitchen and we head out the back door.

It takes fifteen minutes to find Sampson. He's in the same neighbor's yard, near their garage.

I carry him home in my arms. Larissa talks to him the whole way. "You shouldn't have gone out of the house," she admonishes Sampson. "We were worried. I made you a house, just for you, and it has a pink pillow. You were a very bad cat to run away. I was very scared. You'll like your pillow. It's slippery and soft and pink."

Safely inside, Larissa looks up at me. "Can we give him the house I built now? Show it to him? Do you think he'll like it?"

I close my eyes, trying not to sigh out loud. I am just not a morning person. "Can I have my coffee first?" I ask.

She nods, but her eyes say she had hoped for better.

"Okay, let me just get the coffee started, okay? But we do have a lot to do today. We can't take all that long with Sampson."

She nods, as if she perfectly understands.

There is no way, once we bring in the parts of Sampson's house from the car, that Larissa is going to leave here to go on errands without our putting it together first. Of course, it has to go in her room. I'm charmed by the way she says *my room*. I agree to put the house together. I tell her she has to have a good breakfast first. "Okey dokey," she says, and I almost choke laughing. She giggles because I'm laughing so hard. I come this close to hugging her.

When we're done putting the house together, Sampson takes right to it, curling up inside on the pink satin pillow. I doubt he will ever leave his little house again, let alone my big one. Larissa has to lie on the floor with one hand inside the house, petting Sampson for a good fifteen minutes before I can lure her away with the promise of new school clothes.

We go shopping at Kaufmann's and get pants, shirts, shoes, and a new dress. The clothes set me back more than I expected, but they're so much fun to buy. One clerk keeps looking at us, and I know just what she's thinking. She's trying to figure out how we're related. It bothers me, her looking at us like that, but she works in the section where we find a dress Larissa loves. I'm cool to the clerk to the point of being rude, my point most likely going right over her head. Hadn't I looked at other people the same way a few times in my life?

We eat lunch at McDonald's and I get Larissa a Happy Meal. No one at McDonald's looks at us funny.

After that, we go to the elementary school and meet Larissa's teacher, Mrs. Cummings. Finally someone older than me, and all I can think is that she's *too* old to be teaching first grade. How can she possibly have enough energy for a room full of six-year-olds? I'm beginning to understand just how much energy that would take. Larissa has talked nonstop all morning, but she becomes silent as soon as we walk into the school and she hardly says a word to her teacher.

Mrs. Cummings shows us all around, pointing out the room for after-school care. "We'll have a wonderful time together, Larissa," she says, as if Larissa will be the only child in her class. She is certainly a sweet old lady.

At the day care house, Larissa stands behind me at all times and won't answer the simplest of questions. I take Larissa's silence personally, as if it reflects on me. It's three o'clock by the time we leave there, and Larissa is yawning and rubbing her eyes. This would be a great time for her to take a nap and for me to call Yolanda about Michelle if we were home, but we still have to go to the grocery store.

By the time we get home, she's asleep in the car.

There's a message on the machine. Michelle Benton. "I'm sorry," she says. "I'm really sorry. Please forgive me. I shouldn't of never said those things. I shouldn't of never called you a name like that. I thought maybe you took her away so I'd never see her again. I'm really, really sorry. Please forgive me, will you? Please don't hold it against me. I came to your house to say I'm sorry, but you weren't there. I left something on the porch for Larissa. I hope that was okay. I left you somethin' too. Really. I'm sorry."

Jesus Christ. I go out to the front porch and there's a cardboard box, and next to it, a store-bought cake, one of those ones with pudding in them. There better as hell not be some dead animal in the box I think as I gingerly unfold the top. It's Barbie dolls, and Barbie clothes, and some other things. I see the yellow of the stuffed banana. My hand spells *shit*.

They're just toys.

No, *they're a Trojan horse.*

Hey, Alice, toys bother you, you're in for a really bad time.

The cake could be poisoned, I tell Vince. *Did you think about that?*

Getting more like Mother every day, aren't you?

Oh, shut up. I put the cake on top of the box and bring them both inside. I know it's not poisoned; I'm sure she knows Larissa will eat it too. But she was here again. I need a dog. The dog could eat the cake, too.

I call Children and Family Services. Yolanda says I need to make an official report. She tells me who I have to call.

"How could they not have me on record as being Larissa's foster mother?" I ask. "How could that happen? I really didn't appreciate a policeman coming to my house."

"These things happen, Alice," she says. "I'm sure they'll get it fixed."

She transfers me to the new social worker, and I tell her the same story. She sounds as if she's too busy to talk to me, which gets me even angrier. Isn't this all her fault? I let her know exactly what I'm thinking. She says she'll remedy the problem. I don't like the tone of her voice at all.

"Will Michelle Benton still be able to visit with Larissa tomorrow?" I ask, as if this is surely out of the question now.

"Yes, she will," the new social worker says.

"Well, I hope she behaves. Larissa is getting so much better. She's talking up a storm. Did you know she wasn't talking before?"

"Before what?"

"Before she came to stay with me."

"For how long wasn't she talking?"

Don't you have this on record? I want to shout. "Almost six weeks," I say.

"And now she is? Talking?"

"Yes, quite a bit."

"Well, that's good."

"Yes, it is. You will fix those records, so the police don't come pounding on my door again?"

"I certainly will, Mrs. Marlowe."

"It's *Miss* Marlowe. Please get that right too. Write these things down if you need to."

"Yes, ma'am."

I huff. I actually huff. "Thank you." And I hang up.

My hand spells *bitch,* but I don't mean her.

When I show Larissa the box of toys, she runs to the front door.

"Mommy?"

"She's not here," I say as she looks out the door. "She just left the box."

"She didn't wait to see me?" Larissa asks.

"She probably was very busy. She probably just stopped on her way to—"

Larissa whirls away from the door. "Who cares! Who cares anyway! She sucks! She stinks like poop! I don't want her to wait for me anyway! I don't want her to be my mommy!"

Larissa runs up the steps. Her bedroom door slams. Then more things slam. I take the cake and put it in the refrigerator.

Larissa comes down an hour later when I call her for dinner. Her jaw is so clamped shut she doesn't even put her thumb in her mouth. We don't speak as we eat, but just as she's finishing her macaroni, I say, "You know, Larissa, your mother does love you." Michelle owes me big-time for this. Her name tastes like spit.

Larissa looks up at me, dry-eyed. She shakes her head back and forth. I nod once. "Yes, she does," I say.

Larissa's face stays stony. Outside, the Bonchek children play badminton. "Get it, Margo!" "Yes!" "Watch this!" Someone laughs.

As Larissa brushes her teeth for bed, I bring the box of toys up to her room. The top is opened, not folded shut the way I left it. I look inside. All the Barbies' heads are missing, the plastic formed bodies even more grotesque with that nubby little neck naked and headless. They look less broken than purposely obscene. They are the embodiment of the words *Fuck you*. I close the box, put it in the closet. School starts tomorrow. What will she learn there that will help her?

Chapter Twenty

The next morning, we wake at six-thirty. Larisa has to take her shower while I pack her a paper bag lunch, then I get her dressed and fed. It takes forever to braid her hair just as she likes it, and she changes clothes three times. She's nervous and quiet. I like the quiet at this time in the morning.

As I drive, I tell Larissa how I'll pick her up right after school and take her downtown to visit with her mother, and that after that she'll spend a bit of time talking with a counselor.

"What's a counselor?" she asks.

"Just someone to talk to."

"I don't want to talk to no one."

"Then don't," I say, then hear what I said. "I mean, you don't have to tell her anything you don't want to, but she may be very nice. Just see how it goes, okay?"

She doesn't nod, just pinches her lips together. *Maybe the counselor knows sign language,* I think.

I walk Larissa over to a group of students standing outside by the flagpole, near a balloon with her teacher's name. "There's your teacher," I say, pointing to the elderly lady who's chatting with a little girl. Her face shows more animation than I'm even capable of at this time in the morning. "Remember her from yesterday?"

Larissa nods, a small, hesitant nod.

"You'll do great. I'll wait here till you go inside."

She's brought Lucy. Her teacher said she could. She is, though, the only child with a stuffed animal. I'll tear apart any kid that teases her.

My first job of the day, Ed's theater class, doesn't start until ten so I go home and shower, then try to catch up on my paperwork. Only when I sit down at my desk, feel the familiar shape of my life, do I remember Polly. Her mother's funeral is today. I haven't even sent flowers. *Please forgive me,* I think. *Please.*

I try calling her mom's house, but there's no answer. I order a huge bouquet.

When I pick up Larissa after school, she's standing in the spot we agreed on, alone, children playing behind her on the playground. She's holding Lucy, thumb in her mouth. Her narrowed eyes and pressed lips say she is mad at the whole world.

"How was it?" I ask, and offer out my hand. She doesn't take it. She doesn't even look at me. "I'm sorry if it didn't go well.

First days are always tough. We have to get you downtown now, to visit your mother."

Larissa starts walking quickly in the direction of my car. I follow her, catch up, and we walk side by side. I open the back door, and she climbs in.

We make it to the Metzenbaum Center just in time and I park right in front of the building, illegally, so I can run back out and get to my next job. Looking around the waiting room, I don't see Michelle Benton. I'm torn between hoping she doesn't show up, and knowing that I'll kill her if she doesn't. I leave Larissa with her social worker, who assures me that everything's fixed with the records, and that I won't have any more problems.

Want to bet, I think as I rush back out to the car.

I've got a ticket. The policeman is just walking off. I make it to the bank ten minutes late and apologize to everyone a hundred times.

Back at Metzenbaum, I find Larissa sitting with a woman whom I've never seen before. Younger than me. She explains that she's Larissa's counselor, and asks if I can talk to her just a moment. I want to say, *Make this quick,* looking around for Michelle Benton. I can't go ten minutes without thinking about that woman.

We move away from Larissa. "She didn't talk much," her counselor tells me, to which I just nod. She gives me this look that says, *I understand why you nod instead of talk to me.* I want to roll my eyes, see what she thinks of *that.* "But, from what I did get, she likes you, thinks you're taking good care of her." Now I like her, and smile. "She does want to go home to her mother, but most children do." Now I'm just tired. Really tired. "Just keep doing what you're doing," she advises, and I nod. We make an appointment for the next week. I have a job I will have to cancel to get here on time.

"Did her mother show up?" I ask.

"Yes, she did. It seemed to go fine."

"Her mother's been a bit of trouble for me," I say.

"Yes, I know. I talked to her about it. It's understandable, what she's going through right now. It would be nice if you could be as understanding as you possibly can, but don't allow her to interfere with what you need to accomplish for Larissa."

Mumbo-jumbo, I think. Easy to say.

"Fine, thanks." Larissa and I leave. She doesn't say a word in the car, no matter what I ask. I give up pretty quickly.

I want to make something healthy for dinner, but when I suggest veggie burgers and green beans, Larissa looks at me as if I have suggested we eat eyeballs.

"My mother made me eat tongue once," I say.

She cocks her head and squints one eye.

"Yeah, tongue," I say, sticking mine out at her. "A cow's tongue. They're bigger than ours, and gross." I say all this with my tongue still out, and she smiles a little.

"How about pancakes and scrambled eggs?" I offer, and she nods.

Larissa helps make the pancakes. I never ask her about her visit with her mother.

After I put Larissa to bed, I call Polly's mother's house. Polly answers the phone.

"It's me," I say. "How was it?" I don't say the word *funeral,* but my hand spells it.

"Well, it was really very lovely, if you can say a funeral is lovely. It was in the small chapel she always liked so much. The minister knew her pretty well. He did a great job."

"I'm so sorry I wasn't there."

"I understand," she says.

"Did anyone else speak besides the minister?" I remember Polly's mother had a brother, but I can't remember if he's still alive.

"Yeah," she says. "I did."

I hang my head down, close my eyes.

"It's okay," she says. "I understand. Really. So, how is she? Is she really living with you?"

"Yeah. She is. It's tough, though. It can be really tough."

Now she doesn't say anything.

"I'm so selfish, Polly. Here you're going through . . . through your mom dying, and I'm not there for you, and I'm thinking about how I need to talk to you about all this stuff that's happening with Larissa."

"I want to hear all about it. I'll be coming home Friday. We'll talk."

"And I want to hear about . . . you know. How you are."

"Yeah."

"Can I make you dinner? Sunday? Could you and Patrick come then?"

She doesn't answer right away. "Maybe," she says. "That would be nice. I'll call you when I get back."

We say good-bye, and I sit on the couch, unable to read or watch TV. *Sorry,* I spell out with my hand. Then I sign it, a circular motion of an *A* against my chest.

Once again we wake early, get ready, and I drive Larissa to school, walk her to the playground. She doesn't bring Lucy today. We haven't talked about yesterday, how school went, we haven't talked much at all.

You've been an interpreter too long, Vince says. *Just say something. Don't be so Goddamn worried if it's the wrong thing.*

Yeah, I think. *Like I should definitely tell her to look both ways before crossing the street.* I wince.

"Do you want me to wait with you until the bell rings?" I ask.

She nods.

"Okay. I will." We sit on a bench. There are a few mothers with young children, and we nod to each other. Do they know I'm only a foster mother? How quickly will that news spread?

"Give them a chance," I say to Larissa. The bell rings. Kids line up. Larissa walks to a line of kids, and I hope she's in the right one.

Ed's Thursday class isn't until eleven-seventeen, and once again I work through the pile of notes and messages. There's a message from Elaine, and I call her back, agree to two more jobs, cancel one, and refuse another because it's when I have to be at foster parenting class next Tuesday morning. Then I call Yolanda Walker at work. I ask her if she wants to come over for dinner tonight. "I'll order pizza," I say. "Larissa loves pizza."

"You two doing okay?" she asks, instead of answering my question.

"Yeah. We are. I think. She likes my cat."

"It's good you have an animal. Kids like animals."

"Yeah," I say.

"I can't tonight," she says. "Maybe next Thursday?"

"Oh, that would be good."

"My kids will be with their dad that night."

This stops me. Jesus, I never asked her if she had kids. I know she's married—*was* married at least. They refer to her as *Mrs. Walker*.

"Oh, you have kids? I didn't know. How many?"

"Three."

I ask her their names and ages. They're all under ten. "Well, can you come when you have them? Maybe that would be fun for Larissa?"

"No, it wouldn't," Yolanda says. "She'd feel threatened by three strange kids. She feels threatened by me enough already. You sure you want me to come?"

"Yeah, I'm sure."

"Okay. I will."

Around ten forty-five, when I go out to my car to leave for John Carroll, there's a piece of paper on my windshield, tucked under the wiper. It wasn't there two hours ago. I open it and look at the bottom of the page. It's from Michelle Benton.

Jesus, she's been here again! My skin crawls. No wonder she can't find a job; she's spending all her time stalking me. I look around, but don't see anyone.

The lined notepaper has a yellow mum in the top corner. She prints the letters like a little kid.

*I'm sorry about calling you and comming to your house.
I no I shouldn't of. Please forgive me. I miss my Larissa
so bad. Shes all I have and now I have nothing. They
took away my asistance because Larissa dos not live
with me anymore and I cant pay the rent. I work at
Dunkin Donuts now. Im there noon to 6. If you bring*

Larissa to see me, I can give her some donuts and just say hi to her. Its on Mayfeild. Im sure you could get there easly. It would make Larissa happy if you bring her. I know you want to make her happy. This is very hard for me, asking you to bring my own child to me at a donut shop. I cry at night and hope Larissa is okay. I don't know how I can pay the rent and maybe I will move in with Larissas Aunti. Its a small place and I have to sleep on the couch. They won't let Larissa live there with me. They say I have to find a place where she can have her own room. Our apartment is nice. Its to bad I might have to move out. So much bad stuff has happened sinse that day you called the police. I'm not blaming you but its true. I am sorry I swore at you and called the Police. I shouldnt of. Please forgive me and please bring Larissa to Dunkin Donuts sometime. My heart is dead when she is not with me. I feel dead inside and that is why I swore at you. Please forgive me.

Larissa Bentons mother,
Michelle Benton

I have to be at John Carroll University in fifteen minutes. I can't think about this now. Tossing the letter into the car, I look around again. She could be hiding behind anything. She could be in my backyard behind a bush or the garage. I double-check that the back door is locked and leave, telling myself not to think about the letter, but it's all I think about. I interpret badly, screwing up several times. As we walk to Ed's next class, he stops walking and asks me what's wrong. He can read me too well.

Sleep restless, I sign.

Why? Restless? Ed signs.

I explain about Larissa and her mother. He nods as I sign, waiting till I finish. Students walk by, giving us curious glances.

Ed makes a face, considering this. Then, his eyebrows pressed down, mouth a straight line, letting me know he's thinking this through, he tells me that Michelle is feeling alone and scared so she wants to make me scared, too, to even the score. He thinks that she seems pretty smart to be doing that, and I ought to talk with her.

This is not what I want to hear, but I nod anyway, my nod conveying that I understand what he's saying, even though I don't want to do that. What I *do* want to do is give Michelle back her note, all the spelling corrected with a red pen, then punch her in the nose. I always wanted to sock someone in the nose, just once. Ed knows I'm thinking something I'm not saying, but he lets it go—only because he'll be late for his next class.

It's his Shakespeare class. A lot of finger-spelling. I shake out my hands, crack my knuckles.

"Can we have a hamster?" is the first thing Larissa says when I pick her up from after-school care.

"A hamster?"

"Would Sampson eat it?"

I glance into the rearview mirror when I talk to her. This backseat stuff is stupid. "Well, maybe, if it got out of its cage. Why do you want a hamster?"

"We have one in our class. His name is Tom. Tom's a stupid name. I want a hamster and name it myself."

"Well, a hamster would be very afraid of Sampson."

"A boy named Jeffrey pushed me on the swing. He has a bump on his head."

"A bump? Did he get hurt?"

Larissa points to her forehead, above her right eye. "A big bump that sticks out. He says it grew there. It doesn't hurt him."

"Well, that's good."

"If we got a hamster, he could stay in a cage up on the TV."

"I don't think so. Let's just stick with one cat for now. Okay?"

She pinches her lips together and shrugs. We're almost to my house, but I don't want to go home. I love that she's talking to me. There's something about driving around in the car, I think, that brings out this chatty part of Larissa. If we go home, she'll head upstairs and pet Sampson, who has hardly left his little house in three days. I decide to take Larissa to Dairy Queen, a good fifteen-minute drive.

"Did you meet anyone else you like?"

"Uh-huh. There's a girl with a big round face. Her tooth fell out on the playground."

"Did she find it?"

"Uh-huh. I helped her look. It was little. She found it. She spit blood."

Well, school is going to be interesting, it seems. Larissa tells me about everything, even the bathrooms with sinks that spray water out like a fountain, which I don't quite understand. We're at Dairy Queen in no time. We drove right by Dunkin' Donuts to get here.

Larissa and I both have vanilla cones dipped in chocolate. We eat in the car because the wind is kicking up and blowing old napkins and leaves around in the open space where the cement tables sit squat and firm like old men who refuse to move. I see it as a modern dance, those napkins, those old men, and miss who I was when I was young.

Hardened chocolate falls off into our laps and the ice cream melts all over our hands. We use a dozen napkins, but our hands are still sticky. I go back to the window and ask for a cup of water and more napkins. We stick our fingers in the water and wipe up as best we can. "I've invited my friend Polly and her husband to have pizza with us on Sunday. She's been my best friend for a long time. Sometimes she talks with her eyes closed, and she has a mole on her cheek, by her nose." I point to the spot on my face where Polly's mole is. I haven't thought about that mole for a long time, but it seems like the best way to describe her to Larissa. "She's very nice, but her mother just died." I know I shouldn't have said that the moment it's out of my mouth. Larissa's face goes blank. I've missed a smudge of chocolate on her chin.

"Can my mommy come? She likes pizza."

My hand on the key in the ignition, I say, "Gee, not this time, honey."

"When?" she asks.

"Well, sometime," I say.

"And we can have pizza?"

"I guess."

"Okay, I'll tell her."

I drive home a different way, not past Dunkin' Donuts. Larissa goes upstairs to play with Sampson. I have so much work to do. I sit in front of the TV and watch *Judge Judy*. Judge Judy would tell me I'm nuts to invite that woman into my house for pizza.

Chapter Twenty-one

Growing up on Oak, in the same house year after year, there was safety in familiarity. I loved watching thunderstorms from the window near the head of my bed, thrilled with the shock of white light, the *boom* of thunder, the buffeting rain against the window. When I wanted to be alone I'd go up to the cluttered attic, sitting in a corner by a window, surrounded by boxes of Christmas ornaments, *National Geographic*s, fabric, and old shoes. The basement, which frightened me as a four-year-old, became, for me at the age of eight, the best place to hide in a game of hide-and-seek. And in this basement there was a small room with a latch across the door, filled with cans of tuna, soup, condensed milk, peanut butter, crackers, jars of water, blankets, pillows, cardboard boxes, and a white box with a red cross. It never occurred to Vince and me that this room was unusual until one day when we were sitting on the living room floor playing pick-up sticks, and Mrs. Patterson and our mother were out on the front porch, talking. As soon as they lowered their voices, we began to listen to them. Our mother was listing the things in the basement room. "You should do the same," she added.

"You're getting carried away, Hillary," Mrs. Patterson said. "Certainly they're not going to bomb a suburb of Columbus." That night, Vince and I would not go to bed until she explained exactly who might *bomb* us. She called in our father.

We played in the basement more often after that, building a fort from old chairs and faded sheets, as close to that stocked room as possible, imagining ourselves spending weeks and months in there as the bombs fell, the only ones in the world to survive. (Certainly the Pattersons would never make it.) We bought lollipops and string licorice with our allowance for my mother to store next to the jars of water, boxed up a few stuffed animals and packs of cards. We were never to go into the latched room by ourselves, and respected that rule, until a few years later, when nothing at all had happened, and we sneaked in to steal our own licorice. By age thirteen, we'd eaten all of the peanut butter, and used the jars of water for science experiments, placing crackers in the stagnant water, noting how many days it would take saltines to disintegrate, as compared to Ritz. By age fourteen, the closed-off room was only a reminder of our mother's foolish fears.

In our senior year, Vince became involved in the antiwar protests, and I studied for the SAT. My room was a place of comfort; I knew where every pen was, what pile a particular book was in, what was under my bed. On the other hand, to Vince, his room was a place where he was sent when his voice or actions got out of hand, a room to confine him—except that he knew exactly how strong the porch roof was, how to hang from the edge, how to drop and roll.

I've lived in many other places since then, each one growing familiar as I inhabited it; being alone much of the time, the places I've lived in took on the personality of a close friend. Those times when a man lived with me it never felt safer, only fuller. Then I found this house, larger than any other space I've ever inhabited alone. Jimmy Bain lived here for a while, and I've had relationships with men who stayed at times, but kept their own places. It is possible that I've made choices between men and my home, as a single mother might make between her child and a man. I have my spot on the couch and at the kitchen table. I know how to drain the boiler, reconfigure the electrical box, find candles in the dark.

And yet, there were things in my home from those men who I thought, for a while, I loved; even the man I did love left things behind that I moved with me time after time. Some of these things were large, like a TV cabinet, a bureau, a coat rack, a bookcase. And these men had given me gifts: the hand-carved mirror with the golden sunrays, a pair of brass elephant book-ends, even some of the earrings I wore. I grew angry with myself for having so much of these men whom I had somehow failed, and I gave away everything, buying myself presents to replace the presence of men. This house has become my home, as much as the one I grew up in.

But with Larissa living here and Michelle calling, showing up, leaving notes on my car, maybe watching me from behind a bush, my life no longer feels familiar, nor my home comforting. I feel the need to learn how to drop and roll.

Friday morning, after taking Larissa to school, I walk around my house, checking for broken windows or boxes left on my front porch, or someone—Michelle—hiding in the bushes. That I actually do this appalls me. I go inside and plug in my phone. I'm going to stop acting so Goddamn afraid to let the phone ring, to mention Christmas or mothers dying, and we're going to start eating healthy food. There's my garden, too, those potted plants I haven't gotten into the ground yet, turning yellow from lack of care. I will finish that garden this week. And I'm even going to ask the Rothburghs' daughter if she can babysit after Larissa's asleep, and go back to Pilates. I need my life back.

I have three interpreting jobs today: a class for Ed, a class for Shaun, and interpreting for a deaf man who wants to buy a new car. Larissa will have to stay in after-school care until a little after four. I sign wonderfully all day, finding joy again in the process of interpreting, of knowing instinctively the way to rephrase English into ASL, and ASL into English. My hands and face come alive—as a dance, as art, as science of words and grammar, and once again I feel proud of what I can do.

How much of this good feeling comes from the fact that I am simply me alone, doing my job, not at my home? I turn off that part of me that allows Vince's voice to answer me. That part of me that *is* Vince's voice. I concentrate on interpreting. I do my job well. My client decides the financing is not good enough and we make plans to go to another dealership next week. He thanks me. *Helpful you,* he signs.

After picking up Larissa from after-school care, she once again chats nonstop, telling me about the hamster, which apparently gets to go home with a different child each holiday.

"Can I please, please, please take care of him just one time?" she asks me. "Please?" She uses a sweet little baby voice that I seldom hear, and I'm charmed by it for a moment, then question her ability to use her voice that way. Is it some inborn instinct to manipulate with tone? Has Larissa learned that kind of thing from Michelle?

Jesus, Vince says, *it's just a little girl asking to bring home a hamster,* and I know he's right. I'm overthinking things. *Relax,* I tell myself.

"Maybe," I say, and Larissa claps her hands as if I said yes.

At home, Sampson's on the couch and Larissa sits next to him. "Would you like a hamster?" she asks him. "He would be in a cage, but you better not scare him." I'm about to head upstairs to check my fax when she says, "Why's it doing that?"

"What doing what?" I say, but see right away what she's looking at. The phone and answering machine are on the table next to the couch. The answering machine is blinking red.

"It means there are messages on my phone," I say calmly, remembering I'm taking my life back. "People who called while I was away."

"Maybe my mommy called?"

"Maybe," I say, thinking, *Doesn't she remember her mom smells like poop?* "Probably just people who need me to interpret."

"Can we see if my mommy called?"

I brush my left hand through my hair, keeping it from spelling *shit.* "Okay, we can do that." There are four messages. The first is a phone solicitor. The second message is from my mother. "We had such a great time with you and Larissa," she says. "Your father and I hope you can come again soon. The boys got back fine and called to thank us. We hope you're doing okay, and Larissa had a good first week at school. Please call." The implication in her voice is that the boys called to say they got back safe and sound and to thank them; why didn't I?

The third message is Larissa's mother.

"Mommy!" Larissa shouts, rising up onto her knees. As Michelle talks, I watch Larissa. Her whole body listens to her mother.

"Miss Marlowe," Michelle Benton says, "please honor my request and bring Larissa to visit me at Dunkin' Donuts on Mayfield. I will be there until six tonight. I will behave properly. I just want to see her. Ten minutes is all I'm asking. It would mean so much to me and to Larissa." She sounds as if she's reading something she wrote out first, but then she adds, "Oh, Jesus, please, please let me see my baby." Then she hangs up.

I should never have plugged in my phone. I'm not ready for my life.

Larissa gets off the couch, Sampson forgotten. "Oh! My mommy wants us to go to Dunkin' Donuts to see her! Can we? Can we?"

How can I say no? How can I explain my not letting her see her mother for ten minutes? I can't.

"I guess," I say, with a shrug.

She jumps up and down. "Oh good! Oh good! Let's go!"

Her enthusiasm makes my teeth ache. The last message is from Adam, the home study guy. He wants to let me know that he doesn't have to come back. The receipt for the fire extinguisher and the fire escape plan that I turned in are good enough. He's pleased to hear I've become a foster parent. "Good luck!" he says.

Michelle stands behind the counter next to a gray-haired woman, both of them wearing aprons stained with powdered sugar, jelly, and chocolate. The shelves behind them are almost empty. As we walk through the door, Michelle leans over to the other woman. "That's my little girl," she says.

"Take your time, honey," the gray-haired lady says. "It ain't busy. Take your time and talk to her."

I assume she means Larissa. I stay by the door as Larissa runs forward. A bald man sits at the small U-shaped counter to the left, his head bent down over his mug of coffee. He looks like someone who wants to be left alone.

"Mommy, we came!" Larissa sings out, raising her arms. "We got your message and we came right away!" Michelle leans over and scoops up Larissa. I wince. She'll be covered in powdered sugar. Michelle's hair is pinned back with large black hairpins, and she wears a hairnet. Her face is still pale, but now it seems puffy. There are dark circles under her eyes. She's probably eating donuts for all her meals, to save money.

"I'll wait outside," I say. "In the car."

"You want a donut and something to drink? On me?" Michelle offers. She sounds kind and speaks softly. Each time I see her, she acts differently. I can't get a handle on what she's really like. Is she on drugs? Bipolar?

"No thanks," I say.

"Maybe some to take home?"

"Maybe," I say, and Larissa grins as if I said yes. I had better watch those maybes. They're going to get me into trouble.

In the car, I plan out the weekend, and none of those plans involve coming here. I'll take Larissa along when I interpret for story hour on Saturday, and I want to take her to Shaker Lakes to see the ducks. Maybe she can help me with the garden. Sunday night Polly might come to dinner. Would Larissa like her? It's hard to think. What are they talking about in there? My house? What we eat, what we do? Or are they not talking about me at all?

I wait fifteen minutes, then get out of my car and go back

inside. Larissa has chocolate frosting all over her face. Chocolate and a huge smile.

"Mommy says we can come every day and get donuts! Can we? Can we?"

She set me up. I wonder if she got a job at a donut place with just this in mind.

"Thanks so much for bringing her," she says. "It meant so much I could give her this treat. They don't mind me giving out some donuts after four. I made a bag, too, to take back. You like donuts, don'tcha, Larissa?"

"I do, I do," Larissa says, hopping up and down, full of sugar right before dinner. The older gray-haired lady stands behind the counter beaming as if she's watching *The Christmas Story* or some tearjerker. Even the bald man over the cup of coffee is smiling. He's missing a few teeth. Too many Goddamn donuts, I bet.

"You know, honey," Michelle says, "I don't know if Miss Marlowe can bring you every day. She's a busy woman and has lots to do, but maybe a couple times a week? How about that? I'll save you the fuzzy ones every day, just in case you come." She looks at me. "She calls the ones with coconut fuzzy ones. Don't know if you knew that."

"I didn't." My hands are in fists to keep from spelling out very nasty words. I don't eat donuts, fuzzy ones or otherwise. I eat lean meats, vegetables, lots of fruit, although I sure haven't for the last week. Standing here surrounded by the smell of donuts and bad coffee, the isn't-this-wonderful look on the gray-haired lady's face, Larissa's wide smile, I think of just walking out without her. Let Larissa stay in this world if she wants. I can feel my eyes begin to well up and I turn toward the door.

"Don't forget your bag of donuts," the gray-haired lady says brightly.

I turn back and look at Michelle Benton. "Can I talk to you for a minute?" I say. "Outside?"

For a moment there's silence while everyone trades looks. The glance between the bald man with the cup of coffee and the elderly lady really sets me off.

"Now. Right now."

"Sure," Michelle says, wiping her hands on her apron as if that might do some good. As if we might be shaking hands out there. "Larissa, you can help Margie put out napkins. Can you do that?"

"Uh-huh."

"Come here, sweetie, and help me," the older woman says. I turn and walk out the door, even more pissed. My wanting to talk with Michelle has now turned into Larissa helping to put out napkins. She'll probably want to put out napkins every time we come. She'll probably want to work at Dunkin' Donuts when she gets older. *Fuck you,* I finger-spell. *Fuck you all.*

I walk over to the next building so Larissa can't see us talking. Michelle comes out and stands a few feet away. Wise choice.

"I will not be bringing Larissa here more than once a week. Do you understand? You lost your right to control her life when you left her all alone. The law is on my side, do you understand that? I could refuse to bring her at all. Do you want that? Don't push me. You better find some way to make Larissa understand she can't come every day, that you won't be saving her donuts every Goddamn day."

"Why shouldn't I save my own baby donuts?" She stares right in my eyes. I stare back. "Why should *I* tell her she can't come, if you're the one in charge now?"

"Because if you don't be the one . . . if you don't tell her she can't come every day, then we won't come at all."

"I just told her you can't come every day. You heard me."

"Yeah, and then you said you'd save her donuts every day, just in case. I'm not stupid. I see what you're doing."

Michelle folds her arms across her chest. "Two things," she says. "One, I'm not stupid, either. You're her *foster* mother. You're supposed to take care of her till I get her back. Her social worker says reunification is the goal. Re-un-i-fi-cation. It's a big word, but I understand it. Do you? And second? I thought you liked Larissa. I thought you want to do all this shit to make her happy. Seeing me makes her happy. Don't tell me you don't see she loves me. Look at her in there. You see her smiling like that a lot recently?"

"She smiles," I say. "We're doing just fine, thanks."

"Yeah, I heard. She likes your cat, don't she?"

"Yes, she does, *doesn't* she?"

Michelle uncrosses her arms, swings them at her sides. Now *I'm* glad she's standing a few feet away. "So now we're correcting my grammar, are we?"

"Not *we*. Just me, apparently." A man walks by, goes into the donut shop. I imagine Larissa handing him a donut, saying, *You're welcome,* when he thanks her. I grip my hands together and crack my knuckles. "Look. I'm not bringing her here every day. You're right. I am busy. And I don't want her eating a bunch of donuts right before dinner. And I don't want to see you at all. You're not supposed to come to my house or call unless I say you can, and I'm saying you can't. That's what Family Services told me, and I'm sure they told you that, too. We need some stability, quiet time, time to do homework, eat, play Chutes and Ladders, go grocery shopping, read bedtime stories without you interrupting us, she's just started first grade for God's sake and she needs . . ." I stop talking. Tears are running down Michelle's cheeks.

"*I* wanted to be doing those things with her," Michelle says in a hushed voice, so quiet I hardly hear her. "*I* want to be helping her with homework. *I* wanted to take my baby to school. We been talking about it, planning it. She's my little girl and I miss her so bad. I'm sorry what I did to her, leaving her alone. I'm so sorry I got mad at you. It's not your fault. You're doing a good job. I know you are." The tears are thick and don't stop. She keeps wiping at her face and her eyeliner is smeared all over her cheeks, making her look like a soldier in camouflage. Yet, even though she's crying, she's trying not to. I can tell. I've been there before.

We stand there, looking at each other. The man walks out with his donuts.

Finally I speak up. "I can't bring her every day. Don't make me the bad guy."

"Me too. Don't make me the bad guy. Please don't tell her I'm a bad mother or nothing. I made an awful mistake. I'm paying for it big-time." She pauses and pulls up the collar of her T-shirt from under the top of her apron, wipes her face with it. "How often can you bring her? Could you come twice a week? Just for ten minutes. I'll only give her one donut, and one to take home. I promise. I'll tell her it's my idea. I'll tell her they won't let me have visitors that much."

I pause. Have I been played, to agree to twice a week? But she looks so Goddamn sad and pitiful. I shake my head, but not in disagreement. I understand her loss, these tears she hates to cry. "Okay," I say. "How about Mondays and Fridays, but it might be other days, if I have a job, or maybe only one day a week. You see her at Metzenbaum on Wednesdays. You could bring her some donuts then, too."

"Thank you," she says. "I 'preciate it. Thank you so much."

She looks behind her, back at the donut shop. "I better get back." She shrugs, a childlike one-shoulder shrug that says *Don't you think so?* I nod. She smiles at me. "Thank you," she says again. "You're good for my little girl. I know she likes you. I can tell." She walks into the store and in a couple of minutes, Larissa walks out with a bag of donuts.

On the car ride home Larissa says, "That lady had a funny ear."

"What lady?" I ask.

"The donut lady. She had a funny ear. She was nice. She let me give that man a bag of donuts. He got six jelly donuts and I picked them out. And I got to take a donut over to that man. He didn't have teeth. He was sad."

Yes. The gray-haired lady did have a funny ear, a cauliflower ear. I don't say anything back to Larissa. Something about her words nags at me. I try to think. I stop at a stop sign and wait for it to turn green. The driver behind me honks. Stop signs don't turn green. They just stay *stop* and you have to know when it's time to go. I drive on, more carefully now. I don't try to think. I have a little girl in my car.

That night, in bed, it hits me. Larissa sees the bump on a boy's head, and the cauliflower ear on an old lady, just like we all do; they define what these people look like to her, but she doesn't judge them, she sees inside them right away. Is this something kids do naturally, or is she an exceptionally wonderful child? All I know is, if I'd been like that once, I no longer am. It isn't just the terrible mistake that Michelle Benton made that defines her for me, it's her bleached hair and that skunky black stripe, her gaudy fingernails, her overdone eyeliner. If I saw her anywhere, I would think of her simply as the girl with the bad dye job and dismiss her as anyone with a brain, as if being smart is all that matters. And now I have a new image of her I can't shake, as much as I want to. I see her now as Larissa's mother. Flawed. Confused. Angry. Possibly inept. But she loves her daughter. It kills her to hear me talk about helping Larissa with her homework, taking her to the grocery store. How can I hate her? She loves Larissa, and Larissa loves her. I am only the person standing between them, until I am no longer necessary.

Over the weekend, Larissa and I do all the things I planned. It's a gorgeous weekend. The sky can't possibly be bluer, the temperature more pleasant. Larissa takes to digging holes in my garden with a seriousness that makes me smile all day. She calls her mother Saturday night and they talk for an hour.

Polly comes to dinner Sunday. Patrick can't, he's too behind on work and has to catch up before he goes back on Monday. Polly brings a box of enormous chocolate chip cookies, the type where the chocolate chips are really large flat squares. By now I know Larissa's favorite cookies are Oreos.

After she puts the cookies down, I give her a hug and we both get a bit teary-eyed. Larissa's upstairs in her room, cutting out pictures of lions and tigers from old *National Geographic*s to tape inside the cat house. The scissors are children's scissors, with blunted tips. Again, I tell Polly how sorry I am about her mother. She thanks me. "So she's really here?" Polly asks.

"Yep. She is."

"So how's it going?" she asks, her voice almost a whisper.

I think about everything that's happened since Polly left, and it's too much to tell her standing in my kitchen. It would take an hour, and I'd have to whisper. Polly and I have never stood around my house whispering. "Well, it's good and . . . it's hard. I guess you know that. Want to meet her?"

Polly's silent for a second, taking in the fact I haven't really told her a thing, knowing there's something I'm avoiding. "Sure. Where is she?"

I lead her upstairs.

"Larissa, this is my friend Polly. Polly, this is Larissa." I step into Larissa's room. Polly stays in the doorway. Larissa looks up but doesn't say hello.

"Hi, Larissa," Polly says, smiling—not just the smile you make to a little girl, but the kind that shows surprise and amusement. She's looking around the room at all I've done. "Pleased to meet you. What are you doing? Cutting out pictures?"

Larissa looks at me. I explain about the project to put pictures in the cat house.

"Oh, my," Polly says. "Look at that! Where did it come from?"

Larissa looks at her lap. I explain about her and my dad building the cat house, how we put it together when we got home.

"That's a very cool house. Does Sampson like it?" Polly says. Larissa's thumb is securely in her mouth. I tell Polly how Sampson has taken to his house, how much he loves the pink satin pillow. The doorbell rings. Everyone looks at me.

"It's the pizza," I say, hoping to God it is. It is. We eat dinner. I've prepared a salad and cut up a pineapple for Polly and me. I put four baby carrots on Larissa's plate. That's how many she'll eat. I offer her pineapple, but she shakes her head no. Polly asks questions, and I answer them. Everything is conducted with pleasant voices. My shoulders ache and I have to roll my neck to relax.

When dinner's done, Larissa looks at me. I tell her she can go back up to her room and keep working on her project.

"She's adorable," Polly says as she helps me wash the dishes. The sound of the water running helps hide our voices and we don't quite whisper, but almost. It's begun to rain outside.

"She does talk. You should see her when she gets going."

"I'd like to," Polly says, handing me a plate to dry. Polly always washes the dishes when she comes over, and I dry and put away. She pretends she likes to do dishes when she's here, and I pretend I like to do dishes when I'm there.

"She'll warm up to you," I say.

"So, anything you want to tell me?" she says.

I look toward the stairs. "A lot," I whisper. "But not now."

"When?" Polly asks.

I laugh. "Good question." I take the last dish from her. "I want to hear about your mom's funeral. Let's go to the living room."

Polly tells me all about it, starting from the phone call she got from the hospital. We talk in hushed tones, but it's because we're talking about death. When she tells me about how she sat in the hospital room for a half hour after her mother died, not knowing how she could ever get up and leave, I once again say how sorry I am that I wasn't there. I say the same thing when she describes the funeral. This time she says, "Yeah, I wish you could have been there." There is not an iota of reprimand in her voice, only sorrow.

"The coma was the hardest," Polly says, rubbing a hand

against the back of her neck, then closing her eyes. "The slightest sound would give her seizures. We couldn't speak to her, or each other. Even touching her. I did once, and she moaned. Did you know that? The brain does this strange thing. It's why they keep the lights low and make sure every one is quiet in intensive care. I learned all this stuff I really don't want to know."

She pauses, looking past me toward the stairs. "Larissa's there," she says, raising her chin. "At the top of the stairs. Just standing there. I can see her feet."

I turn around. She's there. I look at my watch. We've been talking for an hour. How fast the time has gone. "Larissa? Do you need me?"

No answer. I look at Polly. "It's almost her bedtime."

"You should go get her ready," Polly offers.

I put my hand on Polly's thigh. "Thank you for your help getting her, asking the mayor. Did I thank you enough?"

"Yeah. Yeah, you did. I'm glad I could help."

When I walk her to the door, it's still raining. I think about Michelle Benton walking away from my house in the pouring rain. I haven't mentioned her to Polly at all. Ever since Vince got killed, Polly's known when I've gone to the grocery store, when I've picked up books at the library.

"Drive carefully," I say.

"Call me when you can talk," she says.

Monday after school I take Larissa to visit Michelle at the donut shop. I stay in the car, letting Larissa run into the store by herself. It's still raining. I wrote a note for Larissa to give her mother. *Dear Michelle,* I start it, not knowing any other way.

Does Larissa have rain boots and a raincoat you might bring to Metzenbaum tomorrow, or should I buy some? Also, she could use a few more pants, if there are any more at your house. I just think she'd like her own things, if possible. Thank you, Alice.

It took me twenty minutes to write that note.

Tuesday I start back on my foster parenting classes after missing two weeks. The session is titled Separation and Attachment Impact. Three foster parents have come to this meeting to share their advice. The woman who wore the lavender outfit now wears an outfit with large red flowers. I listen to everything she says. I take notes. I raise my hand. "Is it ever a good idea to get involved with helping the birth parent?"

She smiles, but almost sadly. "In what way do you mean get involved?"

"I don't really know," I say.

"Well, it depends on your relationship with the birth parent, and what their obstacles might be, such as drug addiction, alcohol abuse, anger management, and your ability to deal with those issues. How much can the birth parent be included in the foster parent's activities? Any suggestions?" She hasn't answered me, just deferred the question to everyone else.

Several people in the audience suggest inviting the birth parent to their church, buying presents for the foster child to give to the birth parent for birthdays and holidays. But two of the visiting foster parents tell stories about getting too involved. "I'd never do that again," one woman says. "Me neither," says another. "I take care of the child, and leave rehab to the experts. No way she's coming to my home." The third says she's never had a problem and has invited many birth mothers to her house for dinner. It's two to one.

I don't even know why I asked. How could I help Michelle?

The next day, Wednesday, is the first anniversary of September eleventh. I keep the TV off, telling Larissa this is a special day that people are supposed to read and play games. After school, we play parcheesi and Chutes and Ladders, which I'm beginning to despise. I show Larissa how I clip Sampson's nails. We walk around the neighborhood. I teach her how to play war with cards. We play more parcheesi. I read her *Goodnight Moon* three times and *In the Night Kitchen* four times, then a good dozen poems from *The Children's Book of Poems,* and then play one final game of parcheesi. I'm exhausted by the time she climbs into bed. I have never worked so hard in my life.

In the morning I wonder if I did the right thing, if maybe Larissa should understand the importance of yesterday.

When Yolanda comes for dinner on Thursday, Larissa frowns the entire time. My jaw is tight. I'm getting mad at Larissa; I want her to show Yolanda how well we're getting along. I excuse Larissa from the table as soon as she's done eating. "Please carry your dish into the kitchen," I ask her, and she glares at me.

After dinner, Yolanda and I sit in my living room, listening to music.

"Should I have mentioned September eleventh to her?" I ask.

"Only if she asked," Yolanda says. She's dressed more casually than I've ever seen her before—jeans and a long-sleeved T-shirt— yet still her clothes are tight-fitting, her shoes trendy. She doesn't have any stray movements. How does she stay so calm with three kids and a full-time nine-to-five job? How does she find time to shop for those clothes, get dressed so carefully, do her hair? I feel stupid and dull in my comfortable shoes.

"What do your kids know about it?"

"Racine's only three. The other two, they know bad people came from far away and flew airplanes into buildings and killed a lot of people. It scared them at first. I took a week off work and kept them home from school. But a year later? I don't think they care about it much now. They're young. They got other problems."

I'm not sure if it's too personal to ask what she means, and I'm afraid to look like I don't care if I don't ask. "Problems? Are they okay?"

"It's just the damn testing at the schools. They don't sleep, thinking about them. Those tests make them so worried, they can't learn. They're more scared of those tests than bad men flying airplanes into their house."

Yolanda's face comes alive when she talks about her kids. Does Larissa show on my face? How can I protect her from being afraid of those tests?

Yolanda says she has to leave to pick up her kids. She thanks me for having her over, compliments my house, and says that I'm doing a good job. I wonder how soon I can ask her over again.

The next day I'm home at noon when I get a phone call. It's Larissa's teacher.

"I'm sorry," she says, and I stop breathing. "But we have a problem. Larissa is pinching some of the children. She's a very sweet child, and very bright, but these incidents are quite inappropriate."

"What incidents?" I ask. "How many times has she done this?"

"She pinched a girl yesterday and again today. Two different children. I had her take a time-out and told her I'd be speaking to you. I like her very much, Mrs. Marlowe, and I just want to stop this behavior before it gets out of hand. Maybe you can find out why she feels the need to hurt another child, and help her understand that this kind of behavior is not beneficial to anyone."

I don't answer right away. I'm torn between brushing the whole thing off—it only happened twice—and bursting into tears. Everything I've done has been wrong and Larissa's taking it out on other little kids.

"Thank you for telling me," I offer. "I'm sorry it happened. Do you have any idea why she did it? Someone else pinched her first?"

"No, Mrs. Marlowe. Not that I know of."

"I'll talk to her," I say.

"If she does it again, I will have to write up a report."

"They were mean to me," Larissa says, when I bring it up on the way to Dunkin' Donuts.

"What do you mean, mean to you?" I ask.

"That little girl spits at me," Larissa says. I almost smile at the way she describes a girl her age as *that little girl*.

"When did she spit at you?" I ask.

Larissa shrugs.

"Your teacher says you pinched two children. Did they both spit at you?"

Her bottom lip goes out. "Jimmy says I can't have Tom ever because I touch him too much and I'll kill him."

It takes a second to remember that Tom is the hamster. "Larissa, you can't pinch people, no matter what they say. And if someone spits at you, you should tell your teacher." *Believe me, I will,* I think.

She just sticks her thumb in her mouth.

"Larissa, do you hear me? If someone does something to you, you need to tell your teacher, not pinch them or hurt them."

She takes her thumb out of her mouth. "I'm not tellin' no teacher." She puts her thumb back in.

"But I thought you liked your teacher?"

She shrugs.

The shrug annoys me. "Maybe we should talk about this with your mother?" I say, then bite my lip, wanting to reverse time and take the words back.

"No," she says, popping her thumb out of her mouth so I can really hear her.

"Okay," I say. "Then I don't want to hear about it happening again." I pause, collect my thoughts. "It's not nice to pinch people. If they do something mean to you, they must have problems we don't understand. We have to try to understand what their problems are. Sometimes you have to be very nice to the people who are mean to you, so they understand what love is." I add all this to make sure I've put in a little philosophy along with my threat to tell her mother. She nods. My words stay with me for the rest of the day.

Chapter Twenty-two

A routine begins. Rising early each morning I take Larissa to school, come home for an hour to shower and do paperwork, throw Larissa's wet sheets into the wash, then interpret for Ed and Shaun and any other jobs I can fit in before five o'clock, when I have to pick Larissa up at after-school care. There are visits to the donut shop, trips to Metzenbaum, foster parenting classes, grocery shopping, errands on the weekends—and very occasionally getting the Rothburghs' daughter Nelly to babysit. I refuse most night jobs and I'm not making as much money as I used to. Elaine at the Hearing and Speech Center doesn't seem to call me as often anymore. I feel as if I'm running a marathon wearing only one shoe.

The TV news and papers are filled with the story about the woman who got caught beating her child in the car. No gray areas here; the video of her leaning into that backseat and smacking her daughter are played dozens of times. She's a bad mother, a horrible person. We can so easily hate her. There is one moment though, in the beginning, when she pleads, "I love my daughter. I'm so sorry," that I actually wonder if this was just one awful mistake, that she had never hit her daughter before, and never would again.

Michelle Benton is always on my mind.

Larissa's social worker tells me that Michelle is trying, but failing. She's lost her assistance, and the job at the donut shop is part-time without benefits. She constantly misses or is late to her parenting classes and drug abuse classes because she doesn't have a car, although sometimes, when she really wants to, she can borrow Aunt Teya's. When informed she isn't meeting her goals, she kicked a desk, her shoe going right through the thin veneer, and now she has to go to anger management classes also. It could take a long time until she gets her daughter back.

Larissa's teacher calls to say that Larissa hasn't pinched anyone again, but she's drawing pictures of the kids she doesn't like, printing their names on the paper, then making big black *X*'s over their faces. I want to ask if she's spelling their names right. "She needs to see a counselor," the teacher says. "She is," I tell her. "You need to mention this behavior to the counselor," she says. "I will," I say. "We'll have to keep an eye on her," she says. *That's what you're being paid to do,* I think.

When I ask Larissa why she draws the pictures of her schoolmates and *X*'s them out, she says she doesn't like them.

"Are they mean to you?" We're in the bathroom and I'm combing out her hair before she goes to bed. She runs her fingers inside the sink, chasing water droplets, and shrugs.

Drawing pictures and crossing them out seems harmless, but I've seen what's happening in schools and know it must worry the teacher. "Does it make you feel better?" I ask. "Does it make you feel like you have some power over people who don't treat you nicely?"

She waits a minute before she shrugs again. I know her shrugs now. This one means, *Yeah, a little, but I don't want to talk about it.*

"Then can you draw them at home, instead of at school? If it makes you feel better to draw them and scratch them out, it's okay with me, but do it here so it doesn't worry your teacher. Okay?"

She shrugs. It means okay, I think.

I don't hear from the teacher again. Two weeks later I buy Larissa a plush teddy bear with the softest fur I've ever felt. They're making stuffed animals out of some new material that is so silky, I want one for myself. I sit the bear on the seat next to me in the car and strap him in. Driving to school with the strapped-in bear to pick up Larissa, I am happier than I have been in a long time. I am full of a great moment, and want someone to see what a wonderful moment this is. I think about the home study guy. Maybe he should come back out and just make sure everything is all right.

Larissa's charmed when she sees the bear. She hugs him as we drive home. That night she plays in her room quietly while I work in the computer room. When I check on her, she's sitting in a circle with her stuffed animals, talking softly with them. Sampson is one of the animals in this circle, and he seems to be listening to Larissa. "You must all behave when I'm at school," she says, then notices me and stops talking. I wave to the circle.

"Hello, everyone," I say. "I'm going back to my office now. Have a lovely evening."

A perfect day. I wish my mother could see me now.

I'm watching you, Vince says.

Are you really? I ask. And I believe he is.

One evening in early October, Michelle calls the house. Our deal is that Larissa always calls her mom after finishing her homework, and she already did that. "You still need to talk to her?" I ask. "She's brushing her teeth."

"No. I need to talk to you."

I tense.

"I'm moving in with Teya and her husband. I'm getting kicked out of my place 'cause I missed rent last month."

"I'm sorry." If she asks me for money, I'm going to say the same damn thing.

"Can I ask you something? I got all this furniture. That bedroom set in Larissa's bedroom? That belonged to Charlie when he was little. And that rocking chair in my living room? That's his grandpa's, who's dead. Charlie's parents just have a trailer now, and no way am I gonna let my dad have any of it. We don't speak no more. And there's all Larissa's toys and stuff. There's no room for them at Teya's. Can you take some, and maybe some of the furniture? I know Larissa misses her stuff. She said you made her a nice room, but I know she misses her own bed. I can't afford to put it in storage. They're going to put it out on the street if I don't do something with it. The couch and the dining room set I bought off the lady was here when I moved in. They say I can leave them, but they won't give me more than fifty dollars. Do you have room for them, too? It won't be for long. I'm going to find my own place soon as I can."

Larissa walks down the stairs, teeth brushed and wearing her pajamas. It's time for her to go to bed. She looks at me. I hold up one finger. How can I talk to her mother without her knowing who I'm talking to? How can I say no to this in front of her? How did I get to a position where my decisions are made by the look on a child's face?

"I can't take all of it," I say. I did like that dining room table, but where the hell would I put it? I could take the bed that's in Larissa's room down to the basement so she could have her own, and of course, all her toys should come here. The rocking chair would fit nicely in this room. The couch? I'll say no to the couch.

"Not the couch," I say. "And I'm not sure about the dining room table. How do you plan on moving it here?"

Larissa watches me intently. Does she know I'm talking to her mother? Had they planned this?

"I don't know," Michelle says. "I can't pay nothin' to get it moved. I'll give the couch to anyone who moves the rest of the stuff, if you know someone wants a couch. I could give them the couch and the bookcase and a lamp or something, but I got to do it Saturday. Do you know anyone would want the couch and could move the stuff?"

I do. Ed has just moved into an apartment with Shaun and another deaf guy, and I know they don't have much furniture. And he drives a truck. "I'll see," I say.

"Thank you, Miss Marlowe. Thank you so much. It means a lot to me to keep my husband's stuff. You can have the dining room table. I won't make you pay for it."

I close my eyes and sigh. "Okay. Thanks. I'll see what I can do. You look for someone too."

"I will. Thank you. Thank you again, Miss Marlowe. I mean it." She's just about the only one who gets the *Miss* right.

"Call me Alice," I say. "We'll talk tomorrow when I bring Larissa to the restaurant." Calling Dunkin' Donuts a restaurant is a stretch, but hell, I just told her to call me Alice. What difference do a few words make?

Larissa jumps up and down when I explain what the phone call was about. "Yes, yes, yes! I get my bed! I get my kitchen! I get all my toys!" I don't have to read her a bedtime story. Instead she lists every single thing she has missed so badly, down to a stick of pink lip gloss that was on her bedroom bureau. *I could have bought you lip gloss,* I think. As the list goes on, I see this room fill up, this house, the circle of stuffed animals becoming an army.

Ed says he'd love the couch and whatever furniture he can have. He'll meet me at my house at nine A.M. Saturday morning with Shaun and Joey, and they'll follow me over to Michelle's apartment. I have no plans whatsoever of going to her apartment and almost say so, but then realize the problem. I should offer to interpret for them. The situation will be even more complicated since they'll be carrying furniture.

I don't want to go there. Even less, I don't want to take Larissa there with me. We'll be moving everything out of her apartment. Won't Larissa take one look at me, and one look at the boys moving her stuff out, and remember I started all this? I came to her apartment, called the police, and now I'm taking the furniture? Shit.

I call Polly and ask her if she might take Larissa to see a movie. "At nine in the morning?" Polly asks. "You know where one's playing at nine in the morning maybe?"

"I'm not thinking too well."

"No, you're not. I can't anyway. She's got a big PR thing and I have to be there." Polly always calls the mayor *she.*

"Okay, okay. I'll handle this somehow."

"I think you're nuts to take her furniture."

"It's a nice dining room table," I say. "And, you have any bright ideas how I can tell Larissa I won't take her bedroom set that used to be her dad's, you let me know."

She doesn't have an answer for that one. "Hey," she says. "You ever going to call me just to chat again? I miss that."

"Me too," I say.

Before Ed, Shaun, and Joey show up, I explain to Larissa that all three of them are deaf—that they speak sign language like I do, but don't talk with their voices, and that they can't hear her if she speaks, although Shaun is pretty good at reading lips.

"If you want to say something to them, I'll interpret for you," I tell her as I zip up the purple windbreaker that Michelle brought to our last meeting at the donut shop. It's a little too small.

"Yes!" Larissa says. "That would be so good! But I can spell my name! Don't you do that. I will. Okay? I can spell my name to them."

"You betcha."

"Oh, oh!" she says turning in a circle. She's just started doing this, this spinning when she gets really excited. "I want to spell them my mommy's name! Teach me that! Oh, please teach me that before they get here!"

Larissa knows how to sign the letters in her name, but that's about all. I tried teaching her how to spell Sampson, but she got so frustrated we gave up and gave Sampson a personal sign, like you would give a friend; an S on top of her head where a cat's ear would be. I know that teaching her how to spell her mother's name, a name that has none of the same letters except *L* and *I,* will not be easy. The guys will show up in a few minutes.

"How about you just sign *Mommy?* You know that sign."

"No! They can't call her *Mommy!* That's dumb! Michelle Benton! That's her name! They have to know her name."

Just testing the waters, I ask Larissa how to spell *Michelle.* She looks at me, then realizes she can't spell it even with her own alphabet. She looks so defeated, I feel like a shit.

"Okay, okay, I'll teach you," I say. I sit on couch and she stands directly in front of me, a serious, determined look on her face. In less than five minutes, tears are forming in her eyes.

"Okay," I say. "I have a better idea."

Her thumb goes into her mouth.

"How about we give your mom a special name, her personal name, like we did for Sampson?"

The thumb comes out, and she wipes at her eyes. "Okay."

I can think of a few choice signs, none of them that I could tell Larissa. "How about an *M* to your chin? Where you sign *mommy?* Then it can mean she is both a person with a name that begins with *M,* and a *mommy?*" I show her what I mean.

Larissa thinks a while, as if she's contemplating all the alternatives. "That's good," she says, and copies the sign.

The doorbell rings.

I introduce Larissa to Ed, Shaun, and Joey, and she signs her name perfectly, proudly, not stepping behind me as she usually does when she meets new people. They smile and nod to her, showing her how they spell their names, and she smiles and nods just as if she understands.

Pretty smart girl, Ed signs, and I interpret for Larissa.

Larissa blushes and starts to put her thumb into her mouth, but stops and lowers her hand back down. Then slowly, carefully, she signs *Thank you,* and I know if I ever have to give this girl back, I will die.

We go outside and get into my car. The boys follow in the truck.

"They smile a lot," Larissa says to me in the car.

"Yeah, they do. They're happy, so they smile."

"They're happy they're deaf?"

Wouldn't it be nice to be able to ask simple questions like that? "Ed, Joey, and Shaun are happy with who they are," I answer. "And they should be. They're nice kids."

Larissa nods. "Do you think they'll like my mommy?" she asks.

I look at her in the rearview mirror, buckled in the back as Michelle has taught me to do. "Sure," I say. "Of course they will." And they will like her. Michelle has a happy, friendly personality, when she wants to. It's people with clipboards she seems to piss off. And me, but not as often as she used to. Still, no matter how she acts, I can't shake the image of her shouting *Baby stealer!* at me across a wide busy street. I can't get rid of who she thinks I am, and who I thought she was.

We park out front of Michelle's apartment. You can park in front on Saturdays and Sundays. Larissa hops out of the car and runs to the front door. She's pressed the buzzer and is standing there holding the door open for us by the time we all get there.

"Come on," she says. "Come on! This is where I live. Tell them to come on." Has she forgotten I'd been here before? I sign *Come on,* and we all follow as Larissa dashes up the steps.

Three floors, no elevator. And Ed's truck is not all that big. This will take several trips, and most of the day. I rub my hands through my hair, thinking I could just pull it all out right now, hair by hair.

Michelle stands in the doorway, holding Larissa in her arms. She's dyed her hair. No more black stripe. "Thank you," she says. "Thank you for doing this."

"They are, not me," I say. I sign what she said, and what I said, then introduce everyone.

Larissa pokes me with one finger on my hip. "Tell them my mommy's sign." I make the *M* to my chin, and explain what it means.

Michelle smiles almost shyly. "Well, that's sweet of you. Thank you. Come on. Come on in."

We move into the dining room. The table does have strong legs. It probably weighs a ton. How the hell will it even fit out the door?

All around the apartment are boxes, taped shut and labeled with black marker. TAKE TO TEYA'S some say, with a list underneath of what's in the box. FOR LARISSA, with more lists. STORAGE, and a list. STORAGE is me. I've moved a few times in my life and never been this organized.

"Let me show you guys what you can have if you want it," Michelle says, waving them into her living room. She's wearing tight jeans and an open jean jacket over a striped T-shirt that shows her bellybutton. She's still wearing too much eyeliner for my taste, but the deep mauve lipstick she has on makes her pale face look like porcelain. I see Shaun eyeing her and think *You'd better not.*

With me interpreting, the guys decide what they'd like, which is everything Michelle offers them.

"They'll take the stuff you're giving them on the last trip," I interpret, "so they can just go home with it. They'll take the table first, and fit the other stuff around it." Shaun nods, then signs, and I voice for him. "Do you have tools to take the table apart?"

Michelle grins and nods, goes into the kitchen, and comes out with a socket wrench and two screwdrivers. "I looked underneath already," she says to Shaun. "I think this'll do it."

Larissa runs out of her room. "There're seven boxes for me!" she says.

"I've got root beer and donuts for everyone," Michelle says. "They're in the kitchen if you want some." When I interpret this, all three guys nod. *Donuts,* Joey signs, then kisses the back of his hand.

"I love donuts," I say to Michelle, interpreting for Joey.

"Who doesn't?" she says. I realize she thinks *I* love donuts. God, this is going to be a long day. And how do I tell her now that I hate donuts, now that she has established that *everyone* loves donuts. I don't *always* want to be the odd man out. Odd woman.

When they finally get the table into two pieces, Ed and Joey carry it down while Shaun gets the doors. Larissa, Michelle, and I are left standing in the dining room, half the table lying upside down, its legs sticking up like a dead animal.

"They talk with their hands, Mommy," Larissa says, interrupting the silence.

"I know they do, honey. Do you want some pop and donuts?"

Larissa nods. "Can you come to her house and see the little house I made for Sampson?" Larissa says as she and her mother head for the kitchen. Their backs are to me, but I hear everything.

"I don't know, honey. That's up to Miss Marlowe."

I stay in the dining room, standing by one thick upside-down table leg.

Michelle has borrowed her aunt's car, and we load that up, and my car too. Back at my house, Ed, Joey, and Shaun take the bed in Larissa's room and move it to the basement. Michelle and Larissa carry in boxes. I'm trying to catch Sampson and lock him in the attic before he gets out, but he knows something is up and hides under the couch, so I just stand by the front door, a cat guard, opening the door for Michelle and Larissa as they carry in boxes.

"He's really a nice cat," Larissa tells her mother as they pass by me. "He'll like you a lot." My jaw gets even tighter. I'm going to have a hell of a headache. It's lunchtime by now. Am I expected to feed all these people?

Well, we'll have to eat. But first I have to catch the damn cat. The front door closes for a moment, so I get a broom and sweep Sampson out from under the couch. He runs into the basement. I can't close the basement door—it has to stay open for the guys to carry stuff down there. At least I'm in the kitchen now. I pull everything that I can find out of the fridge.

Michelle comes in. "They're trying to tell me something," she says. "About my bedroom bureau? Should they take that to the basement too?"

"Sure," I say. Hell, maybe they should just move *my* stuff down there so Michelle can move in, I think, banging the lid of the jelly jar on the sink. It's stuck tight. The fact that she's being quite nice, treating the guys great and pulling her weight with carrying stuff, only gets on my nerves.

"Oh, you got food out! You didn't have to do that."

"We've got to eat," I say, still banging.

She reaches out, and automatically I hand her the jelly jar. She gives a quick twist and hands it back to me. "There." She looks around the kitchen. "Nice place you got. I'll pay you back for this someday, really. I can't believe how nice you are." She says this like she really can't believe how nice I am.

"Thanks," I say, and get the Excedrin out of the cabinet.

"You know kids can't have aspirin, right?" she says, turning to look behind her as if Larissa might come shooting around the corner and grab the bottle out of my hand.

"Yes, I know that," I say. But I don't know what she's talking about. I make peanut butter and jelly sandwiches for everyone.

It takes two trips to get everything to my house, and by the time we're done it's four o'clock. The guys are heading back to Michelle's apartment to get the couch and things they want. They say I don't have to come this time, they're doing pretty well with Michelle all on their own.

Yeah, I bet, I think.

"Can I go?" Larissa asks.

Michelle picks her up and they nuzzle noses. "I'll bring her back as soon as the guys get the stuff in the truck. I promise."

I say sure. They leave, and the house is wonderfully quiet. It would feel good, this silence, except the sight of Michelle's rocking chair in the corner is like a loud sign, a red flag, something I can't quite interpret but I know it's not a good thing.

By nine o'clock at night, they haven't returned. I call Michelle. Disconnected. I try Ed, but he isn't answering his TTY. I try to stay calm. What could I tell Children and Family Services anyway? Her mother asked if she could take her and I said yes?

I pace. I swear with my hand, then out loud. At ten, the doorbell rings.

"Sorry, sorry," Michelle says, holding a sleeping Larissa in her arms. "I got pizza for the guys, and then they showed Larissa how to play pool, and we took my—"

"You took Larissa to a pool hall?"

"No, no. They got themselves a pool table. That's about all they got! And mattresses on the floor!" She laughs. "I like them. It's so nice they did all that moving. What took so long was I decided to give them my bed, too, 'cause I'll be sleeping on the couch at Teya's. I was going to sell my bed and bedroom stuff to the landlord, but screw him, I'd rather give it to the guys. So we went back and got it, and then they said they'd take my stuff over to Teya's for me. Well, they didn't *say* it, you know. We did a lot of writing stuff down. Can I take her up and put her in bed?" She shifts Larissa in her arms.

"Sure," I say.

Michelle carries her up, knowing just where Larissa's room is. I stay downstairs. She's up there ten minutes or more. I stop myself from going to see if she's rifling through my jewelry box, but I keep my ears open and pretend I'm cleaning up the stuff on the table by the bottom of the steps. When she finally comes down, her eyes are bloodshot.

"Sorry," she says, and this sorry has none of the vigor of moments before. "It was real hard to walk out of that room," she offers, when I don't say anything. "Her old bed, her sleeping." She wipes at her nose. "Sorry."

What the hell can I say but, "That's okay."

"You're very nice," she says and heads to the front door. "It's been a long day. Thanks for letting me take her."

"Sure," I say.

I watch Michelle walk down the front walk to the car parked on the street. It's dark now, and windy, a cold front moving in. She has to be freezing in that T-shirt and thin jean jacket. I wonder what she has left, now that she's given everything away.

Chapter Twenty-three

Larissa is a little witch for Halloween. In early November, she catches strep throat. Michelle and I both show up at Larissa's fall concert at school, and she comes over and sits next to me, elbowing me when Larissa files out with her class. They sing "Catch a Falling Star" and "It's a Small World." Larissa wets her bed only two or three times a week now. Sometimes I go into the donut shop when I take Larissa there, and talk with Michelle, ask her how her classes are. Sometimes I eat a donut and drink bad coffee, sitting at the counter. Nothing makes Larissa happier than when I do this.

One evening as we eat dinner in the kitchen, Larissa asks me if her mom can come for Thanksgiving. My parents are driving to Arizona to visit Bruce and Dylan.

"Isn't she going to have dinner with Auntie Teya?" I ask.

"She's going away. My mommy will be all alone." She looks so sad about her mom being alone that I say yes.

"As long as she doesn't bring donuts. No more donuts."

"Yes! Yes! No donuts! Can I call her?"

"After you do your homework." This is standard now, and Larissa nods.

"Yolanda Walker's coming for dinner tomorrow," I remind her as I get up and carry my plate to the sink. I had a vegetable burger; Larissa had a regular hamburger.

Larissa frowns. She still doesn't like Yolanda. Yolanda is one of the people who held her down on the doctor's exam table. She puts her thumb into her mouth.

"No thumb," I say. She takes her thumb out, but those eyebrows lower. She wants to stop sucking her thumb—kids tease her—but she still gets mad when I remind her.

"Can we make apple pie?" she asks.

"For Thanksgiving?"

She nods. "My mommy loves apple pie," she says, crossing her arms when she says the word *love*. We don't uses signs as much anymore now that Larissa talks so much. Really, she can just be a gush of words and open longing, that wariness of exposing herself forgotten for the moment. These times, I see Michelle so clearly in Larissa: Michelle's innocent energy, her need to be loved and give love, a raw way of exposing herself that would make me cringe. Still, I envy that in both of them, that they can let loose those boundaries I have made for myself.

"When you say you love something, like a pie," I tell her, "you kiss the back of your fist instead. Crossing your arms against your chest is usually meant for a person, and maybe animals. You could say *I love Sampson* by crossing your arms, but if you were going to say *I love pop,* you would make the other sign, kissing the back of your fist."

"I *do* love Sampson!" she says, making the sign for *love* across her chest. "I do! And my mommy loves apple pie!" She kisses the back of her fist. I hardly ever have to teach her a sign twice anymore. She's a smart kid. I want to tell her that I love her, ask if she loves me. These limitations stand like an electric fence between us.

"Can we make apple pie?" she asks again.

"Sure."

She smiles and runs off. "Sampson!" she calls. "Sampson! My mommy's coming for Thanksgiving! We're going to make apple pie! Do you like apple pie?"

I decide to invite Ed and his friends. I really don't relish the idea of sitting around the dining room table with just Larissa and Michelle, especially since it's her table. A few weeks ago, I'd had Ed and Joey come over and switch the tables, and now mine is in the basement. I like her table better.

Larissa has me teach her how to sign *Happy Thanksgiving* and *You want apple pie?* Ed, Shaun, and Joey bring potato chips and four cans of cranberry sauce. Michelle brings green beans.

I spend much of dinner interpreting. The guys make silly jokes and Michelle and Larissa laugh. "Hey, hey, I got one," Michelle says, "Okay, there's this blonde, a real blonde, not like me, who's driving somewhere, Connecticut, I think, yeah, a place starts with a *C,* and this blonde don't know how to get where she's going so she pulls over at this gas station, and . . ." She stops, squints her eyes, and chews at her bottom lip. "No, not first. First she goes to a Seven-Eleven or something, and asks where's Connecticut, and the guy, he points down the road and says, 'Just keep going that way,' then she gets lost again and pulls over to a gas station and . . . Fuck. I forget. I missed something." She laughs, rolling her eyes. "There's supposed to be this bear." She holds up both hands, still laughing. "Sorry."

Shaun watches Michelle, smiling ear to ear. I'm so busy interpreting that I'm the last one to finish eating.

"I think Shaun likes me," Michelle says as we wash the dishes.

"You picked up on that, huh?" I say. The friendliness in my voice shows and I rub harder at the cutting board I'm drying.

"So he does? Really?"

"Yeah, I think so. He's younger than you, though, I think. How old are you?"

"Almost twenty-four."

"I think Shaun's twenty-two. So when do you turn twenty-four?" I'm trying to figure the math out in my head, how old she was when she got pregnant.

"December twenty-fifth."

"Christmas? Your birthday is on Christmas?"

"Yeah." She shrugs one shoulder and hands me the turkey pan she just washed. The drainer's full. Her nails are chipped.

"Oh." This is going to get complicated—her birthday on Christmas.

Michelle brushes the bangs out of her face. "I like him," she says. "But it would be weird."

I nod.

"Not just 'cause he's deaf. That, too, but I don't know. I haven't gone out with a guy since Charlie died. That mistake I made, that wasn't going out. That guy was such a shit." She picks up one of the wineglasses that's drying in the drainer. "These are so pretty," she says.

"Thanks," I say.

"He's nice, though, don'tcha think?"

"Shaun? Yeah. He's sweet. But being with a deaf person is going to be different because of the language barrier."

"You think I shouldn't?"

I think about it for a minute. "No, you should. If you're ready."

"I might be." She puts the glass back. "I still wear my wedding ring. I don't know if I could take it off. Am I supposed to?"

"I don't know," I say, putting the pan down on the stove. All that's left to do is wipe the counters. We've done a good job of cleaning up. We work well together. "I don't know about stuff like that. You'll know when you're ready. I told Ed some about you, and he probably told Shaun. I'm sure he knows your husband is dead. Leave your ring on, if it makes you feel better."

She dries her hands on the dishtowel I hand her. "Thanks," she says.

"Sure."

She wipes the counter one last time and we go back out to the living room. Larissa and the guys are watching *It's a Wonderful Life* with the sound turned off and the captions on.

"Okay, Larissa," I say. "It's time."

She gets up off the couch and stands in the middle of the room, facing Shaun, Ed, and Joey. *You want apple pie?* she signs. I didn't teach it to her in ASL. One step at a time.

Yes, they sign. *Apple pie. Love.*

Larissa claps. "They said yes!"

"Okay, let's go get the pie," I say. Larissa follows me into the kitchen. The pie looks wonderful. I never knew I could make an apple pie. Larissa has asked things of me I never knew I was capable of.

. . .

After the guys leave, Michelle puts Larissa to bed while I finish straightening up. When she comes downstairs, she's humming something. I'm standing in my living room; if I sit down, it will be an offer for Michelle to sit down too.

"I sang her a little song," she says. "I used to do that when she was little. I forgot that song, till tonight. It's been a long time since I felt like singing."

I sit down on the couch. Michelle walks over and sits in her old rocking chair. I knew she would sit there. She likes to keep moving, even while sitting.

"I got a letter yesterday," she says.

"Yeah?" I say. "From who?"

She laughs, a brushing-off-her-thoughts kind of laugh. I wonder if other people can read laughs like I do. I want to pretend it's my special skill. "I never get letters, 'cept bills," she says. "I don't think I got a letter in maybe two, three years. It was my dad."

She never talks about her dad. I wait. Sometimes the best way to get people to say something is not to ask.

"He's an asshole," she says. "I guess I didn't know it till after my mom died. I think she musta kept him from being such a jerk, or maybe I just thought all dads were that way, you know, full of themselves and all. But after she died, I got to know him better. He was opinionated. Just told you what he thought and never asked what I was thinking. But it wasn't that bad till I fell in love with Charlie. He spit on the floor and told me to leave if I was going to 'fuck a colored.' He still calls black people coloreds. Niggers sometimes too, but his sister, she slapped him right across the face one time he said that, then when she was dying of cancer, she made him promise he'd never say that word again." Michelle shakes her head, smiling now. I can't believe she's smiling. I can't believe she's ever been able to smile. "His sister, she made him promise all sorts of shit, like giving money to cancer doctors and going to church every day. She died of breast cancer, just like my mom, but my mom had died of it when I was little. Nine. I don't remember her much. I guess it's something I got to look out for, breast cancer. It's in my family."

"Jesus," I say.

Michelle shrugs with one shoulder. "Oh, don't worry about me. I'll be fine."

"He sounds like an awful man. I'm sorry you had it so bad."

"Oh well, it doesn't matter."

"So, you got a letter from him?"

"Yeah. He wants to talk. Says he tried calling, but there was no listing for me. He say he wants to make up." She rubs her legs, doesn't look me in the eyes.

"What are you going to do?" I ask.

"Dunno," she says. "Guess I'll think about it a while."

"Good idea," I say.

"I gotta go," she says. "I got work tomorrow." She's borrowed Teya's car to get here.

"Well, thanks for helping clean up," I say.

"Hey, look," she says. "It was really nice you asking me here to dinner. I had a good time. Shaun gave me a piece of paper. He wrote out he's going to call me some special way, so someone will talk for him. That would be weird, but I nodded when I read it. I guess he'll call. It was a good dinner. Thanks for showing Larissa how to make a pie. Maybe you'll show me sometime?"

"Sure," I say.

"See you," she says.

Brushing my teeth before I go to bed, I roll my eyes at myself in the mirror. I had fun. "Watch out," I say to my reflection.

A week later, I get another call from Larissa's teacher. She tells me Larissa used the word *fuck*. I apologize and tell her it won't happen anymore.

The next time we go to the donut shop, I tell Michelle I have to talk to her outside. It's really cold, so she knows this is serious. She even gets her coat. "You can't swear around Larissa anymore," I say when we get outside. "She's picking up your bad language."

She stares at me for a while, cocking her head, angry that I'm telling her what to do. I'm angry that she's making me sound as if I'm superior.

Finally Michelle nods. "Fine," she says. "I'll watch my mouth."

I don't get any more notes or calls from Larissa's teacher. I tell myself that problem is solved.

But as well as I believe Larissa is doing now, I'm falling apart. I seldom get exercise; I say no to a third of the jobs I'm offered; I can't get used to waking up so early; I make two meals for dinner, a healthy one for me and the healthiest version I can come up with of something Larissa likes. I haven't gotten to a book group meeting in months and I never have time to read anyway. Larissa ignores Polly whenever she comes over, and glares at Yolanda Walker through yet another dinner. My parents invite me down for Christmas, and when I mention this to Larissa, tears well up in her eyes.

"It's my mommy's birthday," she says. "We can't leave my mommy on her birthday." I saw this coming.

Michelle is not doing so well either. She's still sleeping on the couch at Teya's, and in order to keep her job at Dunkin' Donuts, she has to miss half the meetings and classes she's supposed to attend. Larissa's social worker, who has come to my house only once, tells me that Michelle is trying, just not trying hard enough. When I complain to Yolanda that I don't know how Michelle can get to all those meetings without a car, she says I'm becoming a bleeding-heart liberal.

"No, I'm not," I say, not sure why I'm defending myself. We're meeting at a deli downtown for lunch. She called me to get together, and I was so pleased.

"That woman needs to bend over backward to get that little girl back," she says.

"Well, how's she supposed to do it, working at a donut shop?"

"She's not," Yolanda says. Her hair is different, again. Now she has a bob with bangs. Last month her hair was braided. I touch the back of my neck. I need a new look. I've had the same haircut since the late eighties.

"What do you mean, she's not?" I ask.

"She needs a better job."

"Well, how does she get a better job?"

"Job training."

"Have you guys told her that?"

"Yes, but she's afraid," Yolanda says. She picks all the cucumbers out of her salad and lays them on her bread plate. How could anyone not like cucumbers? "She's dyslexic, you know."

"She never told me that," I say, embarrassed by the hurt tone in my voice. I clear my throat and bite into my turkey wrap.

"Hey, Alice, there's a lot she isn't telling you. It's part of her game."

I want to shush her. The place is crowded, the tables too close. "But why not tell me that?" I say in a hushed voice. "It's not like it's her fault."

"She's *afraid* to take classes, get a better job, buy a car. It's called growing up. You're making it easy for her, Alice. You bring Larissa to see her, have her to your house. She says she wants her kid back, but she knows she has a year. A year is a long time when you're twenty-three."

"Jesus, Yolanda, you're what, thirty-one, thirty-two? You're pretty damn young, too. What makes *you* so wise?"

"How come you're defending her, Alice? Don't you want to keep Larissa?"

That stops me. "Yes. No. Not if Michelle can be a good mom. Larissa loves her."

"Is a good mom one that leaves a child alone for nineteen hours? Corrects us when we say twenty-four, like nineteen is okay?"

"You never made a bad mistake?"

"Not like that. She can't make mistakes like that if she has a kid. I've had it tough, but I never left them alone for nineteen fucking hours."

The buzz of voices and clanking plates makes my body tense, as if I'm being attacked by sound. As I have before, I wonder if deaf people are more relaxed because they are not bombarded by the noise of everyday life. I motion to Yolanda with my hand to keep her voice down. "You've seen a lot of bad stuff. You're bitter. I wouldn't want your job for a million dollars. I think you do great things, but I think you're wrong here."

"Well, then good thing I'm not her social worker anymore, huh?"

We look at each other. I don't want to argue with her. I want to be friends. But I understand something, looking at Yolanda. We *are* friends, and I have stopped defining her as black when I think of her. And now we're arguing, and yet suddenly I'm smiling stupidly. For almost fifty years I've never had an argument with a black person. I'm always as nice as I can be, as if being pleasant proves I'm not prejudiced. Here, in this crowded deli, I understand what I have been doing for so long.

"I think you're wrong about Michelle Benton, Yolanda," I say. "Yeah, I'd like to keep Larissa. You're right. I can't even think about the alternative. But don't get mad at me because I'm a bleeding heart, and I won't get mad at you for being young."

Yolanda puts a hand on the table. I put my hand on hers.

"Friends?" I say, and she nods.

She gets the check, and I insist I get the next one. We plan on meeting in two weeks, same place. I don't invite her to my house for dinner. I want to enjoy myself.

One day, when I take Larissa to the donut shop, I fill out some client forms while I wait in the car for Larissa to come back out. It's almost Christmas but there's no snow on the ground and the temperature is mild, in the fifties. The holidays have always been hard for me, especially Christmas. I grit my teeth seeing Christmas displays in early November, stores decorated with puffy white cotton, bulbs hung to distraction on fake glittery white trees. I try to ignore it, stay out of stores. But Christmas is all Larissa can talk about. *Christmas is coming!* She skips and twirls with expectation. Her feet hardly touch the ground. She's even getting me excited.

Larissa and Michelle walk out of the donut shop, and Michelle waves to me. I wave back. She stands in front of the door and bends down, taking Larissa's face in her hands, and kisses her right on the lips. Then, as I sit watching from the car, Larissa points to herself, crosses her arms across her chest, fists held up, then points to Michelle. *I love you.* I taught her that. Then I see Michelle sign it right back to her.

My head up, I breathe evenly through my nose, lips closed. I want more than I will ever have. And right now I want to be alone.

But Larissa skips over to the car, opens the door, and hops in, fastening her own seatbelt. In less than a minute, we're talking about Christmas. She wants to get the gray-haired lady a present. I wipe the dry space under my right eye and say, "Sure. But something small, okay?" Larissa starts to list all the small things she can think of. Hair clips, rings, candy, bows, pencils with fluffy things on the ends like the one I got her last week.

"Christmas is coming!" she says, clapping her hands together.

How can I deny her this, or anything? How can I not know what love is? It's going on, doing what I'm doing; taking care of Larissa until her mother gets her back.

Chapter Twenty-four

"You need to get another job," I say to Michelle.

She scrubs the pan I used for the Christmas Eve roast beef. We let it soak while Larissa, Michelle, and I ate cherry pie. Larissa cut a smiley face into the crust. I let her use a sharp knife.

"I know," Michelle says with her one-shoulder shrug that feels familiar to me now. It's like Larissa's one-eyed squint. "No one's hiring."

"You've hardly tried."

"I can't fill out the forms without them laughing at me."

"There's places that can teach you how to fill out the forms."

"I like the donut shop."

"You like giving Larissa donuts. Well, let me tell you a little secret. Larissa's getting sick of donuts."

Michelle squints. "Really?"

"Really."

"Fuck. I thought she liked them."

"Michelle, you need another job."

She hands me the pan to dry and leans her back against the sink. Rubbing at her nose with the back of her hand, she pauses before she says something.

"Listen, I called my dad and we talked a long time. He says he's sorry for all the crap he gave me. He says I can work at the shop and he'll give me health care. He said he knows he's a prejudiced son of a bitch, but we're family, and he's too old to be a son of a bitch anymore. He'll give me a car, too. A piece-of-crap car, but it'll get me to classes. The social worker says they could move Larissa down to Cincinnati to live with my dad, if he passes some kind of tests. He said he ain't taking no tests to be able to have his own grandchild, but I think I could get him to do it. I mean, if he only saw her, I know he'd do anything to help, right?"

By the end of this little speech Michelle's looking down at her feet. That stripe of undyed dark hair is starting to show again.

We're both quiet for a moment. From the living room, the tiny colored lights of the Christmas tree warm the house more than heat ever could. Larissa's watching a Christmas special. Ed, Joey, and Shaun went to their own homes for the holidays. It's just the three of us.

"So," I say. "You're *thinking* about it?"

Michelle tears at a cuticle. She recently had her fake nails removed and her own nails are thick and ugly underneath, and she can't afford to get her nails done again. That's what Larissa's giving Michelle tomorrow for Christmas—a gift certificate to get her nails done, along with gloves, a scarf, and a bottle of perfume, some nameless brand in a pink bottle that Larissa thought was pretty. And for her mother's birthday presents—wrapped in birthday paper, not Christmas paper—there's a nice dress from

Kaufmann's, three packs of pantyhose, two bottles of hair dye (my idea), and a little gold heart pin. The money we spent on Michelle's gifts is the hundred and fifty the county gives me to raise Larissa each month. The money always bothers me, but it helps.

The closets in my house are filled with presents for Michelle and Larissa. I signed FROM SANTA on most of Larissa's. On my mantel is a picture of her in Santa's lap.

"I don't want her to be with another foster mother," Michelle says. "But it would be bad for me, being down there, not being able to see her."

It's around eight in the evening. Outside snow falls steadily. There are six inches on the ground with another three or four expected. It's time for Larissa to get ready for bed. Michelle is supposed to come back tomorrow, late afternoon, for her birthday dinner.

"Then find a job here," I say.

"How? Don't nobody give you jobs unless you have experience, or they know you. I don't know nobody but you and Teya, and she's on disability. She's no help. She's not happy, me sleeping on her couch, either."

"I'll find you a job," I say.

She looks up now, right at me. "How would you do that?"

"I don't know, but I will."

Michelle brushes the hair out of her face, just like Larissa does, with the back of her hand and a twist of her wrist, tucking stray strands behind her ear. They have the same small ears. "That would be nice, if you could. I'd like Larissa to stay here with you, until I get her back. I don't know what kind of job you can get for me, but I'll do anything. I can't spell or fill out forms, but I'm not stupid."

No, you're not, I think.

. . .

Christmas morning, I feel Larissa poke my shoulder, and although I'm sleeping, I'm not startled by her touch. This is how she calls my name, this poking. She won't say Alice or Miss Marlowe; she just pokes me with a finger. I keep my eyes closed, not wanting to rush this day. She pokes me again. "Did Santa come?" she whispers.

I open my eyes. She's peering intently into my face. I want to put my hands on her cheeks, cup her face. "Let's go see," I say.

We make a big deal of tiptoeing downstairs. There are dozens of packages under the tree. My parents sent a boxful of stuff too, even a few for me. This is the first Christmas in a long time that I haven't spent with them. I said I'd come down a few days after Christmas, but they're going to Florida with friends.

"Oh look, oh look, oh look!" Larissa says, her voice hushed with wonder.

"So, should we open them?" I ask.

"Yes. Yes, we should open them!" She twirls once, but then stops. She wants to stay facing all those presents. "Oh, look! That's my name! That's my name right there. And there! That's my name!" She kneels down on the floor. "Look at all the presents!"

"Hey, look, see Santa's name there?" I point to the box closest to her. "Santa starts with S," I say, signing the letter. "Let me get your picture before you start opening them. Here, sit down and turn around and look at me."

Half of Larissa's face is covered by her hair. In the four months I've had her, it's grown another three inches. "Tuck your hair back," I say, and she obliges, but it won't stay that way for long. I move back into the dining room to get the whole shot: Larissa, the tree, the packages scattered artistically about. It took me forever to arrange them haphazardly. I take the picture, and a second one just in case she blinked.

"Are there any presents for you?" she asks. I smile. Smart me, I bought a few things for myself and signed FROM SANTA on them. I'm good at this. Who would have known?

"Yep. I think I see my name. There. See? But you first. The big one?" It's a large box, about two feet high. "It's from my parents." Larissa nods solemnly, quietly. I haul it over closer to her. She peels off the paper carefully, hardly ripping it at all. I imagine Michelle teaching her this, so they could reuse the paper.

I don't know what the present is—my parents wouldn't tell me—and when I see it, I have to turn away for a moment. It's a house for Lucy, with her name across the door, paintings of carrots on the walls, and gingerbread carvings across the eaves. There's a green satin pillow inside with the word *Lucy* embroidered in pink thread. It is the largest present under the tree, in size and heart, and I suddenly realize that I will never have grandchildren. "Oh, look!" Larissa says. "Oh, look what they did!" She picks up Lucy, who is on the floor beside her, and gently places her inside on the satin pillow. Larissa is smiling hugely, her crooked teeth splaying forward like a little rabbit herself. I take another picture. I take a lot of pictures.

I open a present from Santa. Cotton turtlenecks, in dark green and blue. "I needed these! How did Santa know?"

"Didn't he get you anything fun?" Larissa asks.

You, I think.

Larissa loves the pink mittens I got her. They're made out of a fuzzy material with kitten faces on the backs. She puts them on and rubs her cheeks. "Oh, they're so soft!" She likes the Groovy Girls and the clothes to dress them in, and the art kit, and the plastic food for her kitchen set, but she loves those mittens and puts them back on when she's done opening all the other presents.

"Wait a minute, wait a minute! Stay there!" Larissa shouts and hops up. She runs upstairs then comes back down, holding two packages. "You have two more presents!"

Handing them to me, she sits back down next to me on the floor, her knee almost touching mine. She won't wear slippers and her bare feet stick out from under her flannel nightgown. I reach over and touch her foot, give it a little squeeze.

"That one first," Larissa says. "I made it."

The package she points to is small and crumpled-looking, with a piece of red yarn tied around it. The other present is wrapped carefully, the edges neat, the tape in precise measures, and I know Michelle wrapped that one—the same way my mother wraps presents. This thought distracts me for a second.

"Open it!" Larissa says.

It's a pot holder made out of loops of cloth. "I made it in school," Larissa says. "You didn't know I did that, did you?" I didn't. The pot holder is made with a multitude of colors, all woven together randomly without regard to pattern. It's beautiful. It reminds me, in reverse, of my cup of white beads. I lean over and give her a hug. I can count the times I've hugged her on one hand. This time she doesn't tighten up at all.

"Next one!" she says. "Next one. It's from a store!" She's so delighted about this that she can't hold still, bobbing up and down on her knees.

I look again at the neatly wrapped present. It reminds me of all those boxes in Michelle's apartment, neatly taped and labeled. She was so careful wrapping this present, packing those boxes. Why hadn't she been more careful with her child?

It's something I've wondered about for months, and am finally beginning to understand; she lost control for one terrible moment that lasted nineteen hours. I never lose control. I was the one who arranged Vince's funeral, wrote the eulogy, stood up in front of people and said what I had to say without breaking down. I cried only when alone so as not to upset my parents or anyone else. I took off three days of work, then went back, did my job. Although I had lost part of myself in Vince's death, I never lost control, like Michelle did. And here Michelle has lost her husband, her daughter, her life as she knew it, and wrapped me a present. I pick it up and hold it in my hands. I am afraid to open it.

It's the same pink bottle of perfume we picked out for Michelle. "I told her what to get!" Larissa says. "I remembered where we went and told her where to go! Isn't it pretty? I think it's so pretty! Open it up. Try it!" It's sealed in plastic. We hadn't been able to test it for her mother, but Larissa was sure something so pretty had to be wonderful.

I open it up and dab it behind my ear. It smells of roses. I put some behind Larissa's ear, too.

"Do you like it?" she asks. "Do you think my mommy will like hers? Doesn't it smell pretty?"

"It smells lovely. I love it. Thank you."

"I'm glad you like it," Larissa says. "I told her where to go, and she found it!"

Her mother is *her* too. We are both *her* sometimes. It is nothing to take offense at. Larissa likes me. Sometimes we giggle together. Sometimes we hug. I take her to school every morning, and I feed her, and drive her to the donut shop.

And I love her.

Chapter Twenty-five

By the end of January, I find Michelle a job at a small indepen-
dent pharmacy in my neighborhood. The pharmacist is a woman
I know who has a deaf brother, and she's very active in the Deaf
community. Michelle works the register and puts merchandise
on the shelves. Although the pay isn't great, it's full-time with
benefits. She has to take two buses to get to work, but she's
hardly ever late. She's rescheduled her parenting classes, anger
management classes, and substance abuse classes for evenings
and weekends, but getting to them is almost impossible. Sometimes Shaun drives her. She's learning sign language and she and
Shaun date, although they don't have sex very often because
Michelle sleeps on the couch at Teya's, and Shaun lives with two
guys. He teases her that Ed and Joey won't hear them, and they
make love a few times in his bed, but she still feels uncomfortable. They've decided not to be exclusive, and Shaun is seeing

other girls. Michelle tells me all this about her and Shaun, asking me what I think, as if I am someone to her now. Even though I'm uncomfortable with all this, I ask her if she's using birth control. "Condoms and foam," she says. I've never known anyone who used foam.

Sometimes I pick Michelle up after work and bring her to my house to watch Larissa while I go to a late job, such as teacher conferences or a study group for Ed or Shaun. The only problem is that when she babysits, there's no one to stay with the sleeping Larissa while I drive Michelle home. The first time Michelle watched Larissa, we didn't think far enough ahead. She had to sleep on the couch and go to work from my house the next morning. The next time, she packed a few clothes.

February fourteenth is the first anniversary of Vince's death. The word *anniversary* reminds me of the sections in card stores that I avoid. And there aren't cards for this, I'm sure.

It's Valentine's Day, to boot. At least he got killed on a holiday that meant nothing to me. If it weren't for Larissa, I think I might not survive today. I don't want to wake up, I don't want to get out of bed. But Larissa has to go to school. She has twenty-two Valentine cards to hand out. She wrote her name on the back of every card, then wrote the name of each student on the front of each envelope. This took hours. She is so excited.

Happy Valentine's Day, I think to Vince, lying in my bed, my eyes still closed.

Same to you, he says.

Miss you, I say.

He's silent. He's dead.

. . .

I take Larissa to school, then head down to Akron and the marsh. The temperature is in the fifties and last week's snow is slush, the sky gray and heavy above me. Just fine with me. I don't want anything to be pretty today.

Leaning on the wooden railing, I look out across the marsh at the bare trees.

Hey, Vince, where are you? I want to believe in heaven, that I'll see him again. I wish I could.

"I'm sorry," I say, out loud, and take a breath. "Really sorry."

I haven't heard his voice in my head as much recently. I can go through a whole day without thinking about him, just as I would have when he was alive.

I try to put together a picture in my head about everything that's gone on, trying to send him my life in a thought, send it out to the marsh where I pretend Vince now lives, the King of Frogs or the biggest baddest carp in the whole pond. It's a jumble in my head. *I have a life now, Vince,* I think. *It's a little crazy at times. It's a fucking mess, really. You happy now?*

Where's the fucking part? he says back. *You're not dead yet.*

I grin. He's still here, part and parcel of me, like an invisible arm or a leg, keeping me off balance just a bit, or, maybe more balanced.

Thanks, Vince, I think. *It's time to go home. You may like this place, but my feet are getting cold. Come on. Let's go.*

That night I call my parents. My mother starts crying as soon as she hears my voice, and keeps crying until my father takes the phone from her. "It's a sad, sad day," he says, the slur of his words obvious. "We miss him so much. Your mother's having a pretty bad time tonight, honey. It's sweet of you to call. We're so thankful you're our little girl. We're so glad we have you. You just take good care of yourself and Larissa, you do that for us, won't you?"

"Sure, Dad," I say.

"Why don't you call back tomorrow, when your mother can talk?"

"I will," I say. "Love you both."

"Love you too, honey." Then he hangs up.

I never tell Larissa about today being the anniversary of Vince dying. She has twenty-two Valentine cards from schoolmates, one from me, and one from Michelle that came in the mail. Michelle also sent two boxes of small pastel candy hearts. One for me, maybe? Larissa and I spend the evening trying to decipher the words on those little candy hearts.

On the twentieth of February, Michelle moves into my attic. It's filled with old junk I really don't need, like pictures in broken frames, a chair I always meant to fix but really isn't worth the effort, wallpaper reams that were here when I moved in. Michelle and I carry it all out to the front lawn, where she stacks these broken, useless things in a neat tidy pile as if it's a puzzle that will all fit into one perfectly square section of my tree lawn. Ed and Shaun carry up the bed in the basement that Larissa slept in before she got her own bed, and Michelle arranges things so the room seems cozy and inviting. Although it's a small space Michelle occupies up in my attic, I can feel the weight of her above me at night, not as an ominous presence, but as a curiosity, as if her own possibilities are mine. I charge her fifty dollars a month for rent.

Larissa is so happy she skips and twirls around the house for days. Her teacher calls just to tell me what a joy Larissa is in class these days. Polly thinks I'm crazy, and tells me in no uncertain terms, closing her eyes as she lectures me. When I tell Yolanda at lunch that week, she says, "Ah, did you tell Larissa's social worker yet?"

"Not yet. Why?"

"Because you can't do this," she says. "You're not supposed to have Mom stay at your house with the child."

"Why not?"

"Rules."

"Well, that's stupid. Larissa's doing great in school now. She's happy. Michelle helps me. What could be wrong with that?"

Yolanda looks at me with a steady gaze. I like the way she thinks before she speaks. It's like me, organizing a translation of an English sentence into ASL to make sure I have the essence right. I should do the same with everything I say. But I *did* think it over before I asked Michelle to move in. It just makes sense.

"Okay, listen," she says. "We're at lunch. I'm off the clock. We're two people just talking. My advice, as a friend, is don't tell her social worker right away, unless she asks somehow. See how it goes. Maybe it won't work, and she'll move out. Maybe it'll work, then you have some justification to continue. Now, we're going to change the subject. Seen any good movies?"

I smile. "Movies? How about videos? *Shrek* is great. Did you see that yet?"

"Girl, I loved that movie. Did you see *Harry Potter and the Sorcerer's Stone?*"

"Three times in three days."

We talk children's movies for the rest of the meal.

Michelle makes it possible for me to take evening jobs again, and she does most of the cleaning and laundry. She scrubs woodwork hidden by furniture and washes the walls. The inside of the fridge shines.

There is a contentment I didn't expect, having another woman around. One day I pick out a bracelet that I haven't worn for years because I can't clasp it myself. "Can you hook this for me?" I ask Michelle.

"That's a nice bracelet," she says. "And those earrings are so cool." I feel chipper all day; someone so young thinks I'm wearing "cool" earrings.

Still, Michelle is gone a lot. She leaves at eight-thirty for work and doesn't come home until five-thirty. She has all those classes, and her dates with Shaun. Sometimes I am exhausted with her constant motion. Sometimes I turn to say something to her, and she's not there.

Michelle never answers the phone, and she never asks if Shaun can sleep over. I don't tell my parents that she has moved in.

Larissa still talks to me about school as we drive home. She asks me if we can make cookies. She'll ask me to read her a book, fix her hair. If Michelle is around, she'll ask her.

On a Saturday in early March the snow falls fat and lovely. Michelle volunteers to shovel the driveway.

"There's a boy down the street I can call," I say.

"Oh, I want to. It reminds me of when I was a kid. I always

had to shovel. My dad said it was my job since I was like eight."
She licks her chapped lips. Her skin is constantly red and dry.
She doesn't use my lotion, and she doesn't buy her own.

"Didn't *he* shovel the drive?" I'm sitting on my bed. Michelle
has come into my room after taking a shower. She has a towel
wrapped around her head, and another one wrapped around her
skinny body. One towel is hers, one mine. Larissa's downstairs
watching cartoons.

"Not since I was eight. Fuck, I did everything. I cooked and
cleaned. We moved like ten times and I was always the one
packed and unpacked the boxes. He taught me to drive when I
was fourteen, and he'd give me the car to go to the grocery even
though I didn't have no licence yet. Not that we had much
money for food. I can make you soup from any bone you give
me. Hey, you want me to cook some? I can cook. I just don't
know if I make things the way you want them."

"Thanks. Sure. You can cook anytime. What *did* he do?" I ask.

Michelle rubs the towel over her head. "What do you mean?"

"Well, if you did everything?"

"Oh, he worked. All the time. Like ten hours a day. The rest,
he drank. He got pissy but he passed out quick. He slept in the
chair more than his own Goddamn bed!"

I take a breath as if I'm going to say something, but then
nothing comes out; *I* worry that my father has a few too many
beers at night.

Michelle looks down at the floor. "Oh, I'm dripping. Sorry."
She reaches down and runs a hand upward on her leg.

"Don't worry," I say. "So he didn't like your husband?"

"No. He wouldn't even come to the wedding. We had the
wedding at my best friend's house 'cause she had a big backyard
and her parents weren't prejudiced and they liked Charlie. He

was a football player at my school. He played quarterback. Half the school was black and we got along, mostly. I mean, there were fights, sometimes. Most people liked Charlie 'cause he was such a good quarterback. He was the first black guy I ever kissed. The only one, really. I couldn't believe I liked him as much as I did. He was the second guy I ever slept with. He could kiss me and make me wet in a second." Michelle's face reddens, even more than it had from the shower and the winter. She rolls her eyes. "I can't believe I just said that."

I smile. "So he was a good kisser and a good quarterback. What did he do, after high school?"

Michelle's look changes to anger. Did I ask something wrong?

"He went and got fucking killed," she says, then shakes her head. "No. Sorry. He got a job at Wal-Mart. He was thinking a' joining the army but I wouldn't let him. I was scared he'd get killed." She rubs her bare arms, like she's cold. "Look, I didn't mean to get morbid or shit."

"That's okay," I say. "Sounds like you have a good reason."

"It was a nice wedding. I still have my wedding dress. Janey Potts, my best friend? She made it for me. You want to see it?"

"Sure."

"She moved to West Virginia, and I haven't seen her for a year. We talk on the phone sometimes. I should write her a letter. Could I give her your address? I don't want to call her long distance on your phone."

"Sure, give her the address," I say. I stand up, but Michelle doesn't move. Maybe she didn't mean she wanted to show me the dress now. I wonder if I'm supposed to give her a hug or something, show some female support. I pick up a receipt off my bureau, fold it in half. "You could call her, if you want. Your friend."

Michelle is quiet for a moment, as if she's confused, trying to figure out what I've said. "From here?"

"Yeah. If you want. You know, just don't make it too long."

Once again, she thinks first. "Thanks, but I don't want to owe you nothing like that. But thanks." She turns and looks out the window. "I saw a shovel in the garage. I can use that, right?"

"You really want to?"

"Yeah, I do. I'm gonna make Larissa shovel the walk. She needs to do more work. You spoil her, you know."

There's an awkward silence while we both look away. "Sorry," she says.

"You don't have to be sorry," I say. I pause. "You think I spoil her?"

Michelle tugs on an ear. "No, not spoil her, I guess. You're just really nice, that's all. Real moms aren't always nice."

Now there's another silence. I tuck the receipt into my pocket.

"I guess I'm putting my foot in my mouth all over the place," Michelle says. "Sorry. You're doing good. Better than me."

"No," I say. "Not better than you. Differently, maybe. I'm new to this, so I'm extra careful. I make mistakes . . ." I spell *help* with my hand, then make a fist.

"Not like I did," she says. She backs toward the door. "You always do that thing with your hand. You sayin' something behind my back?" She tries to make it sound like a joke, but the accusation hangs there. "I better go shovel the walk." She leans out the doorway. "Larissa! Get on your snow stuff! We're going outside to shovel!"

"Don't go out with wet hair," I tell Michelle.

"Yes, Mother," she says. There is, again, silence. "It's a joke." Then, "You'd make a good mom." She says this with more importance than her description of her drinking father, her mother dying. I feel my throat swelling up. I am so uncomfortable standing here with Michelle, and yet I want her to stay, to keep talking with me.

"Thanks," I say.

A little while later I look out the front window. Larissa and Michelle are making snow angels in my front yard. I'm unmarried, Vince is dead, my parents are hours away, and these two peculiar people are in my life and I am strangely happy.

One day, I can't find the garnet heart necklace my mother gave me for my twenty-first birthday, but I don't remember when I saw it last. And now, sometimes, there's less money in my purse than I thought, but I'm not sure. I start counting it more closely. One day there's definitely ten dollars less.

March twenty-eighth, Michelle gets fired for stealing.

Chapter Twenty-six

"What the fuck were you thinking?" I yell at Michelle as she climbs into my car when I pick her up at the corner by the pharmacy. They're not going to press charges. It's only ten dollars. They just want her out of there.

"They don't pay me shit," she says. "And they make me clean the bathroom. No one else has to do that." She looks petulant, not mortified. She is someone I don't understand.

"Jesus," I say. "It's a job. You do what they tell you. I can't believe you stole money from them!"

"Everyone takes something. I've seen them. Like toothpaste, or deodorant."

"That's your excuse? Someone else took deodorant?" I'm so pissed. Pissed that I'm driving toward *my* house to take her *home*. I have to be at John Carroll in twenty minutes. I do not want to drop her off at my house and leave her there.

It's March and it's snowing these big fat stupid snowflakes that looked beautiful in December. I take a sharp right and the car skids just a little, and that skid feels good. Michelle knows this is not the way to my house.

"Where you going?" she asks.

"I'm taking you to Teya's and you can Goddamn well stay there." Larissa isn't the only one who swears the more she's around Michelle.

"What? What if she's not there?"

"She's always fucking there, Michelle. She's housebound. Did you take my garnet heart necklace? Tell me the truth or I will never forgive you."

"Jesus, Alice. Calm down. I just took ten dollars. I was gonna pay it back."

I pull over to the side of the road. "Own up to what you did! Stop making fucking excuses. You left your daughter alone! Left her sitting in an apartment that could have gone up in flames or something. She could have lit a candle. Turned on the stove and caught her pajamas on fire. She could have been so scared she opened a window to look out for you and fell right out. You didn't have locks on them, or screens! She could have drunk Drano, or bleach, or taken your pills!" I'm getting good at imagining the things a little girl could do that might get her hurt. "And you left her for nineteen fucking hours. Didn't you wake up once that night to go to the bathroom and think, shit, I gotta go home?"

"I thought Teya was going to get her!" Her eyes are welling with tears. *Good.*

"Bullshit! She's almost a cripple. She can hardly get to her car. I don't believe you thought she was coming. You took a chance, and you blew it. Yeah, it was a bad day, and I'm sorry your husband got killed, but don't fucking lie to me. Did you take my heart necklace?"

"No," she says quietly, looking down at the floor of the car. "I just took some money from your purse once."

"Right," I say. "Get out."

"Here?" she says.

"Yeah, right here. There's a bus stop someplace, I'm sure."

"I don't have money for a bus," she says. "It's all at your house. I got seventy cents. Look, that's all I got." She opens her purse, starts digging out her wallet. "I'm saving all my money to get Larissa back. It's in a box, in the attic. I'm trying to save money, so I don't take it with me places."

"Yeah. You're saving it ten dollars at a time. From my purse and the register."

She's opening her wallet. "Look, this is all I got. I'm sorry I stole from them. It was stupid. I'm not smart like you. I don't own a house or a car or have an education—"

"And that's a reason to steal?" I turn around in the cramped space and grab my purse from the back of the car. "Here. Here's two bucks. Take the bus to Teya's. We'll talk later. I got to go to work. Goddamn, I'm so embarrassed you did that. You know how bad that makes me look?"

She's crying now, one hand on the door handle. She takes my two dollars. "You never look bad, Alice. You help deaf people, you take in little black girls, everybody thinks you're just great. You eat good, you read books. You work real hard being good. Nobody's gonna think you're not, never."

"I don't take in little black girls! Jesus Christ, Michelle. I took in Larissa because she needed someone. She needs *you*. You just don't know how to be an adult and take care of her. Taking care of her means cleaning the bathroom at work and not stealing. From me or anyone."

"I didn't take your necklace," she says. "I never saw it. I did take some money from your purse. I was going to pay you back."

"Go to Teya's," I say, too worn out to shout any more. Too depressed. "I've got to go to work."

"What will you tell Larissa?"

I look at her, and her mascara's a mess. I hand her a Kleenex from my purse. "I'll tell her Teya needs you."

"Thank you," she says, and opens the car door, gets out. I drive off. I know why I'll tell Larissa that Teya needs her—because I'm so fucking good. What's so bad about that? Why do I feel like shit?

Because I feel stupid. Because I let myself like Michelle, and I still do. I want to believe she never saw my heart necklace.

Larissa takes my explanation about her mother staying at Teya's like a trooper. "When will she come back?" she asks.

"I don't know."

"Can we go to the store and see her?" Larissa loves visiting her mother at the pharmacy. They have candy and cheap toys.

"She doesn't work there anymore," I say.

Larissa looks at me a long time, then nods. It's a wiser nod than just eight months ago.

That night, she cries in her bedroom. When I knock lightly on the door she tells me to go away. In the morning, I find Lucy on the floor, one ear torn off. I sew it back on and put her into the bunny house. Larissa never mentions it.

Polly comes over that night after Larissa's in bed. "Hey, you did your best," she says.

"Yeah, I'm a good person," I say.

She looks at me for a while. "Yeah, you are," she says. She doesn't know why I don't smile, and I don't explain. I need to talk to Michelle and tell her how she hurt me. Instead, we watch the war in Iraq, stunned into silence by it all. Polly leaves by eleven, and we plan on getting together again soon.

That weekend I call my parents, but I don't tell them I kicked Michelle out, since I never told them she was here. I tell them everything's fine, and we make plans to come down on Memorial Day. I call Bruce and Dylan, and they cheer me up for a little. Yolanda buys me lunch and says she's sorry. I'm quiet around Ed and tell him that I'm just depressed by the war. Who wouldn't be?

I tell Larissa we can have the hamster for one weekend if she wants, and she says he died a month ago.

Two weeks later, Michelle calls me. She's called Larissa every day, but we haven't spoken. "Can we meet someplace?" she asks. I spell *no* with my hand, but my mouth says yes. I tell her to meet me in the parking lot of the nature center. I don't want to meet her at a coffee shop or someplace where we sit facing each other.

Michelle's waiting in a corner of the lot by a tree. I don't see Teya's car. I've never seen Auntie Teya. If Larissa didn't speak about her now and then, I might believe Auntie Teya never existed at all; I have come to doubt anything Michelle has ever said. I'm embarrassed by my memory of thinking we were friends.

She's wearing a coat I've never seen, and immediately I think she must have stolen it.

"Let's walk," I say, pointing to a wooden path that's a short loop through the marshland. It's April now and still cold. It's been a longer winter than most people remember.

"I got some stuff to tell you," Michelle says. I slow down, watching my step. The boards are icy in unexpected places.

"I called my dad and I told him I want the job, the one he said I could have if I come down. He says it's perfect timing and all. You won't believe this. The girl that answers the phone? She's getting married and moving to Florida with some guy. Anyway, he says I could stay in the room above the garage. No rent. He'll pay me good, better than the pharmacy."

I take all this in, not saying anything. I head toward a place where, in the summer, there's millions of cattails, higher than our heads. Right now they lie flattened from the snow. Michelle doesn't say anything for a while. There's just the sound of our footsteps. I spell *leaving* with my hand. We stop in a railed-in area about ten feet square. There's a bare tree to the left with a big black crow on a branch. He makes a clacking sound with his beak like a woodpecker. *Rat-a-tat-tat*. I turn around and face Michelle. "Why are you doing this?" I ask.

She ignores my question. "I talked to Larissa's social worker, told her about my dad's house. She says I could get Larissa placed with him, but he has to have that home study thing and get a criminal check and fingerprinted. He said he would."

There's a bench here, but I don't sit down. I lean against the railing. "I thought you said he's a drunk."

"Yeah, but he sounds different this time, really. He says he wants to see Larissa, be part of her life and all. He says he's really sorry for kicking me out. He never said that before. I told him he's got to go to AA meetings with me. I'd be doing something good, if I went down there, like you did. Help him get better." She does her one-shoulder shrug, and my teeth clench. Only now do I notice she's not wearing as much eyeliner. She looks older, without it. My hand spells the word *strange*.

"They may not let her go there, if he's a drunk."

"Not unless someone tells them," she says simply, but I know her now. There is nothing simple about what she says. "He never got arrested for it or nothing. I think he's better. I wouldn't do this if I didn't think so."

I close my eyes and sigh.

"He says, I come down now and he'll give me the shop when he dies."

"It's a body shop," I say. "They fix wrecks, right?" I'm imagining this place, dingy and smelling of grease and oil, a few grungy guys with tattoos. "What do you know about running a place like that?"

She lifts her chin. "You sayin' I can't, 'cause I'm a woman? You think women can't run body shops, or you think I'm stupid?"

I don't answer. Talking seems like a waste of time. She's made up her mind.

"I gotta do this, Alice, and I don't want to fight with you. I feel bad. I know this is gonna hurt you, taking Larissa away and all, but I could own a business. Shit, that ain't gonna happen here." She's running her fingers along the wooden railing. She'll get splinters, but I don't tell her that. I want her to hurt herself, just a little, and see for herself.

"You should go to college," I say. "Learn a trade."

She laughs. "Right."

"Why don't you go down there first? See if he's really changed?"

Michelle looks up at the sky before answering. "I gotta do

this," she says. "I gotta get Larissa back with me. He's gonna pay me good. He'll give me a car. I'll be able to get to my classes. I don't know why I didn't do this before."

"Because you said you hated him." I want to remind her of this, and so I say it a bit nasty. I want to remind her of her past, and all I've done for her. She just smiles a half smile.

"Yeah. Sometimes I do. He's an asshole, really. But he's gonna give me a job and a way to get my baby back."

How can I argue with that?

"When are you going? How are you getting there?"

"He's having some guy drive up for me two days from now."

I nod, start walking back to the car. Michelle follows.

"What about Shaun?" I ask.

"Shaun's a nice kid," she says. "He can do better than me."

I stop and turn to her. We're too close. "Don't dismiss him. Don't hurt him, or Larissa. Do what you have to do, but stop hurting people."

In the distance, the crow makes that *rat-a-tat-tat* sound. Michelle tucks her bangs behind her ear, then shakes her head and her bangs come loose again. "*Dismiss*. That's one of your words, isn't it? People like you. I'm not dismissing nobody, and I'm not trying to hurt nobody. Say what you mean, Alice. Don't hurt *you*. Well, I don't want to. I want us to be friends. That don't mean I shouldn't do this, though, do what's right for me."

The breeze is cold against my cheeks. I cross my arms. "Tell me something. Are you telling me all this hoping I'll ask you back to live with me?"

"No, Alice," she says. She sounds sad. She sounds like she pities me. My hands ache. "That won't work. I'm not stupid. We're nothing alike. I got to be with family now."

I feel like I've been dumped. Now my cheeks are hot, despite the breeze. "Well," I say, "I hope it works." I have no idea if I'm telling the truth. I always thought the truth was such an easy thing to know.

Michelle moves down to Cincinnati. It takes a while for her dad to get the home study done, then they tell him he has to bring the house up to code first. Apparently the bathroom sink doesn't work, the basement is a fire hazard, and the door to the room that Larissa would sleep in is missing. Michelle's dad gets angry at the home study people, telling them that they've got a lot of nerve to say he can't have his grandchild come stay with him till he fixes up his place. He says the people next door live like pigs but they got all their kids living there, and their grandchildren. The home study person tells him that might be true, but he has to fix up his house. He doesn't do this as quickly as Michelle would like. Whenever she can, she drives up to Cleveland to visit Larissa. She always stays at Teya's.

The next months go quickly; night comes before I'm ready for the dark. May is gone in a blink. We visit my parents for Memorial Day. Bruce and Dylan can't come and it rains most of the weekend, so we put together a five-hundred-piece puzzle of stuffed bunnies my mother found in a catalog. My parents hug Larissa good-bye, saying, "See you soon." I tell Polly and my parents that I'm ignoring my forty-ninth birthday, that I really can't handle this right now, and that they are not to even bring it up. I must say it with such seriousness that they actually believe me, because all I get is a card from both of them.

I'm not turning forty-nine without you, I tell Vince. *I'm certainly not going to turn fifty. If you don't have to get old, neither do I.*

And the alternative is? he says.

Yeah, yeah, I get your point. But I'm sticking at forty-eight. Period.

Well, sis, I died at forty-seven. I'm younger than you. I win.

I roll my eyes. We're both crazy as loons.

Happy birthday, he says.

Same to you. Damn you for leaving me.

Love you, too.

Larissa graduates from first grade.

Walking to the car with Larissa on that last day of school, I want to turn to someone. *Look,* I want to say, I have gotten this child through a whole year of school and she has an art folder the size of Alaska, a pot with marigold seedlings, and a lined notebook with the alphabet written as neatly as any child has ever written. Sometimes I miss Michelle.

For Larissa's birthday, we invite Michelle and Auntie Teya for dinner, and this is my idea. "Should we invite some of your friends from school to come, too?" I ask as we plan her birthday party on a piece of paper. She wants me to write everything down. She likes lists, like my grocery lists. We mark all Michelle's upcoming visits on the calendar, trusting the promise of written words.

"No, no," Larissa says to my question. "Just Mommy and Auntie Teya. Can we have a cake with a picture? I saw cakes with pictures. Can we have one?"

"A cake with a picture?" I ask. "I don't know what you mean."

"I'll show you. I'll show you," she says. "They're at the place you get those big cookies. Can we get one?"

"Sure," I say. And I'm damned, they do have cakes with

pictures on them at the bakery. It's like a painting sprayed on top of a cake. Larissa orders one with a picture of a castle and a dragon and a princess. The woman behind the counter asks her if she would like the princess to be an African American, and I am swelled with that woman's goodness all day. The cake turns out to be wonderful. Aunt Teya is huge. She wheezes with every word, and hugs me tightly. She says she can't eat cake, and then she does.

"Oh, honey," she says. "Don't you worry about me. I don't." She laughs hard. I want to ask her if she really was supposed to be at the apartment that day. The whole time she is at my house, that question is in my chest like a flutter of hands. I keep thinking the words will fly out and change everything with the knowing who is at fault. I am a good hostess and never would embarrass her that way. It doesn't matter, I tell myself, watching Michelle as she encourages Larissa to blow the candles out, Michelle looking for all the world like a kid who wants her own cake, her own candles. It doesn't matter because despite everything that has happened, I like Michelle, and I like Auntie Teya, and knowing might change my mind, but not my heart.

In early August, Michelle's father gets the okay to be her foster parent. Larissa's social worker, who thinks I'm the greatest foster parent of all, is the one who tells me. "Guess what!" she says, as if I might be thrilled by the news. "Larissa's going to go live with her grandfather!"

In August, almost one year to the day since Larissa came to stay with me, Michelle drives up from Cincinnati with her dad to get Larissa.

Her father is a small, wiry man with a fast smile and a quick laugh. He makes a breathy *ha-ha* sound after everything he says. "So this is my little granddaughter," he says. "Ha ha." Larissa hides behind Michelle, just peeking around her mother's legs at this odd little man. I stand between my back porch steps and the old, rusty car that will take them away.

"I got some presents in the car for you, little girl," Michelle's father says. "Ha ha. You want to see them?" He sounds like a man offering candy to a child and I shudder. I want to run and grab Larissa, but she's with her mother.

Larissa shakes her head no, and Michelle's father *ha-ha*'s again, rubbing at his chin. I'm a good five inches taller than him. I can take him out, I think. I actually think that. I make a fist, but not to stop myself from spelling something.

Larissa tugs on her mother's sleeve and whispers something in her ear. "Sure, honey," Michelle says. "Go ahead." Larissa runs over to me, circling wide around her grandfather. *Stay,* she signs to me, and runs up the steps into the house. I burst out laughing. Not a *ha-ha* sound, but a gurgle of laughter that takes over until I have to turn away. When Larissa comes back out of the house, she's holding a small package. All the rest of her stuff is outside already, by the driveway. I didn't want Michelle's father entering my house.

Inside the wrapped box, so obviously wrapped by Larissa, is a stone the size of my hand. It's shaped like a heart and painted red. My eyes get hot and I am afraid I'm going to cry.

"I found it at camp," she says, "when we went to the creek. It looks just like a heart, doesn't it? I painted it red."

"Thank you," I say, giving her a hug. "You come visit sometimes," I whisper in her ear, and she looks up and nods seriously.

"We will," she says.

I gave her a good-bye present last night, an album with pictures of her, most of them taken during the last two and a half months. I also gave her a camera and showed her how to use it. I loaded film in it, and told her to send me some pictures. I gave her twenty dollars to pay for the developing.

"I got to hug Sampson good-bye," Larissa says to her mother.

"Go ahead, honey," Michelle says. Her dad loads Larissa's stuff into the trunk.

Looking at me, Michelle tilts her head in the direction of my backyard, then begins walking that way. I follow her. My perennial garden is at the end of its peak; only black-eyed Susans and some yellow mums are still blooming. The ground is hard now from so little rain this summer, the grass brown.

"Hey," Michelle says, looking down at her feet then back up at me. "Thanks. I owe you. You did good by her. I know you did. She really likes you. She's gonna miss you, I know it."

"Thanks," I say.

"We'll call you. You call, too, anytime, okay? It's okay with me, you call her and talk. You're like her grandma now. We're gonna come visit you, you wait and see, we will. It's not so far away." She rubs her nose with the back of her hand. Her fingernails are done again in a soft pink with a glittery stone in the center of each nail. She has no stripe of dark roots in her hair. Her dad is paying her nine dollars an hour with health care benefits, and she doesn't have to pay rent. She has money for hair dye.

"Yeah, I'll call," I say. "And you call me anytime."

"You done a really good thing," she says again.

I look at her, at her honest admiration. We stand in my backyard, on this rectangle of my yard. Anyone looking at us would think us mother and daughter. "I hoped you wouldn't get her back," I said. "A lot of times."

"Yeah, I know." She smiles a half smile. "You didn't like me much."

"No, I didn't."

"But we're okay, now?"

"Yeah, we're okay, now."

"Okay," she says. "I'm going to give you a hug then. Don't freak out or nothing. You don't have to hug my dad."

"I wasn't planning on it."

She hugs me, and I hug her back. Larissa comes out of the house, as if on cue. Michelle's dad is rummaging around in the backseat.

"Had to move some of those presents over, so they'd be room for you," he says to Larissa. "Ha-ha. You can open them as we drive."

Larissa stays by her mom, going no closer to the car despite the presents. *Good girl,* I think.

"Do you need to use the bathroom?" I ask Michelle.

"Naw, we stopped before we got here," her dad says. Michelle looks at me, and I know she made sure they did that.

"Miss you," I say to her.

"Yeah, we'll miss you, too," she says, looking down at Larissa. I hug Larissa good-bye again, but can't say anything else.

They climb in the car and drive away. Larissa waves Lucy's arm out the car's window. *Careful,* my hand spells. *Careful Lucy doesn't fall out,* I think.

I keep the dining room table, the rocking chair, and Larissa's bedroom set. Michelle's dad is buying them all new stuff.

I go down to my parents' house for Labor Day weekend. Bruce and Dylan can't come. My father looks older than last year. My mother moves more slowly. At dinner we talk about the old days, then go to bed early. Sunday morning I wake with a terrible backache and stay in bed for the whole day. It feels as if my muscles are fists around my spine, that they have broken every bone in my back. It still hurts Monday, but I get out of bed. I'm walking crooked.

"This is how you mourn," my mother says. "It's your body talking to you, telling you you're sad. It's how you cry."

"Really?" I say. "I thought it was my body telling me I'm in Goddamn pain." I hear what I've said, and she smiles.

My body interprets for me. It's what it's good at.

"Love you," I tell my parents as I get into my car. My mom leans over even farther than she already is and kisses me on the forehead. I close the car door and cry half the way home.

Michelle and Larissa call me every Sunday night, and I call them every Wednesday night. They come and visit once in late October. Michelle says things are going all right. Larissa is a second-grader now. She hardly sucks her thumb at all. Lucy is a mess. Together we patch her as best we can.

Two weeks before Christmas I pick up the phone and call Yolanda at work. "Do you have anyone who needs a home?" She's asked me before if I wanted to do this again, and I always said no. Those times, she'd nod and say, "You may be right. Larissa was a great foster child. They're not all that easy." *Easy.* Not the right word at all.

"You sure?" she says now. "You might get a kid who's difficult, you know. You might not fall for this one the same way."

She's probably right. "Yeah, I'm sure. I've got this extra bed-room set, and all these fire extinguishers. I was just thinking there might be some kid who doesn't want to spend Christmas down there with you guys."

"Yeah, Christmas can be a hard time. You thinking about a girl again?"

"No," I say. "Whoever you think might be best."

"Any particulars?" she asks. "Age, race, religion?"

"No, Yolanda. No particulars." Then I think of something. "Wait. Yeah. Siblings? A brother and sister? Kids you don't want to separate? Are there any?"

"Yeah," Yolanda says. "There are. You sure?"

"Yeah. I'm sure. Hey, they can play Chutes and Ladders to-gether. I'm never playing that game again."

"There's a lot of kid games, Alice. Might be easier buying bingo or something than taking in two kids."

"If there are siblings you need to place, I'll take them."

"Okay, Alice. Trust me, there are."

"And, Yolanda?"

"Yeah?"

"That guy, Adam, the one who did my home inspection. Does he still work there?"

There's a pause, and then, "He does."

"Is he seeing anyone?"

She laughs. "Hey, girl, I don't know, but hold on." She puts me on hold for a few minutes, then comes back. "All I can tell you is he's not married."

"Okay. Thanks. Could you give me his direct line?"

She has it all ready for me. "You call me right back," she say. "All the details. I'm not kidding."

"I will."

I call the home study guy. I can hardly remember what he looks like except he was shorter than me and had a friendly way. "Hi," I say. "It's Alice Marlowe. Remember me? I needed a fire escape plan?"

He chuckles. "Yeah, I remember you. How's it going with that little girl?"

"It went well," I say. "She went back with her mother a few months ago. I'm going to take in a new foster child, maybe two, hopefully before Christmas. Do you need to do another home visit?"

"Not really," he says, but I can hear the possibility in his voice.

"Can you come anyway? For coffee maybe? Just tell me if everything's still okay?"

He doesn't even pause. "Yeah. I could do that."

I call Yolanda back. Then I call Polly.

"You'll never believe what I did now," I tell her.

"Try me," she says. "Unless it involves breaking and entering."

"Not that," I say. "I just called a guy and asked him over for coffee."

She shrieks. Right there in her office, she shrieks. "Alice! You didn't! Who?"

"Adam, the home study guy. And I'm going to take in another foster child. Actually two."

"Good for you," she says. "Good for you."

"We'll get together," I tell her. "We'll find time."

"Sure," she says. "Of course we will."

And that's me, the woman you saw yesterday, the tall, white woman walking toward the playground with the short dark-haired man and two children walking with us. It was such a lovely day, the sky blue, the grass green, yellow daffodils and purple crocus blooming, a red cardinal singing from a bush, and you, you were wearing a lavender skirt, or pale pink blouse, or blue jeans, and someone laughed, one of us. You looked back at us. You looked curious. I thought I'd tell you who I am.

Adam doesn't live with me, but he might someday. The children are Doreen, five years old, and Donnell, seven. They've lived with me for seven months now. It's not easy. Yolanda was right. Larissa was special.

Some people say I saved Larissa. But they've got it wrong.

Acknowledgments

I would like to thank the many people who helped me with the research for this book. For their kindness, knowledge, time, and expertise I thank Detective Bartee of the Cleveland Heights Police Department; James McCafferty, director of the Department of Children and Family Services; Harold Harrison, John Lympany, Deborah Crawford, and Jackie McCray, all of the Department of Children and Family Services; John Lawson, Esq.; Judge Peter Sikora, Bailiff Theresa Nugent, Magistrate Patricia Yeomans, and Magistrate Nancy McMillen, of the Cuyahoga Country Juvenile Court; Sam Moore and Joey Heine, my teachers at the Cleveland Hearing and Speech Center; Lynn Hartman Oblisk, CSC; and Debi Epstein. Any factual mistakes in this book are my own invention.

Also, for their thoughtful readings and generous help, I thank the writers in my writers group: Neal Chandler, Steven Hayward,

Paul Ita, Maureen McHugh, Erin Nowjack O'Brien, Charles Oberndorf, Amy Bracken Sparks, Lori Weber, Jim Garrett, and Charlotte VanStolk.

And finally, a standing ovation for my agent, Christy Fletcher, and my editors, Susan Allison and Leslie Gelbman.

05